Published by
Etched in Stone Publications
Newark, New Jersey 07106

Copyright reserved 2018
ISBN- 978-0-9898907-4-8
Printed in the United States

The Devil's DNA
Robert Taylor

This work and all of its characters are fictional. Any similarities to real life and events are just that. No part of this book may be used or reproduced in any form or fashion, for movies, video scripts etc. without the authors permission.

All rights are reserved by; Etched in stone publications

INTRODUCTION

Robert Taylor will have you on the edge of you seat with this powerful, descriptive and jaw dropping tale. Follow him as he paints this thriller with such passion, you won't want to put it down. Run for your life as you find yourself trapped in the horrific scenes, unable to escape Satan's nasty web of lies and destruction. No one's exempt when the hellhounds, overlords, demons and the devil himself turns up the heat, in an unforgiving *reign of terror*!

Special thanks to God, for giving me the insight and ability to finish this work. To Rabbil Ford for helping me to explore another genre. To my Mother and Father for being the great souls they are, my brothers and sisters for their love and support. To Jessica Wright Tiles for her editing. To Paul and Tony Mclean, Lisa Arrington, Hassan an Joan Rhem, Sharon and Jalen Sykes, to Lionel Slade, Robert Bruce, Tarah Mack, Monasia Parker, Mark and Tisha Mckenzie, Jemmie Adams, Vogel Eliassant, Patrice, Masonie and Dex at the Source of Knowledge, and to all my Facebook friends etc. I love you all!

THE DEVIL'S D.N.A.
SEIGE OF DARKNESS

Siege of Darkness/Robert Taylor

1
PASSAGE TO THE DARK AGE

July 17, 1840

A foggy night deep in a dark wooded area. Everything was calm as an elderly white man whistled while walking with his German Shepard and clutching his hunting rifle. Scanning through the colorful trees and bushes, he heard loud howling as he stepped casually in the moist dirt, through high grass. The howling grew louder and louder, grabbing the man's full attention. Suddenly, a barrage of screams and ear piercing growls stopped him in his tracks; he alertly looked about. Not knowing where or what it was, he didn't hesitate to quicken his pace. He feared there was something real strange about this night, and there definitely was. Looking up into the sky, he glimpsed the full moon, as he moved along; his face still and blank.

Within seconds, the growling grew closer, as did heavy panting and swift moving thunderous steps. As branches and leaves crumbled beneath their feet, these creatures were not going to be denied their kill. The man nervously turned to see this angry pack of wolves trailing him. In fear of his very life, he took off as fast as his old, thin legs could carry him. While in full stride, he turned his head slightly to look back, hollering for his dog that had stopped and started barking. A few of the wolves, revealing their sharp dagger-like teeth, growled just before they savagely jumped on the dog, leaving it squealing for it's life. Their mouths foamed and dripped

Siege of Darkness/Robert Taylor

with blood, as they left the dog maimed and motionless. Seeing this, the man continued to run, horrified as he did so. Tripping over a large tree branch, he stumbled and fell. Before he could even attempt to get back to his feet, the wolves leaped. Without hesitating, he aimed his rifle and shot one after another. The bullets did nothing more than tear holes in their flesh, angering them. In the midst of this madness, a few others sunk their teeth into his chest and legs, tearing his flesh from its bones. He screamed at the top of his lungs, as bones snapped and his face tightened. Blood shot from his mouth and everywhere else, but there was no one to hear his cries that echoed in the wind. All the animals in the woods jumped around, squealed, roared and danced in celebration. As the man lay mangled, drenched in his own plasmic waste, he felt his life slipping away, short of taking his last breath. The full moon illuminated the sky, a testament to the evil that happened beneath it.

    The next day, as the sun brought about light and warmth, and danced in and out of the shadows of the clouds, everything seemed calm and peaceful. There, along a winding dirt trail in Blacksburg South Carolina, the birds chirped and towering trees were as far as the eyes could see. Walking and humming loudly, three sweaty and exhausted slaves carried a large parcel, as they followed behind their slave master, who led them through the woods. The silver and blonde-haired middle aged man, who we'll come to know as Stephen Mason, was on horseback. A mangled body in the road caught his attention, as he scanned the trail visually before him. Growing near, he slowed to a halt and his eyes set sights on the corpse. By the way blood was dried against the tree and splattered about the grass, it was clear a violent struggle had taken place.

    "Whoa, hey, what's that dare boys?"

Siege of Darkness/Robert Taylor

"Looks like what's left of a dead man, Massa Mason suh!" one of the slaves told him after closely analyzing the remains. The mangled torso was soaked in dried blood as it lay severed from its legs.

Mason took off his hat, pressing it to his chest out of respect and climbed down out of his saddle. Slowly kneeling to personally examine the corpse and without warning its hands grabbed hold of his shirt. The eyes of the three slaves bulged, as they quickly backed away out of fear. Mason immediately fought to free himself of its grasp. The head rose as the mouth opened and razor-like teeth were prepared to do the unimaginable. Without pause it sunk its teeth into Mason's left shoulder, causing him to yell out. Mason pulled his gun with his right hand and blew half of its face clean off. As the flesh splattered on the ground, a spirit rose from the body. Maggots immediately appeared from everywhere, causing Mason to hurriedly try to stand, but he fell back to his knees. Instantly, he became faint and fell out, as his blood continued to pour. The maggots slowly dissipated seconds later.

Breaking the trance of the utter shock, one of the bewildered slaves took off his sweaty white T-shirt and ripped it in two. He pressed one piece against Mason's wound while wrapping the other around it to stop the fierce bleeding. After the slaves threw Mason's weakened body onto the horse's back; the larger slave rode off, while the others trotted slowly behind.

Reaching the plantation, the slave brought the horse to a stop. Seeing her husband slumped across the horse's back soaked in blood, Lily Mason hysterically panicked and raced from the porch.

Siege of Darkness/Robert Taylor

"What goes on here? What has happened to my husband?" she cried out. Still in somewhat of a state of shock, the slaves weren't eager to usher a single word.

"Well, one of you best ta tell me something or it'll be your blood spilling next!" Lily demanded.

"Missus. Mason ma'am, we's was comin' through the woods back dere likes we's always do and we saw us a dead body! Ain't that right, ya'll?" The six-foot-three muscular slave went on as the others nodded and answered "um hum" in agreement.

"Massa Mason come down off dat dere horse and soon as he get near, the dead man grab' em and start to bite'n! Massa shoot him dead, yes he did!"

Some of the white field hands rushed over and carefully pulled him down from the horse's backside. As they carried him into the house, blood dripped on their clothes and bare skin.

Lily watched and ran in behind them, but not before shouting, "The lies you tell. I'll deal wit you's later, now gon'!" she finished as Mason's blood against one of the field hand's veins began to bubble.

Hours later, as the humidity rose to a swelting 101 degrees, within the Mason plantation a pale Stephen Mason lay in his bed drenched in sweat. Beneath, his body soaked the sheets. His neck and shoulder area were burgundy and swollen. They were wrapped in adhesive plasters that were stained with dried blood and signs of puss because of its yellowish brown color. As his eyes bore rings, his body seemed to shake, all of this while he was being fed a hot bowl of soup from the loving hands of his wife of ten years. She looked worried as she raised the steaming spoon to his quivering lips. Trying to form words, he held his right hand out and she paused to listen, but his once commanding baritone voice had been reduced to a whisper.

"What is it honey?" she asked with a concerned look as she sat the bowl on a nightstand and leaned in. He cleared his throat before he said anything.

"There's something going on inside of me! I feel so strange, I feel like I'm…ah, dying and changing at the same time. Something crazy… seems to be taking place! My body's on fire!" he forged as his lips met her earlobe.

"It's gon' be okay! The doctor said rest now, you're just delusional, hon, and you done lost a lot of blood. Doc said… he don't understand how you even survived. We sent one of the slave into town to find Priest Bauer, but by the time we all got back and in this here room, you seemed to be breathing normal. Your pressure and pulse are stable and strong! Doc told me he had to go, but if things changed for the better or worse, for me to send for him." She picked up the bowl and spoon from the nightstand. "Here now, eat your soup."

Seconds later, the large slave darkened the doorway.

"Is Massa Mason gone be alright?" he asked out of concern.

"Yes he is. Now you gon', get out of here!"

The slave turned and could be heard walking down the steps.

***

A quarter of a mile out, inside one of the slave's cabins, two of the men became fever ridden. As they lay up, coughing and spitting everything from their blood to their guts, their wives were concocting remedies they figured would be of some help. The men's eyes began to sit still, turning yellow with red veins

Siege of Darkness/Robert Taylor

throughout them. Their mouths began to protrude as they took on the look of wolf-like creatures, while a black canine barked loudly outside the window.

***

Later that evening, long after night fell, a oil lantern flickered while providing the only light within the Mason's darkened bedroom. While Lily was in a deep coma-like sleep, Stephen's skin began to crawl as it grew solid, tight, and vascular. His eyes turned a bright red, his cheeks sunken and he clinched his fist, trying to absorb the painful transformation. The night sky shifted as a strong wind whisked across the land, tossing anything that wasn't secured.

While all this was taking place, things got real strange in the Roman Catholic Church of South Carolina. Father Harry O'Conner, a priest of the cloth, prepped to leave the chapel. As he walked down a long stoned filled corridor to an area that housed the private quarters, there seemed to be the shadow of something following him. Once inside his room, he removed his vestment robe and sat on his bed in his underclothes. His pale skin, that cried for sunlight, hung loosely about his frame, as his gray eyes sat deep in his mysterious yet strong face. Quickly rising back to his feet, he walked over to a large standing mirror that sat between two paintings. He viewed himself as he took a deep breath and pulled in his stomach.

"Hello, Harry O'Conner, I'm Byron Malic, a former priest of the cloth. I have some unfinished business with those of the faith." The voice startled him, causing him to quickly turn

Siege of Darkness/Robert Taylor

around and scan the entire room, from its high ceiling, to its large windows and floor.

"What?" he shouted, as he rushed over to the door and peeked out into the hall area. After not seeing anyone or anything, he closed the door and locked it.

"I know of you and your work. With your help, we can be God's, blessed with immortality! If you're not interested, I can surely find another more-than-willing candidate. I chose you because of your loyalty, plus the others amongst you think so little of you and your eagerness." the voice added. equally scaring the life out of Father O'Conner.

"Who are you?"

"Right now, I am nothing more than a spokesman, a messenger; I am here to place before a deal that will give you great power and, once again, immortality. I was once like you an eager, headstrong priest of the cloth. I couldn't be swayed by anything or anyone and that's when I saw that I could be much, much more..."

Father O'Conner listened, but gave the thought no energy, as he continued to look about.

"There is only one GOD, and I am a devoted servant of his and cannot be persuaded by falsehoods." Father O'Conner recited and collapse to the floor in prayer.

"You fool, you have been in the priesthood for over twenty years and you're much more intelligent than your colleagues, but yet you continue to allow them to take credit for your works and findings."

"The Lord is thy Sheppard, thou shall not want; He maketh me to lie in green pastures and walk alongside still waters." he continued pleading with God.

A loud sinister cry of laughter could be heard as the priest finished his prayer.

Siege of Darkness/Robert Taylor

"You fool!" the voice added in the midst of its laughter. Father O'Conner just sat on his knees praying with his eyes tightly shut.

"There is no one greater than you o-Lord, please guide me away from the evil's that be. I am forever faithful to you my Lord, let not he take my soul!" Father O'Conner begged. Suddenly there was silence, Father O'Conner opened his eyes, looked up and spat;

"Thank you Lord! Thank you!"

***

Morning broke, a rooster crowed and Stephen Mason seemed fine, as he sat on the side of the bed seemingly in thought. After which, he stretched his arms high and walked over to a large picture window draped in gold and blue. He stared out into a large grassy field. Lily watched and smiled from within the tan sheets that laced their king-size bed. After staring out a while and squinting from the sunlight, he pulled the drapes shut, darkening the room.

Climbing back in the bed, with a mischievous look about him, he came out of his shorts and aggressively manhandled his wife, pushing her over onto her back. She smiled excitingly, surrendering as she wondrously stared up into his eyes. In the midst of it all, she happened to touch his bandaged shoulder and could feel warmth. The swelling had pretty much disappeared. He hiked up her night gown, exposing her white flesh and snatched her lengthy legs open, forcibly planting his throbbing penis into her unsuspecting, tight walls.

She pushed away and cried out, "You're hurting me! Please stop, you're hurting me!"

Siege of Darkness/Robert Taylor

He pulled her back close and barbarically drove, grunted, and savagely stabbed himself inside her harder and harder. She began to bleed onto him and the sheets, while scratching and pounded at his chest. Tears ran out the side of her glossy eyes, as she cried so loud the dog outside began to croon.

Flipping her over onto her stomach, he rode her like a wild buck as the bedsheets lay soiled beneath them. Growling sinisterly, he continued to punish her vaginal walls. After a while, the legs to her beaten body gave out and she laid flat in her own waste, dripping in sweat. He lay atop of her, licking her neck and backside, and within minutes, he started back up. Her eyes popped wide open, as he did and she yelled, as she tried to endure the pain once more.

An hour later, his eyes darkened, as his body hardened and began to violently shake. Falling over on his side, he lay out, as his chest rose and fell.

Horrified, Lily rolled from the bed onto the floor, where she clawed her way up the wall to get to her feet. Relieved to be done and away from her husband, she staggered into a bathroom across the hall.

As her nude breast hung over the sink, she cried from how disrespected she felt, and how animalistic he acted. Looking down between her parted legs, she saw a trail of blood from the bedroom to where she stood. As she closed the door, she felt shooting pains throughout her vagina, uterus, and stomach. Reaching down, she ran her right hand lightly across her sore vaginal lips. She could feel the torn flesh as blood dripped lightly onto the floor. Dampening a rag, she attempted to put a stop to it and cringed from pain.

While she was in the bathroom cleaning herself up, a female slave banged on the bedroom door. Stephen walked over and snatched it open, grabbed her by her throat, and

Siege of Darkness/Robert Taylor

pulled her in. As she hollered and screamed, Lily opened the bathroom door only to see her husband ripping the clothes from this voluptuous slave. She yelled to him to stop, as she feared approaching because of the look in his eyes. He threw the half nude slave onto the bed and jumped into the sheets with her. With his hands planted tightly around her throat, he positioned himself as she kicked and screamed.

Against her better judgement, Lily rushed over in an attempt to stop his intensions. As the slave continued yelling, he ripped her drawers from her dark thick flesh, while Lily fought to get him off her. He knocked her to the floor and began to rape his slave. Dazed, Lily slowly found her way back to her feet, screaming, as her husband savagely drove his erected hardware between the slaves quivering thighs. Hitting him over the head with an old steel pail, Lily went into shock when his arm struck her across the face, knocking her off her feet and unconscious.

Thirty minutes later, as the slave's nude body lay out motionless; Stephen climbed from the bed and stood over his unconscious wife. He growled ferociously, revealed his stained teeth, and, with the swiftness, he drove his fist down through her chest as blood shot everywhere. Ripping her heart out, he held it up and squeezed it, allowing blood to drips in his face.

Hours later, sunlight stalked blindingly, as it beat upon the dead remains of the black canine on the Mason plantation. Loud screaming fractured the morning silence, as a female slave, coveted in a brown dress with her hair wrapped, raced up the dirt road bare footed. She hollered as she quickly grew closer to the big white house, with two horses and a wagon out front. She ran clean up on the wide wrap around porch, as the broken down cabin she resided in, sat back in the distance. As she approached, Stephen stood staring out, looking like his normal self, except for all the blood about his clothes, face, and hands. The slave stopped a distance away as she took note of his appearance and frightfully began to speak.

"My youngin' done took sick. He foaming about da mouth and out in the yard dere's blood and ..." She couldn't finish due to her hysterical state. Stephen approached the slave, who tried to remain somewhat calm, but yelled out of fear and took off running from the porch. He staggered slowly behind her, but she was much too quick, as she could be seen kicking up dust along the dirt trail.

No even thirty minutes later, as he stood stone faced just beyond the house, he seemed to be absorbing all that was taking place. Gun shots rung out, as slaves could be seen running and falling everywhere. Field hands ran for their lives, as the fright could be seen in their faces. The scene was pure pandemonium; bodies were mangled and left to die beneath the dust accumulated from all the commotion. Armed with guns, the field hands ran to Stephen's aid, but were immediately halted by his appearance also. Without pause, he snatched one of their guns and shot the three of them as he took an array of pellets from a shotgun. The madness went on throughout the night and continued through the early morning.

***

That following day, in the confines of the Roman Catholic Church, Father Harry O'Conner, Father O'Brien and two other priests discussed different matters pertaining to the priesthood.

Siege of Darkness/Robert Taylor

"I'm leaving the priesthood. I have lost my faith. I've been promised eternal life and immortality by another," Father O'Brien stated loudly.

As he finished, Father O'Conner processed all that had been said and thought about his visit from the spirit world.

"The spirit of Byron Malic has visited you, too, I see? Do not believe the falsehoods he speaks of. Do not allow him to dilute your perception. He is a dark force who is trying to facilitate the second dark war. He is evil! " Father O'Conner cautioned.

"He has shown me in its entirety the first war, from its burning clouds to the expulsion of angels. How he works under the command of a fallen one equal to God in every way," said Father O'Brien.

"Equal to God? You can't be serious? All your years of loyalty, you're willing to throw away for eternal damnation, to side with the serpent himself? To lead a legion doomed for the fire? And to think I respected you! I can't believe this. You know a third of heavens legion was banished for their misconduct and yet, you are willing to sell your soul and join such. We mustn't forget that the human soul is like gold to the devil. He is the twister of fate and perception, the master of deceit. He is adversarial to the Most High and to the very grounds that we stand upon. Forgive us…oh, Lord, forgive us!" Father O'Conner pled.

Father O'Brien sat silent for a few minutes and then spoke.

"I have been in the priesthood much longer than you. I have served as one of the greatest examples this church has ever known. You…though well learned and versed, cannot possibly understand!" Father O'Brien carried on.

Siege of Darkness/Robert Taylor

"What is there to understand, but the fact that you are willing to trade a life within God's kingdom for one of no honor with no one other than the serpent?"

"How dare you judge me! You...who has lived for many years reaping the benefits of this God forsaken world! You came to us, broken down and we raised you back up a saint to be respected. How dare you?" Father O'Brien added.

"God has cleansed me of all my sins, so for that I am immensely grateful. Please...I beg of you, not to go through with this!" Father O'Conner feared the worst.

Father O'Brien remained silent, as he seemed to be comfortable with his decision.

****

Three days later, there was loud talking inside one of the slave's quarters on the Mason's plantation. The three men screamed back and forth, as three children, one girl, two boys sat at a table. A dead woman sat at the head, as an empty bowl sat out in front of her.

"We must leave here! God has come and He do away with the wicked."

"But He killed my wife, Samuel an all da others. Is He not jus? This da devil's work!"

"Whatever it be, it sho scare me!"

"I don't know 'bout y'all, but I's gon' be out 'fore dark." the third man finished, as the kids ate and watched.

Seconds later, there was a knock at the door and when one of the men opened it, there stood three male slaves.

Siege of Darkness/Robert Taylor

"Let's get ta goin' for it get too late," one of them spoke as he held a bible under his right armpit. Without hesitation and without a moment to waste, they hurried into the night.

In the darkness, as the twelve slaves moved through the bush, they were spotted by three white men on horseback. They tried to run, but were halted by a single shot in the air. At gunpoint, they were all gathered and made to stand near a tall oak tree surrounded by patches of grass.

"Where you niggers coming from this time of night?" one of the men asked.

"We's from the Mason plantation. Everybody done took sick and died back dere! We's just trying to be safe," one of the slaves answered.

"I know Mr. Mason personally and I don't think he'd take kindly ta findin' out some of his fine property was out here tryin' to escape in the night. Now you all gon' and get on y'all knees before I shoot you dead! Ya hear? Hurry now!"

"But suh, deres something strange going on back there!"

"Shut ya mouth there boy... and do as I told ya! the man shouted as he cranked his rifle.

"Billy, you gon' down to the Mason plantation and find Stephen and bring him back up here. Tell him we found some of his nigger property trying to escape."

On that note, one of the men rode off.

After waiting about an hour and Billy never returning, the others began to worry. Suddenly, amidst the darkness and trees was loud howling. The men began to look around.

"What was that?" one of them shouted, as they all wondered. A frightened slave jumped to his feet and attempted to run and was shot down immediately.
(ca-poof)

Siege of Darkness/Robert Taylor

"Where in the hell…is Billy?" one of the men questioned.

"I don't know what going on, but something ain't right!" another added.

"We need to go on down to that plantation and find Billy."

"What about these here slaves?

"Hang 'em…they're runaway!"

"I'm telling you's, there's something bad goin' on back dere. Lotta blood!"

"Didn't I tell you's to shut the hell up?" the man on the horse shouted as he raised his rifle and hit the slave in the head with the butt of it. He fell over in the dirt, holding his head, while blood seeped through his fingers.

One after the other, they were hoisted in the air with a thick rope around their necks and left dangling until there was not a breath left in their bodies, kids and all.

2 DEATH AND DESTRUCTION

Months later, as news of random killings throughout Cherokee County South Carolina circulated, people from Draytonville to Cherokee falls to Blacksburg all came together forming a search party. They traveled hours, for miles around, throughout the area, until finally they came upon the Mason Plantation. Noticing vultures circling, hovering and squealing, they were immediately on alert. As men on horses trod through the plantation of bugs, gnats and stray dogs, they watched as they mauled the dead flesh. Startled by all of this, the men raised their rifles and guns, slowing their horses to a casual stroll. Two of the dogs stood and growled, as their foaming mouths hung. One of the men shot the dogs dead. Others squinted as they covered their faces with their shirts. The dreadful smell of death nauseated them, causing a few to vomit. Anything that moved was shot and killed. The few slaves they captured were gathered, tied up in one of the slave quarters, and torched alive. They thought that would stop the killing, but it didn't, it continued. The town people figured some of the slaves had gotten free. Therefore, they executed any slave caught running, deeming them to be dangerous.

During the course of that same month, one day Stephen Mason found himself lying in a grass-filled area with rifles pointed at the back of his head. At the other end of those guns were weary soldiers sent to search the area. One of them spoke,

Siege of Darkness/Robert Taylor

"Is you one of dem there critters or you one of us?" he asked as he cranked the pump and stared down the barrel awaiting an answer. In his eyes there was a merciless look; one could see this man had killed before, many, many times before!

"Get those goddamn guns outta ma face!" Stephen hollered as he rose to his feet, blood about his clothes.

"Hold up, you, why are you covered in blood?" one of the men asked as the others stood their ground.

Stephen astonished himself, looked at his clothes,

"...I just killed a deer...and carried it to my wagon and I... guess I fainted out here in this here heat. Now if you don't mind, I got to get into town." He finished and walked off as the men watched. Afterwards, the soldiers turned and continued their search, they walked through acres upon acres, as quite a few gunshots rang out. They gathered and dragged the bodies into an open field, away from everything and burned them.

That same day, in his room within the church, the spirit of Malic cornered Father O'Conner again, this time while he sat painting at an easel.

"Your soul's one worthy of praise. I commend you! Your honor is noble and just. I am all but astonished by your loyalty. We'll meet again, I'm sure of it."

Startled, Father O'Conner dropped his paintbrush. He looked around and continued to listen, but there was silence. He bowed his head, closed his eyes, and uttered a brief prayer.

Siege of Darkness/Robert Taylor

A while later, Malic made his presence known in the room of Father O'Brien. He appeared ghostlike as he spoke,

"Are you ready for eternal life and power beyond your imagination? Are you ready for your Godly existence? That life which is infinite! If so, stand before me and say these words."

"I call upon you...oh mighty one. I ask for your assistance in helping to prophesize what is to come. I am an ordained priest of the church, who seeks to be a mercenary of your army of disciples."

As O'Brien repeated word for word, darkness blanketed the room, as a bright yellow-like light illuminated from him. He bowed his head in submission and shut his eyes, feeling his pores opening. A powerful force entered through his ears and nostrils taking possession as, his eyes rolled to the back into his head, leaving only the whites exposed. When the atmosphere calmed, he opened his eyes, exposing darkness. An energumen smile made way for Malic's distinguishable laugh spilling from his tongue, signifying the formality of their union.

Within seconds, the priest fell to his knees and sat in silence. From his ears, nose and mouth, emerged the spirit of Malic once again. On the ceiling, a large, red face appeared, and then vanished. Father O'Brien opened his eyes and the spirit of Byron Malic was before him again.

"Why were you killed?" Father O'Brien asked.

"I was never killed! Each of the vessels I inhabited were destroyed! They were accused of practices like sorcery and witch craft. Back then the religious doctrines had fine lines in which they followed. They often burned or hanged anyone that was deemed unholy! I...Byron Malic was approached, by

Siege of Darkness/Robert Taylor

Lucifer one night in the woods. He promised me I could live forever! Eternally! I accepted his offer, and now I am before you extending a similar one!"

"It was said that you were a former priest of the cloth. Why did the church seek to destroy you and think they killed you?"

Because I was the first priest to ever defy the word of the church, and of God! They blamed me for countless murders and demonic occurrences and, without proof, they banished me from the priesthood. Later, they cornered me in a cave sleeping and took me out and killed me. So, they thought! But, long before that, I made a deal with my God for eternal life!"

So...how do I fit in this picture?"

"I shall instruct you as time withers and days pass of the tasks expected of you." Malic disappeared, leaving O'Brien somewhat confused.

The next day, not far away in Blacksburg, White soldiers were crossing the Poinsett Bridge and heard echoing screams. They stopped and raised their guns, as they scanned the area. The ghost of a slave climbed over the edge of the bridge with a noose hanging loosely around his neck. He was then pushed to his death. The soldiers froze, as they watched and in seconds they took off running. At that moment, the air got thin, as this dark and mysterious area took on an evil vibe. The men fell out screaming as bodies appeared and dangled from everywhere. The scene was like nothing ever witnessed. The men took off again fearing for their lives.

***

Siege of Darkness/Robert Taylor

A few days later, not far from a Roman Catholic burial site in Charleston, there seemed to be a supernatural presence. The sky roared thunderously, shedding light on an otherwise unseen act. A man in a black robe stood, bringing his chant to an end.

"It is You, o', Lord, that I am here to serve. Direct me as You so wish, o', Lord!"

A spirit rose from beneath the soil and stood before him; its face was that of a middle aged White man with eyes of emerald green.

"You have made a wise choice, the first of many in our quest to become forces in this vast habitat of falsehoods. You are the wisest of those amongst you and I am honored that Malic has brought you before me. Place your hand on this Holy book that I hold and we shall become one."

There as his hand lay flush on the ancient book, his eyes fluttered, his pores opened and his nostril's flared. He felt a power race through his body like none he ever felt before. His blood seemed to be boiling, as his skin bubbled.

That same evening, walking through the backwoods with his hunting rifle, Stephen spotted a deer. He raced across the field, holding his rifle in the air. The deer took off. Stephen aimed and shot. The deer bawled and fell out; twitching as it slowly began to succumb to its wound. After walking it down, Stephen pulled out his hunting knife and began savagely carving it up. Settling to rest down under a large tree, he barbarically tore into the raw flesh. With his head down and blood about his face, he scanned his surroundings with a look of pure evil.

Siege of Darkness/Robert Taylor

Hours later, some soldiers were searching that same area of the woods. They stumbled onto a site, where it looked like someone had recently been. Beneath a large tree were carved up, half eaten human remains. Not wanting to believe what they were seeing, the soldiers moved on. They were hoping to catch up to the beast causing such a massacre.

***

Days later, on another abandoned plantation, where bodies littered the grounds, Stephen Mason sat at an old oak table, drafting a suicide letter. He seemed confused about his thoughts as he scribbled out a word here and there. Twenty minutes later, he was finally finished. It read:
To whom it may concern,

I, Stephen Mason, have taken my own life, because demons have invaded my soul and I refuse to do the work of the devil. A regular man, or so he looked, bit me and my blood boils with a sickness that is driving me to do heartless, violent acts. I have to escape this ...

He rose soldier-like from the chair, picked up his .44long Colt, closed his eyes, and placed the barrel against his temple. Tears flowing from beneath his fluttering eyelids, as his sweaty hands trembled and his mind was slowly becoming unrecognizable. Without hesitation, he pulled the trigger and in that split second, the bullet exploded from within the chamber of the gun shredded through his skull and brains, blasting blood and tissue out the opposite side of his head. His lifeless body crashed to the floor from the impact, where he lay within a pool of his blood. As he bled out, his blood started to spread as it was moving towards anything warm or that had a pulse. It moved from the stove, went under a door, and into another room where a cat lay sleeping.

****

    Two weeks later, after days of relentless rain, the sheriff, Father James Bauser, and a few men scouted all the plantations. During their inspection, they came upon corpses and dead animals in front of one of them. As they traveled through the muddy grounds of this abandoned plantation, they came upon the big house. The wet unkept grass stood tall, as if someone hadn't cut it in months. Father Bauser blessed the grounds and the dead as he rode through. The sheriff halted the brigade of men. The smell of death was also present as it was on the Mason's plantation. It was an awful stench, one that could make you regurgitate everything resting within walls of your stomach.
    Once inside this old place and after going from room to room, one of the men looked down. There was Mason's body sprawled lifeless on the floor. His eyes widened as he noticed he was standing in a pool of thick, crimson red blood. He tried to step free of the bloody mess, but it was stuck to his shoes. Panicking, he turned and screamed for help. Lunging on the man, a red cat started scratching out his eyes, as the blood turned into a red plasmic web devoured him whole. One of the men wet himself, as he stood in shock. The others ran, all except for one, who took aim, pumped his shotgun, and blew the plasmic blob to shreds, along with the left side of his friends face and shoulder. As the body collapsed to the floor, pieces of the splattered cat landing everywhere, as it was seen moving about the walls and slowly came back together. The

men hopped on their horses and galloped off. The sheriff, who was wondering what had spooked them, didn't hesitate or ask any questions. He and the priest rode off also.

***

That same day, Father O'Conner and O'Brien passed each other in the long empty corridor. Smiles covered their faces as they greeted one another.

Father O'Conner spoke as he gritted his teeth just beforehand.

"I rebuke you in the name of the lord!" there after he tossed from a cup, holy water onto Father O'Brien in passing. Without pause, Father O'Brien shouted,

"Your holy water is nothing but frivolous drops of rain to me! A distinguishing laugh followed catching Father O'Conner's attention, causing him to look back and around. Puzzled, he continued on, looking back every few paces. He rushed towards the chapel where all the priests were gathered and burst in.

"Father O'Brien has sided with Lucifer and is working to bring forth evil forces onto the earth. A representative from the dark world has promised him immortality!" Father O'Conner blurted as he gasped and finished. Father James Bauser and the other priests stopped what they were doing to hear him. They couldn't believe what he said.

"What is this madness you speak?" Father Bauser asked, as the others were all ears.

"A force has invaded the walls of the church, seeking an apprentice to do the devil's deeds!"

"Where is he now?" Father Bauser asked curiously, as he seemed to ponder.

Siege of Darkness/Robert Taylor

"Come..." Father O'Conner led the way.

The group of priests hurried to Father O'Briens quarters. He wasn't there, so they split up and searched the entire place. He was nowhere to be found.

***

Days later, the sheriff had the second plantation quarantined, as he had twenty wagons brought to the site. Right away they shot anything that moved or showed signs of life.

"Shoot them all in the head before you touch them! They may not be dead! You hear me boys? Don't take any chances!" After the sheriff made that statement, gunshots rang out for the next half hour or so. They placed each corpse on a cart, one on top of another. Then the loaded carts headed out, one behind the other. After an hours drive in the hot sun, they finally reached their destination and dug a mass grave. Off of Covington Road, behind an old, dilapidated church, they buried well over a hundred dead souls. A preacher quickly blessed the grounds, jumped on his horse, and rode out. As the sheriff called to his men to saddle up, a few of them seemed possessed. They drew their guns, shot the sheriff and some of the others, and took off down the road.

Elsewhere, deep in a wooded area hidden from sight, as darkness filled the sky, thirty sobbing slaves stood around a massive, open grave. They burned quite a few torchlights, as evening was the only time slaves were permitted to have burials. Body after body, they prayed over, wrapped and dropped into the huge hole.

3 HISTORY OF THE UNDEAD

Saturday, August 24, 1979

Eleven year old Jason, who was white with black curly locks, sat on a large area rug within a small home in Charlotte, North Carolina. A tattered notebook sat in his lap, as he drooled in amazement and seemed to be obsessed with the stories his uncles, Willie and Jimmy, often told him. He wondered if there was any truths to them. As told, their ancestors had great fear of Byron Malic. So much so, that his father, Chris, still kept crucifixes and Bibles throughout the house. He even wore a silver, three-inch cross around his neck that he never took off. He also prayed every morning and every night. Many thought Malic to be a demon, the devil himself. Jason would often beg his uncles to tell him more of the stories and to take him to where the ritual supposedly had taken place. Whenever his father got wind of it, he often gave young Jason a look that frightened him, yet intrigued his curiosity. His little mind would race day in and day out, as he would put together the pieces. He read the details over and over, committing them to memory. He fantasized about what life would be like, if it were all true.

When young Jason was nine, he asked his father to take him to where the ritual took place. Angrily, Chris grabbed him up by the arms and stared him in the eye,

"Look boy…trust me, there's no way I'm taking you anywhere near that gravesite, even if I could find it! The answer is no! You betta not ask your uncles or anyone else either! You hear me?" he shouted angrily, as he continued beaming into Jason's eyes and shook his small frame.

That only made young Jason more curious. Many times he listened, as his uncles would bring up bits and pieces, and each time he took notes. He often persuaded them also, when they didn't feel like doing so. This was one of those days.

Uncle Willie drank his beer while he sat in an old brown recliner and rambled on.

"You know I shouldn't be telling you these stories? Your father is dead-set against it. Did he leave for work yet?" Willie questioned to make sure he wasn't around.

"He left an hour ago!" Jason assured him with a sinister grin.

"Boy...what's with you and these stories now? I'm not going to be fighting with my brother because of you!"

"I know, but I love them! Please, Uncle Willie...please!"

"Okay...okay...man, we all used to sit around and laugh at the stories our grandfather used to tell us, about supernatural beast of some kind in our midst. We thought it was downright funny, everyone but Chris! Huh..." he trailed off in thought. "It really frightened him! Grandpa would speak of vampires, werewolves, all sorts of creatures that one could imagine. He used to really get angry with us if we didn't listen. Dad use to tell us he was nuts! Sometimes he would tell Grandpa to stop making up these lies to scare us! Sometimes he sat and listened too. Who would have thought, something we watched so much on television now...was once a reality? He told us Malic was vicious! He had people scared to go anywhere at night, you hear me? Anywhere! Because that's when he was supposed to have stalked! People thought him to be Satan himself, because of his malicious ways. He was said to have

Siege of Darkness/Robert Taylor

been a former high priest of the cloth. It was also told to us that he somehow found a scroll, the black Sabbath scroll that put him in touch with the four dark overlords, hell's dark angels. Yeah, Grandpa had all of us spooked, especially Chris and Dad!"

Uncle Willie sat up in his seat, as if equally enthralled about the story he was telling.

"During this meeting, Malic made a deal, a deal for eternal life! But what he received was pure hell! He was an animal! He spread his malicious reign of terror and blood wherever he roamed. It became like a sport to him. He hung bodies from street poles, left some with their hearts ripped out and others decapitated."

Jason's eyes bugged as he listened intensely.

"It was also said that as time went on, a few priests from the Roman Catholic Church eventually sought him out, cornered, and dragged him into the woods, where they performed a ritual and killed his demonic soul. Yeah," he moved in closer to Jason and lowered his voice, "when they put his body in the ground, it was said that all the moist soil, hardened and the grass disappeared! The trees even took on a dreary strange appearance. At least that's how it was told to us, isn't that right Jimmy?" Uncle Willie looked to his brother for his stamp of approval.

Uncle Jimmy nodded.

Uncle Willie sat back in his recliner, lighting a pipe. As he puffed and blew smoke, he looked at Jason and smirked.

Jason grew filled with amazement, this time and every time he had heard these stories. He sat with his diary, eagerly jotting down as much as he could capture, writing as fast as his tiny fingers could. Seeing the growing curiosity in him, Uncle Willie smiled and continued.

Siege of Darkness/Robert Taylor

"I know your father doesn't agree with me telling you these stories, but your great grandpa told them to us, so why not?"

"Man...the funniest part was..." Uncle Jimmy interrupted as he sat nearby chuckling with a beer in his hand. "Chris used to crawl up under the covers...literally frightened out of his skin! There were nights he was so scared that he often pissed in the bed. He was too frightened to even get up and go to the bathroom."

"But is it true?" Jason asked, looking up, awaiting an answer from either of them.

Uncle Jimmy chimed in, "That's what Grandpa told us and we all were scared to death."

A baffled look crossed Jason face. "So...why nobody ever tried to find the spot where they drained the blood from Byron Malic and buried the scrolls and altar?"

"I'm sure people have. But, because, it was said whoever dug those things up would be cursed far beyond one's imagination, a lot of people just left it alone. They'd be doomed to hell on earth!" Uncle Willie told Jason, who seemed to glow from the detailed accounts of the horrifying and gory events.

Jason ran off, out onto the back porch where he sat and fiendishly flipped back to the front page of his notes. There he began to read aloud.

"A Sheriff shot him up and he walked right through the attack, snatched up one of his deputies and ripped his head clean from his shoulders. Blood sprung from the neck of his collapsing body, as it also ran from his eyes, nose and mouth. The strength of this beast was phenomenal. Another time, he chased a woman down and she locked herself in her home. He busted through the wall and pulled her apart like a chicken!" Flipping through the pages, he searched further in his notes.

Siege of Darkness/Robert Taylor

"All the traditional methods of killing or executing the supernatural had no effect on him."

The sky lit up and roared, causing Jason to pause before continuing. "It was said that the Roman Catholic Church called in a group of elder priests, led by High Priest Bauser. They all were familiar with spirit exorcisms. They set a trap, cornered Malic under the full moon, and killed him! But it was also said that Malic's spirit may have found another host." After reading, he closed the diary and sighed as he looked up into the dark sky wondrously, his little mind digesting every thought-provoking detail.

***

Father O'Brien sat on a flight from Europe, bound for Newark, New Jersey. The priest was dressed in blue jeans and a striped shirt. He stared out the window into the white clouds, reminiscing. He visually raced through the time he ran from the church out into the woods. With every step, his mind was performing on an elite level. His senses and alertness were extraordinary. On this undeterminable journey, he grew familiar with his new self. As he woke from thought, his nostrils flared. All the different scents from perfumes, foods, and breath plagued his senses. Nauseated by it all, he got up and strolled toward the rear and to the bathroom. He slammed the door shut and sighed heavily, expressed his relief. Leaning against the mirror, images of death clouded his head, causing him to shutter.

Ten minutes later, after gathering himself, he returned to his seat. Passing through the aisle slowly, a few unusual scents permeated his nostrils, familiar only to a few. Once seated, he took another deep breath, smelling the presence of at least three others. He wondered, why so many were on the plane, and if something strange or violent was about to happen.

***

An hour later, in the streets of downtown Newark, New Jersey, Sherrod, a light-skinned teenager standing about 5 foot 10, was returning home from a youth correctional facility after a three year stint. He seemed lost as he wandered upon a bus stop, approaching fifteen people waiting. People walked by as he looked around watchfully. He noticed how much things had changed, the music, the dress and the attitude, but still remained the same.

A man walked past, with a radio, playing an interesting tune; "What's going on" by Marvin Gaye. As the man sung along with Marvin, *"there's to many of us dying!"* A group of young thugs strutted up. They grabbed a young man, dragged him into an alley and commenced to do what looked like a robbery. Sherrod glanced, as did others, but said nothing. Finally, the bus pulled up and he mixed in with the crowd that gathered at the door. Thereafter, two police cars bombarded the scene and the officers jumped out.

As cigarette smoke filled the air, the bus was crowded from front to back. Squeezing between riders to move towards the rear, Sherrod noticed how weary some of them looked. Finding a seat midway, he dropped down into it and the old woman beside him gave him an angry stare, as she moved over slightly. He exhaled and looked forward as the driver pulled away from the curb and continued his journey.

A scraggly man sitting across from him, tapped him on the leg and asked,

Siege of Darkness/Robert Taylor

"Hey, do you know if this bus goes to the Irvington terminal?"

Sherrod shrugged trying to remember, "I don't know, I think so."

Block after block, he looked out the windows, trying to familiarize himself with the area again. Everything was pretty much as it was when he left, except for a few additional burnt out homes.

At 1:30 p.m., as the heat was scorching, Sherrod, who was walking up Clinton Avenue turned down 20th Street. He spotted a sign that read; *Rooms for Rent*. He walked up on the porch, rang the bell, and waited patiently for someone to answer.

A loud, female voice breached the solid wooden door. "Who is it?"

"I'm here about the room for rent!" Sherrod shouted back. The door opened and he stood face-to-face with a sassy, slender, dark-skinned woman. She looked like she was about fifty, wearing a long, red robe, with silver hair covered in a multi-colored scarf.

Her hands on her hips, as a cigarette dangled between her lips, she looked him up and down. "You're kinda young; you don't have any family you can stay with?"

"I'm...I'm not going to lie to you, I just came home from prison and I really need a place to rest my head. I won't bring you any problems, I promise!"

With her head tilted, she surmised him. He looked harmless.

"Okay now, I'm going to give you a chance. The room is fifty dollars a week and I need that before you can move in! How old are you anyway?" She held her right hand out.

Siege of Darkness/Robert Taylor

"I'm eighteen...Look, I need to rest, can I give you the money in the morning? I promise I'll get you the money!"

"Oh hell no! Please, if you need somewhere to sleep for the night, just say so! Don't beat me in the head with all the bullshit! And you ain't no eighteen either! She peered up at him, her arms folded across her chest. "Boy if you get me in trouble, I'ma get somebody to kick ya ass! Now, come on!" She stepped back and allow him entry, before closing the door behind them, turning and heading up the stairs.

***

An hour later, at Newark Airport as the plane landed, passengers were pulling down their carry-on luggage from the overhead compartments and exiting the plane. With his bags in his hands, Father O'Brien made his way to the front to exit also, as his mind produced more images of dead bodies lying in the streets everywhere. Fires burning for miles, nothing but destruction as far as the eyes could see.

Looking around the airplane, his eyes landed on a stewardess standing before him.

"May I help you with something?" she asked pleasantly.

"No, I'm quite the abled body." He smiled and she moved to allow him passage. She watched him with a look of curiosity.

***

Early that evening, as crickets chirped in the south, Jason sat in his room, watching a black and white Frankenstein horror flick. He began to conjure up scenes in his head, monsters leaping through the sky and off buildings, fighting

Siege of Darkness/Robert Taylor

relentlessly and to the death. So hypnotized by his thoughts, he surfed the channels, looking solely for anything remotely horrific. When it got late, Chris walked into the room, turned off the television, and chased him to bed. An angry Jason pleaded with him.

"Please, Dad! I just want to see the rest of the movie and I promise I'll go right to bed!"

"No! You don't need to be watching that stuff anyway. Go to bed, Jason, I'm not playing with you!" he commanded as he walked out. A pouting, Jason mumbling to himself. When he thought his father was asleep, he grabbed a flashlight, along with some of his action figures and created his own movie sequence.

***

About midnight, inside a graveyard in Newark, a few dogs aimlessly roamed. They sniffed around until suddenly, one of them started digging into the surface. The deeper it dug, the more eager it became. The others raced over to help. When they reached a certain point, a ray of light shined through. As the earth opened up, the dogs howled and raced into the ground. The blinding light reached up to the clouds, a loud thunderous clap erupted shaking the very earth. Street lights fell as the pavement cracked, driver smashed their vehicles into each other, trying to avoid falling debris. Then within minutes, it all had seized. Some thought it was an earthquake, but the roaring sky left many to think otherwise.

Newscasters discounted it, as they fell short by calling it a quake measuring an eight on the rector.

Elsewhere, beneath the earth's surface, the heat was unbearable to any living soul. Within the devil's realm, Satan was furious with some of his soldiers. He yelled ferociously.

Siege of Darkness/Robert Taylor

"I need more human souls! You must work through the ones that are filled with hatred, the most devious and uncaring. Work side by side with them to bring about the demise of this insignificant civilization!. Leave me, you fools, and do as I have instructed or I will destroy you as well!"

After that was said, his army could be seen as they transformed back into dogs, wolves and humans. They rose from the depths of hell, back onto the earth.

***

At two o'clock that next morning, Chris was on his knees, praying beside his bed. Visions of him as a kid, seeing his grandfather drinking heavily, while ranting about Malic, consumed him. *I know exactly who you are and why you're here! You can't fool me! I'm not scared of you! My father may have been, but not I! You can take my very life if so wish, but I will never grovel for you!* Another vision of his mother and father, who died mysteriously in their bed while asleep, haunted him. His grandfather cried his heart out, later walking around jittery, continuously yelling. *"That son of a bitch! Show yourself, you son of a bitch! I'm not afraid of you!"*

Chris, the elder of the brothers, saw and understood a lot more. He knew something wasn't right. After that mental imagery down memory lane, he gripped his old crucifix within both hands, while pressing his forehead against it. His bible was opened to, *John 5:18 Whoever is born of God does not practice sin; but he that is born of God keeps himself, and that wicked one touches him not*!

In a tear-filled voice, he began to confessed.

"Dear father, please walk with me through this hell I live in, into the paradise you promise there of tomorrow. I have

Siege of Darkness/Robert Taylor

found myself drinking the devil's nectar. My thoughts are evil, as my mind conjures memories of the past. I beg of you, deliver my soul from what plagues my dreams and thoughts! Dear lord, protect me as you have done for years. Please, keep these demonic forces from around me. I am at your disposal. Amen." He finished, kissed and hung the crucifix just over his bed, next to a picture of his wife Tessa. After which, he piled back the sheets, lied down and closed his eyes.

Between his cracked bedroom door, Jason watched his father's ritual, the same as many nights before. He wondered what his father was so afraid of, and if it could be the stories. Closing the door, he climbed back into bed, closed his eyes and, within minutes, he was fast asleep. Floating off to dreamland, he connected with the stories his uncles told him and the monsters, vampires, and creatures his imagination conjured. He tossed and turned as he fought with them like a gladiator!

Caught up in memories of yesterday, Chris reflected back to a time, when he was trying to strangle his wife while she slept. In this vivid but troubled memory, it was three o'clock in the morning, when he awakened to her beet-red face and her forcefully smacking at him, yelling for him to stop. Afterwards, he remembered telling her, he was fighting a beast, a demon of some sort. That's when he woke up with his hands around her neck. Later, he started acting strange and she left and took Jason with her.

He pleaded with her to come back and swore he would seek help.

They talked back and forth for months, everything seemed to be going well. She decided to give him another chance, as long as he did what he promised. Three days after, she dropped a teary eyed six year old Jason off, and left him standing alone on the porch. Afterwards, she disappeared for a few years and he never forgave her for it.

Drenched in perspiration, he woke up and starting reciting; *"Gracious heavenly father, in Jesus Christ's name...please..."* It was rare that he got a good night's sleep, as it showed on his face.

That next breezy afternoon, Chris was arguing with his brother, Willie, as they sat in Willie's eighteen wheeler.

"Why do you and Jimmy continue to tell Jason these stories? Do you guys even remember what those same stories did to Grandpa? He's in a damn asylum, coo-coo for Cocoa Puffs! Can't you guys see what it's doing to Jason? Do you even care? Because, if you did, you'd stop this nonsense! The boy is taking it to school and the teachers are complaining now! Out of respect for me, could you guys...please stop! I'm begging!"

"Okay, I get it. If that's what you want...then that's what it is."

"I appreciate it." Chris looked him in the eyes, opened the truck door, climbed down, closed the door and walked towards the house. Willie pulled off as the long trailer connected to the semi followed.

Later that evening, as the wind grew stronger, Chris, Willie, and Jimmy sat in the living room, talking about old times. With beer bottles everywhere, they seemed to be getting along fine.

"You know, Willie, when I think about how Grandpa worked all these acres by himself, I'm amazed! He stayed out in that hot sun for hours...sun up to sun down...damn!"

"Yeah...he was a tough dude! Stubborn as hell, though!"

Siege of Darkness/Robert Taylor

"Shit...he scared me! I watched him wring a chicken's neck and take his head off without batting an eye!" Chris stated.

"That's nothing, I saw him gut a cow!" Willie said trumping Chris.

"Old granddad was a special type of dude! I miss him and his stories," Jimmy pondered deeply.

***

That same night, Sherrod sat on a stoop, drinking with his friends.

"Welcome home, my dude!" one of them stated as he passed a bottle of clear liquor to him.

"Glad to be here!" He turned up the bottle and guzzled a third of it.

"Here's some change for your pocket, my brother." Walt, a hefty guy of medium height, told him as he pulled out a knot.

The group hung out all night, taking Sherrod around town showing him a good time. They got him good and drunk and dropped him off at the rooming house. He stumbled up the steps, making all types of noise. His boys sat in the four-door idling car, laughing at him as they watched. The lights in the hall came on and a door opened.

"Could you make a little less noise when you come in? Some of us got to get up and go to work in the morning! " his landlady expressed angrily.

"I apologize...my boys took me out, welcoming me home." He staggered past her and up more steps. At the second level, with a drunken grin, he turned and jammed the key in the door to open it. She walked back in her place, disgusted and shaking her head.

Siege of Darkness/Robert Taylor

4 THE MEETING

Thursday, September 6, 1979

That evening, after a nice dinner, Sherrod relaxed in his parent's living room. He was talking to his father, while his mother was cleaning off the dining room table. His father, a bald, dark skinned man, smiled as he spoke,
"Son, I'm glad you're home. I know our relationship hasn't been the greatest, but I do love you! I just want you to do better. There's nothing in those streets for you. You're a smart kid, get it together!"
"Dad, I know, that's why I stay away. I'm gon' try real hard this time, I promise you!"
"Okay. It's your life now! We're not gon' be around forever!"
"I know…I know. Oh yeah Dad, can I borrow a hundred dollars? I have to pay next week's rent. My boys been helping me out, but I don't want to keep asking them. I'll give it right back. That's, if you can stand it." His father shook his head, rose and headed up the stairs. His mother came in the livingroom, kissed him on the cheek, and followed her husbands lead. When his father returned, he put five twenty-dollar bills in Sherrod's left hand, as he looked him in the eyes and hugged him.
"All I ask is that you get it together, son! Don't worry about paying me back. You getting it together will be payback

enough!" He stared at him with concern. The two smiled at one another and together they walked to the front door.

"There's an opening for a janitor at my job. Come fill out an application and I'll put in a good word, you being my son and all." His father smiled, as they stood on the stoop.

"Okay, I'll do that. Tell Mom I love her and I'll see you guys real soon." Sherrod finished as he walked away and down the street.

***

The sun sank lower in the sky, as the light of the day drained, giving way to the velvety dark of night. Jason sat on the front porch, writing after an hour-long phone conversation with his mother. He looked out, as his father pulled up and jumped from his truck angry about something. Jason hopped to his feet and stood at attention to greet him. His grin broadcasted how happy he was.

"Hey, Dad…I talked to Mom today!"

"Not right now!" he spat marching past Jason and into the house. Following behind him, Jason wondered what had him so unnerved.

Through the house, he rushed, into his bedroom, where he went in his closet and pulled down some books. Seeing young Jason watching, he yelled, "Get ready for bed! It's getting late," and slammed the door in his face.

In his room, Jason, who saw the title before his father closed the door in his face, wrote it down for future reference.

Chris searched through the book, as a recent incident had him flipping the pages wildly.

"Where is it?" he uttered lightly. After finding what he was looking for, he sighed and started reading softly.

Siege of Darkness/Robert Taylor

In the last days, there will be civil unrest. People will become lovers of self and money. They will become arrogant, abusive, unholy, heartless and reckless. A brother will betray his brother to death, and a father his child; and children will rebel against their parents and have them put to death. In this time of unholiness, Lucifer (the light bearer) will come to rest in the clouds along with his angels. He will perform miracles and acts of kindness, as he works to deceive the people. Many will believe he is God!

After reading that passage, he pondered on several incidents that happened over the last few months. One was of children cursing at their parents in the streets. Another, was a fellow worker was killed by his son, as he laid sleeping in a recliner. Finally, as he was driving home, he saw an image in the sky, a red face with a pair of red eyes. After another hour of reading, he was blown away and had to lay back and digest all that he had taken in.

The following Monday over breakfast, Jason stared across the table at his father, who chewed on a slice of bacon. Chris noticed and grinned.

"Dad, why can't you and Mom get back together, so we can be a family again?"

"Your mother and I have our differences. I love her, but it'll never work! We grew apart. Sometimes that happens."

"She says something happened, and you were never the same afterward."

"Eat your breakfast, boy!" he commanded, attempting to cut the conversation short.

It was silent for only a moment and then,

Siege of Darkness/Robert Taylor

"Dad, have any of you ever seen a supernatural being? I mean, since you guys been on this earth?" Jason asked as he looked over and bit a beef link in half.

"Boy, why are you trying my patience this morning? Those were old folk tales, nothing more! Now finish your breakfast, so we can get out of here."

"But, Dad, I keep having these dreams and they seem so real!"

"Don't 'but' me, I don't want to hear another peep about none of this. You hear me? Those damn brothers of mine, they never quit."

Jason tuned him out and got up from the table.

Chris shook his head in disbelief.

Fifteen minutes later, as they drove to Jason's school, Chris struck up a conversation. Jason was quiet the entire time, and stared out the window.

"Son, I don't mean to yell at you, but I just want you to stay focused on your school work. I don't want you to be an old miserable man like me. Do you understand? Make me proud." He rubbed Jason's head.

Jason looked at his father making eye contact.

***

By noon in Newark, at Barringer High School, Elijah Cross, an eager, intelligent, young, Black teen was deep into his studies. The class assignment for the month was Greek mythology. He was doing a paper on Zeus. As he read paragraph after paragraph, he learned of Zeus' brothers, sisters, and wives. He learned of his brother Hades, the lord of the underworld and ruler of the dead. He also learned of his son Aris, a murderous coward. He became intrigued, so much

Siege of Darkness/Robert Taylor

so that his eyes widened. Page after page, he became engulfed, so much that when a fellow student touched his shoulder, he jumped and fell out his seat. The class laughed as he sat on the floor with a mystified look on his face.

Later, as the sun descended, and streetlights came on a few at a time, Sherrod sat on a stoop with his friends, drinking and talking over old times. He grinned as they rehashed some old stories.

"Remember when you got into an argument with that bus driver and he went to chase you and tripped and fell off the bus? He hit his head and was out cold! We thought he was dead and ran like hell!" One friend reminisced.

"But, the funniest time was when you made old man Daniels take off all his clothes and run down the street naked," another added.

"What was the reason you did that, anyway?"

"I don't want to talk about all that old shit!" Sherrod angrily stated, as he jumped up and the others got up along with him and marched down the street.

As they made their way, they turned over garbage cans, swung on poles, and hollered out obscenities.

In the meantime, as Father O'Brien walked down Market Street toward Penn. Station, Newark, he acted totally like a tourist, as he marveled over the fruit and vegetable stands. The proprietors swept and hosed down the sidewalk, preparing to shut down. People were everywhere grabbing what they could beforehand.

Later that night at 10:00 p.m. in a darkened subway, Sherrod and his friends pushed passed people, jumped turnstiles, and bum rushed a train coming from New York

Siege of Darkness/Robert Taylor

City. As the train's doors chimed opened, they raced onboard and began to bother passengers. As some got off, shaking their heads, and others sat in fear, Father O'Brien, who happened to be getting up, spoke.

"Leave these good people alone," he demanded.

"Sit down and mind your business, old man!" Sherrod shouted turning to face him. His boys stood around him, smiling sinisterly.

Father O'Brien also had an evil smirk as he walked up to face Sherrod, his breath savoring tartness fouler than a dead body weeks after decomposing. His eyes were soulless, but yet hypnotic and scary.

Sherrod and his posse backed away.

The man's eyes widened, as his foul mouth opened and his tongue slithered out, launching a clot of plasma, which landed on Sherrod's right cheek. The train chimed again, alerting everyone that it would be moving on shortly.

Sherrod, angered by the man's disrespectful act, frowned, as he wiped his face. The clot, as if a living organism, made its way to the side of his mouth.

Father O'Brien smiled again, his eyes growing dark and mysterious.

Filled with fear, Sherrod and his gang fled through the open door, as did all the other passengers on the train.

Two police officers in the vicinity alertly drew their weapons and cautiously stepped on as it sat. Coming face-to-face with Father O'Brien, they stood before him with their guns pointed outward, ready for whatever should happen.

Father O'Brien smiled as he stood with his arms folded.

"Is there some kind of problem, officers?" he asked.

"We're not sure! Do you know why everyone ran from the train?" one officer asked as they looked around.

Siege of Darkness/Robert Taylor

Suddenly, Father O'Brien's nostrils flared, his eyes grew dark once again and the train started to shake.

Tumbling around, the officers feverously tried to grab hold of anything to keep steady. Stunned by it all, they lost their guns in the commotion.

Father O'Brien never moved an inch.

"I have no idea." Father O'Brien added as the turbulence ceased. "You guys enjoy the rest of your evening!" He casually exited the train.

As the doors closed, the officers watched from a frozen state of fear, as the train left the station.

Thirty minutes later, after walking into a nearby hotel, Father O'Brien stood patiently at the front desk waiting for assistance. A tall, slender, Black man, wearing a shirt and tie, walked up, smiling.

"May I be of some help?" he offered.

"Yes, my name is James O'Brien and I would like a single occupancy room, preferably on one of the top floors."

"I'll see what I can do." The clerk walked away and into an office. He returned, holding a gold key, hanging from a green tag with the numbers 1213 engraved in gold.

"Here you go sir," the clerk passed the key and added, "That'll be $65.00 plus tax which comes to $68.90.

***

Elsewhere, as Sherrod and the gang raced away, he slowed nearly to a halt, grimacing, as he could feel the acids in his stomach become unsettled. Pains began to shoot, causing him to fold over. One of his boys stopped, as he looked around for Sherrod and noticed him a few houses back, holding himself. He hollered to the others, and they all rushed back to his aide.

Siege of Darkness/Robert Taylor

There as he sat on a stoop, his boys gathered around him, voicing their concerns.

"Are you alright, Sherrod?" one questioned, between deep breath.

"What the hell! That man was scary...wasn't he?" another pointed out, as he sat down next to Sherrod. "You don't look good."

"I'm okay. I'll be alright in a minute, just a little indigestion," Sherrod assured them. After this reassurance, the group relaxed and continued on their way.

***

Father O'Brien sat on the bed of his hotel room with an open suitcase beside him. Mental images of the train incident surfaced. He saw the plasma as he launched it, landing on Sherrod's face, where it crawled across his cheek and into the side of his mouth. As it slithered down his throat, making its way into his stomach, it would eventually compromise his bloodstream. Reflecting on episodes of old memories, he recalled the day Father O'Conner confronted him and threw Holy water on him and how it had no effect. How he laughed and told him, "Your Holy water is nothing but frivolous drops of rain to me. I am a god, you fool!" Stunned by his reaction, Father O'Conner ran away and informed the others in the church, but by then, Father O'Brien was long gone. He also recalled his untimely death, where lightning struck him as he sat under a tree, reading the Bible. Coming out of the trance, an overlord caught him off guard.

I see you are one worthy... and it is pleasing to see such loyalty and unbridled contempt for these insignificant beings!

Siege of Darkness/Robert Taylor

Father O'Brien just listened and nodded in agreement. The overlord disappeared as quickly as he appeared. Father O'Brien unpack his suitcase. Not long after, he grabbed a towel and walked into the bathroom.

***

In the wee hours of Tuesday morning, on a darkened street, an older, gray-haired White man, wearing a dark blue suit, had just gotten off work. He gaily walked with a thick, White prostitute into a smelly, dark alleyway. The man smiled as the prostitute pushed him up against a graffiti-covered brick wall, slid her hand down his bulging crouch, and kissed him on the neck. He closed his eyes and relaxed as she dropped down to her knees. At first, her hot moist lips and saliva seemed to have him giddy and dancing against the wall, but then suddenly his eyes popped wide open. As his face tightened up, he let out a loud piercing scream. Blood Splattered the brick wall, as his eyes fluttered at the prostitute standing before him with his blood dripping from her mouth, down her chin. Eyes fiery red, her face distorted as she growled before burying her face in his neck, sinking her teeth deep into his veins. He yelled continuously until there was no strength to do so.

Two-thirty that same morning, on a stoop in the hood, Sherrod looked into his open shaking hands. His face had a scary look about it. The color of his eyes changed from brown to yellow to solid black to normal. His boys, who sat around him laughing and joking, were oblivious to what was taking place. Sherrod looked up at the sky and took a long deep breath. Every breath after seemed as if his first. Closing his

Siege of Darkness/Robert Taylor

fist tightly, his knuckles crackled, his veins bulged, and his chest rose and fell.

That afternoon, Jason was home from school. After washing his semi-truck, Uncle Willie was on the back porch, drinking as usual. Jason walked up on him, startling him.

"Boy, you don't sneak up on people like that, announce yourself!"

"I'm sorry uncle."

"What's going on with you?"

"Not much…hey, uncle, do you mind telling me another story?"

"Okay, boy, but not a word of this to your father. I really don't want to hear his mouth!"

"I promise." Jason crossed his fingers and smiled. Uncle Willie sat down, and got comfortable.

"It was a full moon, because you know that's when you could hear the spirits as they became vocal. The bodies that they inhabited became weakened and couldn't do much of anything. But, check this out! One of the spirit, who was said to be Malic, stayed free of the flesh when the priest burned the old soul that he inhabited. They stood around it, chanting. The louder they chanted, the louder the spirit of Malic laughed. 'You cannot kill me!' he carried on. Everyone, including the townsmen that were there, were never the same after that. They all died with great fear of him. In later years, when the priest by the name of Harry O'Conner was sitting beneath a tree reading from the Bible, it was said a demonic spirit approached him, many assumed it was Malic! The spirit attempted to persuade him again. Father O'Conner started reciting, '*God, our Lord, King of the ages, the All-powerful and All-mighty. You who made everything and transformed everything by Your will,*' and right in the middle of his recital,

Siege of Darkness/Robert Taylor

a bolt of lightning came crashing down. It struck him and the tree, causing him to suffer a massive heart attack and he died right there on the spot. It's not known whether Malic caused it or not. He wanted his soul bad, mainly because he couldn't have him, which made him that much more valuable!"

"Uncle, is this one connected to the others?"

"Yes, your great-grandpa told us a little bit each night until he got sick. I used to love hearing them, just like you! He also told us his father had journals on this stuff. Before he died, he was supposedly chronicling all his notes."

"Who has those notes now?"

"No one knows. He never told anyone where he kept them and they were never found. Now get out of here!"

"Uncle Willie, do you think he was just making this stuff up or do you really believe this stuff happened?"

"Coming from that crazy ol' kook, who knows!" Willie stared at Jason, who sat engaged. With nothing more to say, Willie chased Jason away.

Jason laughed and darted into the house, straight to his room and grabbed a pen and his notebook from his dresser. Flopping across the bed, he started writing.

My great, great-grandfather kept notes of all the events and to this very day no one knows what he did with them. His son, my great-grandfather, told the stories as told to him and is now in an asylum.

***

Bored, Elijah lay across his bed, as rain fell that afternoon. He put aside the romance novel he was reading and picked up a book on mythology. It captured his attention immediately. He began highlighting different parts throughout the book. He grabbed the Bible from the nightstand and opened it to Genesis 1:2. He highlighted passages from both books such as, *"God created man and all living things."* In mythology, there came to be several authorities above all and the most notable was Zeus. In both books, food attributed to the fall from grace and a great flood embarked upon the world. War also had become commonplace. Intrigued by the similar characteristics of biblical understandings, the supernatural qualities and mystical personalities, Elijah continued highlighting. Before he knew it, the birds were chirping, and the sun was rising. With his eyelids nearly shut, he refused to sleep, as he thirsted for knowledge. Page after page, he envisioned every scene. He had gotten to a part where Herod, the king at the time Jesus was to be born, ordered the three wise men to find baby Jesus and surrender Him. When they didn't, he ordered the killing of all newborns in Bethlehem. In mythology, after successfully ridding the world of all his newly born, Cronus' wife, Rhea, managed to bear a child and hide it. This child was Zeus, who later grew up to conquered his father.

Closing the book to rest his eyes, Elijah got up and walked out of his room and across the hall to the bathroom. Hearing him moving around, his father met him after he turned out the lights and was heading back to his bedroom.

"Son, I'm going out of town for a week to see a potential client about some real-estate. I should be back by the middle of next week. I doubled your allowance just in case."

"Dad, you know we were supposed to go see the Giants-Redskins' game Monday."

"I know son, I'm sorry about that. I'll have to make it up to you, when I get back."

Siege of Darkness/Robert Taylor

"It's okay." Elijah was little disappointed as he walked back into his room. He father smiled and walked back into his bedroom and turned out the lights.

***

That evening after sleeping the day away, Sherrod jumped out of bed and ran to the bathroom to vomit. With his face in the toilet, he felt his insides heating up. Hanging there a few minutes, he gathered himself as he began to feel a little better. Back on his feet, he went back into his room, where he flopped across the bed and started to cough lightly. As he lay there, his mind was beginning to challenge him, as he tried to maintain control.

Siege of Darkness/Robert Taylor

5 SUCCUMBING TO THE DEVIL

Wednesday, September 12, 1979

As morning drifted closer to noon, Sherrod lay in bed, curled in a fetal position, with excruciating stomach pain. His body riddled with fever, and sweating profusely, he grunted and screamed. Shaking and foaming at the mouth, he felt as if he were in his last hours. A large, open bottle of magnesia citrate sat on a raggedy dresser, with a stained tablespoon beside it. His phone rang, capturing his attention.

"Hel…lo," he painfully snuffled out.

"Boy, are you all right?" his father asked worried after hearing his voice.

"Yeah Dad, just some serious stomach pains."

"Okay, boy, you taking something for it… I hope?"

"Yes…oh, God, I got to go! I got to go! I'll call you in the morning." Sherrod hung up, not waiting to hear a response.

Minutes later, Walt called him.

"What's going on my brother?" he greeted in a happy tone.

"Not feeling too good; My stomach is still killing me!"

"I hope one of those dudes in prison didn't get you pregnant!"

"You…always joking, this is serious!" He moaned in pain. "This shit hurts!"

"Damn, man, I'm sorry! You need anything?"

Siege of Darkness/Robert Taylor

"No...I'm good, just need to rest. I'll call in a little while." Sherrod hung up on him as well. He closed his eyes and attempted to fall asleep.

Before Elijah left for school, he was talking to his mother.

"Boy, you know your father. He loves what he does. You and I can go to the game, if you'd like?" she offered as an alternative.

"I'd like that...and thanks, Ma." Elijah smiled.

"For what?"

"For being you!"

He grabbed his books and marched out the door. While he was walking, he envisioned all the times his father put work before him. Believing some situations were coincidental and others just flat out lies, Elijah continued to school.

***

That afternoon, Jason was on the phone with his mother. He was happy and smiling from ear to ear.

"How's Mommy's favorite little boy? You know I miss you! When I come back to town, I'm going to make sure to take you out, just you and I...okay?"

"You promise? I can't wait! When are you coming?" Jason's voice projected his excitement.

"I should be there by the end of next week." she told him, guesstimating.

"If you're a good boy, I'll bring you a gift when I come! I love you, son, goodbye!" she hung up. Smiling proudly, Jason turned on the television and relaxed.

****

Siege of Darkness/Robert Taylor

September 17th, Sherrod entered a local grocery store. Browsing through the racks, he grabbed a bag of chips and a soda, then walked to the counter to pay for them. The older black man behind the counter smiled, as he rang the items up. Sherrod, spaced out and sweating, began to look a bit nervous. An overlord appeared in the background, while the man's focus was on the register. Sherrod quickly pulled a small 25 handgun from his hoody pocket. Seeing this, the man froze. Looking around, Sherrod shouted,

"Give me the money, now! Hurry the hell up!" Without hesitation, the man did exactly as told, before he gave Sherrod a cold stare. Sherrod turned and ran toward the door to make his exit. The man reached under the counter, grabbed his gun and raced out to try to catch him.

Sherrod, poppy eyed, gun dangling from his right hand and a fist full of dollars in his left, darted across a street. A woman on the sidewalk stopped and ran back the other way. The storeowner appeared in the doorway seconds behind him with a .22 caliber shotgun. Filled with rage, he shot at Sherrod several times.

Sherrod returned gunfire, and hurried on. A few blocks away, he took shelter and rested in the hallway of an apartment building. He crawled behind a staircase, tucked the gun in his belt, and counted the money.

"Two hundred twenty-four dollars," he mumbled with a slight smile. Sirens blared, as patrol cars raced through the area.

An hour later, he peeked out the door to see if there were any cops or other people around. Seeing the coast was clear, he quickly started making his way to the rooming house, noticing police had taped off the area near the store, with patrol cars positioned in front.

Siege of Darkness/Robert Taylor

***

On a breezy, warm Monday, Elijah and his mother were sitting in the MetlLife Stadium in East Rutherford, New Jersey, as the New York Giants and the Washington Redskins took the field. Elijah looked over at her and smiled, because she was always trying to make things right. As the two of them wore the home team's jerseys, they rooted for them all the way to a 27-0 loss. Elijah enjoyed himself, as did his mother, the loss had no impact on their time together.

***

Thursday morning, a small radio announced the news that hurricane David killed over 2000 people in Dominician Republic, and other parts of the carribean. Then went on to commend Micheal Jackson for his Off the wall album, which was well on its way to being his best ever. With a number of chart busting hits, he was cementing himself as a strong solo presence. As the radio personality played his music, police officers bum-rushed the rooming house Sherrod's resided in. With their guns drawn, They caught Sherrod off guard while he slept. He jumped from the bed to the ceiling, his finger like claws locking into the plaster. His stomach pulsated as the officers immediately aimed their guns right at him. He relaxed, jumped down, and surrendered. As he did, his flesh seemed to change.

"Cuff him!" yelled the bewildered sergeant to the shaken officers in the room. Astonished by his feat, they were reluctant. Slightly nervous, one officer cautiously placed his cuffs on Sherrod's wrist. Arrested for murder, amidst all the gunfire, a bullet struck the storeowner in the head. Led down the stairs and onto the porch, the officer held onto him tightly. The landlady shook her head, as she watched angrily.

On the ride to the precinct, Sherrod began to get violently ill. He cried and carried on as he grimaced from the pains in his stomach. Sweating again, he regurgitated the content onto the floor of the patrol car. Not knowing what to do, one officer radioed it in.

"Captain. The suspect seems to be in a lot of pain and is coughing and throwing up. What should we do?"

"He's probably dope sick or something? Is that him making all that noise in the background?" The captain went on.

"Yeah...he's going through it."

"Shit, bring him in, and if he needs medical attention, we'll take him from here!"

"Got you, captain."

The entire ride to the precinct, Sherrod banged his head against the door and the iron divider.

"Help! Something's happening to me! Somebody, please help me!" he cried with tears running down his face. The officer behind the steering wheel looked at his partner and sped on as he began to get worst.

Twenty minutes later, as they dragged him into the dreary and dimly lit precinct, he looked like they had beaten him up. His face was swollen, his eyes dark and bloodshot red. His mouth hanging as he slurred out,

"Help me!"

"What the hell happened to him?" the Captain asked as he came from behind the desk, looking Sherrod over.

"He didn't look like this when we put him in the car. He kept screaming and knocking around in the back seat as if he were actually tussling with someone! The shit was crazy!"

Siege of Darkness/Robert Taylor

"Get him to a hospital, so he can stop bleeding all over my floor! He needs medical attention!" With their instructions, they headed out the door, dragging Sherrod back to their patrol car. After carefully placing him inside, they sped off in the direction of Beth Israel Medical Center.

***

That evening around six-thirty, Jason was playing in his backyard, when he looked up into the sky and saw a full moon. He released a blood curdling scream as some kind of force picked him off the ground and whisked him back and forth across the yard, as if he was flying with assistance of an unknown source. Finally, he crashed to the ground. Wicked laughter ensued, followed by an unfamiliar voice.

"I see you are an eager young and aggressive soul. Not yet ready, but in time I can see you being the catalyst to my legacy!"

Jason's eyes widened, as he gasped for air, running in the house, yelling, "Uncle Willie, Uncle Willie!" He was amazed at what transpired and lit up as he stumbled about searching for his Uncle.

Jason stood in his doorway of his uncles bedroom, gathering his breath. Startled by Jason's presence. Uncle Willie, who lay resting on his bed, sat up, awaiting Jason's first words.

"Uncle Willie, the craziest thing just happened to me!" he said between deep breath.

"Something picked me up and spun me around and carried me across the yard! I felt like I was flying! You should have seen it. And, after it put me down, a voice spoke to me. It said something about a legacy!" A hyper and astonished Jason ranted dramatically.

"Stop playing Jason," Uncle Willie said in the midst of his laughter.

"I'm for real, don't laugh at me!" Jason pouted realizing his uncle wasn't taking him seriously. Willie continued giggling and laughing, causing Jason to walk away.

***

Two days later, Sherrod woke up chained to a bed in the hospital, and his vision was fuzzy. All he could see was a silver badge hanging on what looked like a blue uniform. The face wasn't clear.

"Officer, what's going on? What happened to me?"

"You flipped out in the back of a patrol car after being arrested." Sherrod's vision began to clear up. Seeing all the tubes running into his body, he started panicking. The rest I can't tell you, because I wasn't there!"

"Call a doctor in here." Call a doctor in here, now! I need answers!" Sherrod demanded confused.

Five minutes later, a doctor entered the room smiling.

"Ah...Mr. Tillman you're awake. Good, now we can talk. You seem to be okay. What you were experiencing was probably a brief psychotic disorder. Have you been under a lot of stress lately?"

"No...not really," he answered after a little thought.

"Well, you're okay now. You just need a little rest." The doctor thoroughly checked him out and got ready to exit the room.

Siege of Darkness/Robert Taylor

"Where he's going he's got plenty of time to rest!" the officer said jokingly under his breath as the doctor rushed past him.

***

That afternoon, after arriving in North Carolina, Jason's mother, Tessa, had rented a car and went shopping. Afterwards, she called Jason and drove to pick him up. Once he was in the passenger seat, Tessa leaned over and kissed her baby boy. Giving him a gift, she waited for him to open it. Young Jason tore off the wrapping paper. Once he opened the box, he lit up immediately. She smiled as he held up the rock'em sock'em robots.

"Thanks Ma, I love it! Aww man, I can't wait until I get home."

"Who are you going to get to play with you?"

"Uncle Willie will play with me. He likes stuff like this!" Jason put everything back in the box and placed it on the floor of the car. His mother smiled as she listened and he was overjoyed.

****

Weeks later, Sherrod was beginning to adjust to the prison life. He was sitting in his cell reading when someone darkened his doorway. He looked up to see who and why. A smile grew on his face as he jumped to his feet.

"Hey…hey, what's good with you?" Sherrod hugged this hefty person tight.

"Ain't too much, I'm here!" he replied as they broke their embrace.

Siege of Darkness/Robert Taylor

"I heard you're in here for murder boy! What the hell happened out there?"

"Money was real funny, and I robbed a store. As I got to the door, the owner grabbed his joint and started shooting at me. I took off, bustin' back and I guess one of the bullets hit him and killed him, so here I am!"

"Word? Damn! Well, I'm in here for a parole violation. I'm done! They broke me! After this, I'm not coming back. God willing. I promise you!" The two talked until a guard yelled for them to lock in.

For the next month, Sherrod was in and out of court. Unable to afford a lawyer, the courts appointed him a state attorney. The prosecutor played hardball due to his priors and was trying to send him away for a long time. Realizing his back was up against the wall, after several visits to see the judge. Sherrod decided to take the offer that was on the table. His only other option was to take it to trial, but if he lost, he was looking at twenty five years. It was a no brainer, there was a witness, so he pleaded guilty to manslaughter and armed robbery. He got fifteen years and he would be eligible for parole in twelve years. Depressed, he sat in his cell.

Thanksgiving Day, as he tossed and turned on his sweat soaked cot, he tried to open his eyes and get up, but it was as if something had him pinned down, while his eyes was sealed shut. Eventually, he forced his eyes open as he flipped over on his back gasping and breathing heavily.

"What the hell?" he yelled as he looked around in the darkness, wondering if there was someone or something else in the room with him.

Up off the cot, he walked to the bars and looked out. To his amazement, he saw spirits, ghostly prisoners moving about as if they were actually there. They were talking, smoking, moving up and down the tiers. Sherrod rubbed his eyes as if he were hallucinating, because he couldn't believe what he was seeing. A voice spoke,

These are deceased inmates that made deals with Lucifer. They are floaters here, whose purpose is to encourage the suicidal and weak-minded to join them. You can see them, only because you have been chosen. Chosen to legitimize my God's presence amongst the living! Welcome...

"How is that?" Sherrod asked, turning his back to the bars and stared into the darkness awaiting an answer.

"There will be a time for that conversation. Right now, there is a more pressing matter at hand...

"...And, what is that?" Sherrod asked after peeking back to watch the floorshow.

At that moment, like a cloud of smoke, all the spirits floated upward and out through an open vent.

"When you leave this place, there will be things expected of you. I cannot tell you what these things will be, but nevertheless your life will depend on it! I will be coming to speak to you again...

***

That same evening, Chris's ex-wife surprised them with a large turkey and all the trimmings. With his mother and father at the table together, Jason was the happiest kid alive. Uncle Willie and Uncle Jimmy were there too. They all laughed and talked like a normal family. After they were finished and watching television, Jason fell asleep resting against his mother's left shoulder.

Siege of Darkness/Robert Taylor

After putting him to bed, Chris and Tessa sat in the living room where they began to talk.

"I know you're glad I showed up with that turkey! That dried out one you made was terrible!" she laughingly poked fun.

"It wasn't that bad."

"So, why is it still sitting there? Why no one ate any of it?"

"Anyway...why did you leave like that?" Chris asked, tired of her ridiculing him about his cooking.

"I didn't know what to do...you scared me! You can't blame me, you almost killed me!"

"You know I was hallucinating! I didn't even know how that happened."

"That's not the only thing; you were acting really strange and scary!"

"So...why did you drop Jason off and leave him...if you thought I was crazy?" he questioned.

"I needed to get a second job or a better paying one and I couldn't do it and take care of him. The job I applied for in Chicago required me to be there in three days. I had to get a last minute flight, pack and figure out what to do with Jason until I got stable."

"It must have paid great, for you to uproot and leave our son behind," Chris stressed to her.

"It did...and I needed the money to get out of debt and get my life back on track. After our break-up, it was hard for me. Really hard for me!"

"Nobody told you to leave, you left on your own."

"No, you were acting like a crack pot and I didn't feel safe around you."

"So, what kind of job was this that you abandoned everything for?"

Siege of Darkness/Robert Taylor

"I sought out an occupation only a desperate person would consider. I, was working as a CPA for this company that was laundering millions of dollars a year. I didn't know that at first, that's why I took the job. After my second month there, I started seeing crazy things take place. That's when I knew I had to ease my way out, before I was caught up in that mess or killed for knowing too much!"

"How did they find you?"

"I sent out resumes, and they were one of the first to call me. For the money they offered me, I didn't ask any questions. I just thought about getting my head above water and living a little. I was tired of struggling."

"So, are you still working with them?"

"No, not anymore. Thank God, I met this guy at my bank that owns an investment firm and he offered me a job." She sighed.

"I still love you," Chris stated, blindsiding her, as his face held a look of sincerity.

"That's sweet, but I'm dating someone now!"

"Is it serious?" he questioned.

"Somewhat…he's a very nice guy," she answered softly, as she stared into his eyes and touched his right cheek.

****

The next day, Sherrod was confronted by a Hatian named Pierre, as they were walking towards the day room to watch television.

"Hey, what's up, man? I'm Pierre and you are?"

"…not interested," Sherrod answered.

Siege of Darkness/Robert Taylor

"I'm not selling anything. I just see you every day sitting by yourself and looking depressed. I thought you could use a friend."

"I'm not depressed and friendship is far overrated!"

"Oh…okay, when you need a friend look me up, I ain't going nowhere, at least not for the next three to four years, anyway!" He turned to catch up to someone else.

***

Day after day, Jason rushed through his homework, so he could read and absorb the material he took time to gather from libraries and bookstores. He was becoming so obsessed that he did his school reports on the supernatural.

On a class assignment, he chose to read an essay on those of a superior nature. After his teacher called on him, he gathered his papers from his desk and walked to the front of the classroom. He cleared his throat and with a smile, he looked out at his classmates.

"My report is on the *Werewolf*. *"From as early as the 1800's, werewolves were thought to have been the ultimate shapeshifters and carnivores. The myth has it that they came about along with witches in the Middle Ages. According to folklore, they didn't only surface during full moons. They are otherwise known as Children of the moon and, like the vampire, they were Downworlders and considered demonic…contrary to popular beliefs, they can only be slowed down by a silver bullet, not killed!"*

Jason went on in an animated voice, with full dramatics and had everyone's attention, including his teacher. When he was finished, the mesmerized students stood and applauded.

Siege of Darkness/Robert Taylor

****

That first weekend, beneath a breeze in December, Chris was driving from his home into town. As he pushed along a stretch of road, he noticed what looked like a human body lying in a patch of grass. He slowed down, looking in his rearview mirror to be certain. Unable to see clearly, against his better judgement, he turned around and went back. The body was gone, but there was blood everywhere. Beyond the trees came a loud growl, which caused Chris to take off running. Jumping back in his truck, he gassed up and never looked back.

He kissed his cross and said,
"Dear God, I pray that wasn't what I thought it was!" scared out of his wits, he thought of his previous encounters.

***

Inside the prison, a few inmates walked by Sherrod's cell and stared him down. Sherrod happened to look up as they passed and went back to browsing through an old magazine. Dropping it to the floor, he rose and walked out of his cell, out onto the open tier. Looking around, he noticed those same guys glaring back at him. He went back in his cell and thought nothing of it.

***

On December,17th, Chris was out on a date with a pretty blonde. They sat in the rear of a local restaurant named Ray's. His pager sounded as they were talking. He stopped to look at the screen. Not recognizing the number, he thought nothing of it. It sounded again, followed by the numbers 911. Excusing

Siege of Darkness/Robert Taylor

himself, he got up, walked to a payphone near the restroom area, and dialed a number.

"Hello," he greeted.

"Yes, is this Mr. Milosky?"

"Yes it is,"

" I'm Mr. Stein, one of you son's teachers. Do you have a minute to talk?"

"Just a minute, is all I have."

"Your son Jason is in class telling some of the other students that monsters and vampires really exist. He's disrupting the lessons, drawing pictures of me with fangs and wings. I just want you to talk to him; he's a very intelligent kid. He just seemed to be distracted."

"I'll have a talk with him tonight. Thanks for calling and you enjoy the rest of your evening."

Shaking himself free of his thoughts, he walked back to his table. Apologizing for the interruption, he smiled while he picked up his menu and scanned it.

"Is there something wrong?" his date asked.

"Just my son being a kid, that's all." He looked across the table into her eyes.

That evening, after arriving home, Chris walked into Jason's room.

"Wake up, boy!" Chris stood over Jason's bed with his arms folded.

"Yeah," he responded as he opened his eyes.

"What's this I'm hearing you're in school being a clown and disrespecting your teachers?

"Dad, I apologized to him and I told him it wouldn't happen again!"

Siege of Darkness/Robert Taylor

"Okay, since you want to be a clown, I've got something for you, wait until tomorrow! Embarrass me... will you?" he carried on as he walked out the room mumbling.

That next morning Jason woke up to his father's knocking on the door and him pushing it open.

"Here you go, put these on, and hurry up so you're not late!" Chris yelled and closed the door. Jason sat up on the side of the bed, where he held up the pants and shirt his father threw at him. They looked a few sizes too small and were faded. Jason got up, opened the door, and called out.

"Dad...these clothes are too small. I can't fit them...and their out of style!"

"That's what you're wearing today! Since you want to be a clown, you might as well dress like one! Now get in the bathroom, wash your behind... and get dress!"

"Dad, you can't be serious!" Jason spoke as stared at the clothes again.

"Don't try me, I'm dead serious! Go-get- dressed." Chris stood at the bottom of the steps.

A few hours later in the school hallway, Chris was walking Jason to his homeroom. All the kids they passed looked, laughed, and joked about Jason's clothes. Jason frowned angrily as Chris dragged him.

"You want to be a clown; this is what clowns do...get laughed at!"

Days later on Christmas Eve, amidst the bitter cold, Chris was sitting in the livingroom, watching the news and wrapping a gift, while the newscaster ranted about some unusual occurrences and killings. Chris stopped what he was doing to listen.

"Never in the history of the United States," said the newscaster, *"have there ever been so many violent and*

Siege of Darkness/Robert Taylor

unexplained deaths. There have been bodies found, from the east to the west coast, mutilated or drain of their blood. There have also been a lot of wolf and beast sightings, but none of them has been substantiated!

An hour later, he got a call from his ex-wife. Just after he greeted her, she hollered through the phone catching his full attention.

"Hey, what's wrong?" he asked out of concerned.

"I can't believe this...he's leaving me for an old girlfriend on Christmas day! Can you believe this?" she ranted and cried out.

"Calm down, it's going to be all right. Calm down...okay?" Chris cautioned while consoling her. She continued to weep, while he listened and felt like God was presenting him with a second chance.

***

In an asylum deep in the woods, Jason's great-grandfather sat in a padded room, talking to himself. While rocking back and forth, he stared at a wall and repeated,

"I'm not crazy, all of you are! You and thy Lord God believe the wicked can change and become righteous. Can you not see? They're all around us. Look around you! The wicked one is winning! The end is near!" he carried on jolting his head from one side to the next.

Siege of Darkness/Robert Taylor

6

March, 12th, 1980

As the spring brought rain and flowers, Sherrod leaned against the bars constipated in thought. He realized that whatever his body was going through heightened his senses and strength. He could feel the difference when he closed his fist. He also wondered why the spirits of the dead prisoners seemed to be guarding his cell. Were they protecting him from something? The overlord hearing his thoughts, answered.

We are one! They are truly their brother's keeper. This is no sarcasm, this is truth! They are connected to you... in life and in the afterlife. Be not afraid... you are amongst family!"

Sherrod wondered how this was so? How did this come to be? He thought back to the incident on the train and wondered if that was what brought all this to a head. The old man's face settled on his conscious while his sinister presence rode his very thoughts. He envisioned him launching what appeared to be blood into his face, over and over again. Massaging his throat, he suddenly began to revisit the pain as it traveled from his esophagus to his stomach. Things became intense, as it mixed with bodily fluids. He could feel his entire vascular system overrunning and burning as something foreign ran

Siege of Darkness/Robert Taylor

through it. Hyper as he came back out of thought, he looked around and the spirits were gone.

***

The next few days, it rained and the thunder roared, lighting up the sky. Each evening, Chris stood at his bedroom window staring out, as if there was something out there. Trance stricken, his focus was on an area; just beyond some trees. There was light of some sort, a beaming and blinding light. However, he knew the area well enough to know there was nothing out there but forest. He wondered if God was symbolically trying to show him something. Suddenly, that light grew closer and brighter; until it totally blinded him. Out of fear, he backed away, shielding his eyes.

A voice spoke as a spirit of an elderly priest slowly appeared.

"I am the spirit of Harry O'Conner, a former priest of the cloth. I was sent here in response to all your prayers. Call upon me as you see fit. I shall be your guardian, as long as you dwell in this god forsaken world!" The light disappeared as did the voice and image. Chris dropped his arm and stopped squinting. He stood in total shock, not believing what just happened.

***

That evening, the demonic spirits stood like watchdogs once again at Sherrod's cell. This time they were nosier than usual. They seemed amped about something. Standing at the bars, Sherrod stared out to see what was going on.

A prisoner began to yelled,

Siege of Darkness/Robert Taylor

"C.O., yo officer...C.O...my bunkie is bleeding to death in here!" There illuminated was a passageway, and the spirit of the dead man rose from the floor and walked through. At the same time, the darkened prison lit up floor after floor and the spirits disappeared. The guards rushed in to see the scene.

Inside the cell, the officers stood over the still body. He had bled out from slashes across his wrist.

One of the officers rushed out of the cell, yelling into his walkie-talkie.

"We got an inmate in here dying! He might be dead! He slit his wrists! There's blood everywhere!"

Four days later, Sherrod's boy, Walt, came to visit him. As Sherrod entered the visiting hall and their eyes met, the two smiled as they rushed to embrace each other. After sitting down, they both sighed.

"Ahhh, it's so good to see you!" Sherrod expressed as he continued smiling.

"It's good to see you, too! How are you doing in here?" Walt asked, as he looked around.

"I'm fine, just fine! How's the crew?"

"Everybody's fine,"

"I just got a construction job and they're paying a brother well! I tried helping the others, but they just don't want to work! I got a family now; I can't play around with them dudes."

Sherrod smiled and nodded in agreement.

"What girl let you get her pregnant?" Sherrod asked jokingly.

"What are you trying to say? Please, man, I taught you how to get girls!"

"Yeah, yeah, whatever!" Sherrod laughed.

"So, what's going on in here? You all right? Ain't nobody trying to take that booty? Walt joked.

"They'll die trying!" Sherrod smirked and stared.

"Speaking on that...an inmate killed himself a few days ago! He cut his wrist!" Sherrod told him as they began sharing their thoughts on different things and people. An hour blew by and over the intercom a guard announced that visits were terminated.

Around that same hour, Chris was talking on the phone to his ex-wife.

"Thanks for being there for me. I don't know what I would have done without you," she told him.

"It did just as much for me, just to hear your voice. I missed how we used to talk all night."

"I'm so sorry, maybe I should have tried harder for us. You just scared me, when you snapped out like that."

"I know, I couldn't blame you! I would have done the same."

"I'll tell you what, let's take it slow, and try to work it out. That's if it's all right with you?" she offered.

"Sure...slow it is!"

"Let me clean up here, pack a few items, and I'll be there to see you guys. Okay?"

"Okay, okay." He smiled and lit up from the inside out.

***

That Monday, as Elijah was walking through the rain, trying to make it home, his mind wrestled with some homework his teacher placed before the entire class. One of the questions was, *What makes humans different from other advanced species?* He bounced that thought around in his head

Siege of Darkness/Robert Taylor

as the rain did on his umbrella. Finally reaching his doorstep, he rang the doorbell.

After seeing him through the peephole, his mother pulled the door open. "Where are your keys, boy?"

"I left them in the library or school, one of the two?" He walked in and closed the door.

"Boy, I don't know who's worse with keys, you or your father! Dinner's ready, and take off those wet clothes, dripping water all over my floor!"

That evening, as he lay on the floor, he had a book on the human anatomy and another on the human behavior out in front of him. He took notes as he read and began to come up with his theory.

What makes humans different is the fact that, we have larger brain mass and, in most cases can outthink all other primates. Technology and the ability to research our differences from other creatures also separate us...

He noted in his thesis and continued on for the next few hours.

He got up to take a break and went downstairs to get to the kitchen. His father was sitting and watching television. Seeing Elijah, he called out to him.

"Son, could you come over here for a minute?"

Elijah walked over and sat down next to him.

"I don't like disappointing you, but in my line of work, I'm forced to travel. I do this so you and your mother can have the finest life has to offer. It's no consolation for my absence, but we all have to make sacrifices."

"Dad, I understand. I really do!" Elijah got up and continued his stroll into the kitchen.

Siege of Darkness/Robert Taylor

***

That following Sunday, Chris was preparing for church. As he stared in the mirror, plucking his nose hairs, Jason knocked at the door.

"Dad, do I have to go?"

"Yes, you do! We all need God in our lives. He keeps us balanced. Now, I made breakfast, so go put something in your stomach, before we get out of here!" Chris put down the tweezers and began fixing his tie. Jason turned and walked from the room, mumbling.

Later as they sat in church, the pastor spoke from the book of Psalm.

"Lucifer became so impressed with himself, his intelligence, wisdom, and power, that he sought for himself the honor and glory only due to God! He corrupted himself because of his pride. He wanted the accolades and respect bestowed upon our Lord. Thereafter, Lucifer was casted down onto the earth, like a bolt of lightning, revealing him to the people. This was his punishment for his disobediences. But, God did not strip him of his power. He was still God's first creation..."

After church was over, Chris and Jason walked through the crowds of people, towards their car. Jason had quite a few questions.

"Dad, the pastor said that Lucifer was casted from the heavens and allowed to live amongst us. Is this true?"

"Yes, Satan rebelled against God and opposed his work as he attempted to destroy all the good He created. He will ultimately be confined for an eternity!"

"Lucifer sounds like a bully!" Jason carried on.

Siege of Darkness/Robert Taylor

"Somewhat. He was the first to hate and show Jealousy. He wanted to be God! So in his angry rebellion, he sought to destroy!"

"Wow…" Jason was at a loss for words. Chris looked at him and smiled, realizing he was trying to get an understanding.

****

Time seemed to be flying as summer was near. The temperatures were warming things up, relief to all who hated the cold. However, on this day a storm was brewing. Jason was out in the park when dark clouds maneuvered to cover the sky, 180 mph winds made it gusty, and scary. Relentless rain poured down, sweeping up and down the streets, sounding off as it pummeled cars and rooftops. Caught in it, Jason raced home, as did a lot of others. Fallen trees crushed cars and littered the streets. Uprooted tree trunks lay across lawns and against houses. Soaked and barely able to see, Jason pulled out his keys. He pushed his hair out of his face and approached his front door.

Once inside, his father hung up the phone and turned to look him in the face. Jason started peeling off his clothes right there on the spot; right before running up the stairs.

Coming back down wearing jean shorts and a yellow T-, shirt, he dropped down in the recliner across from his father.

"I thought you were upstairs in your room. If I had known you were out in that storm, I would have come looking for you. I thought I told you we were going to catch the tail end of a serious hurricane."

"You did Dad, I forgot! It's crazy out there. Whew…man!" Jason began to relax, sniffling and sneezing as he did.

Siege of Darkness/Robert Taylor

"I just got off the phone with your mother and she sends her love," Chris added and seemed to be glowing for some reason.

That same night, a pack of hellhounds were leaving the graveyard and wandering aimlessly through the flooded streets. As they slowly trotted, cars did everything to avoid them. One of the wolves jumped on the hood of a blue Dodge SUV and growled, revealing jagged teeth. The man and the children in the vehicle yelled out of fear and watched as it jumped down and continued on.

Minutes later, the hounds came upon a green Jeep Wrangler, its hood crushed by the trunk of a huge tree, as a lady lay unconscious, bleeding from the head. With its sharp dagger-like teeth, one of the wolves pulled at the handle of a slightly open door. As the others howled and waited, he snatched it open, as another helped him drag out the woman to a nearby lawn. The beasts tore into her flesh like the carnivores they were. Fighting for position, they growled at each other. Horrified, a young Spanish couple watched from their front window. The wife called 911, hoping to get help in time.

"911," the operator answered.

"There's Lobos, wolves in my front yard and they're killing a woman! Please hurry, my address is 15 Saint. Patrick's, prisa!" she shouted hysterically. Refusing to stand by, her husband ran to fetch his shotgun from his closet.

Seconds later, out on his lawn, he angrily and aggressively started shooting. Neighbors appeared in their windows, but dared not to leave their homes or confront the breasts.

Siege of Darkness/Robert Taylor

The hounds stood their ground, growling and revealing their blood-drenched teeth. The bullets only seemed to infuriate them, striking them again and again. Seeing the bullets did not affect the mad animals, the man was truly horrified. He turned and made an attempt to run back toward the open door, but it was far too little...too late.
One of the hounds leaped and jumped on him. He fought and screamed for dear life. The hound dragged him down the walkway to the rest of the pack, that were eager to feast. They tore into his flesh, as blood gushed from everywhere. His wife while still inside, ran, yelling and hollering, closing the door, as she feared for her life also.

The following Friday morning, amongst all the flooding, broken branches and fallen trees, people were assessing damages to their properties and homes. The sound of chainsaws and generators lit up the neighborhood. Ambulances and police cars were prominent. The young woman whose husband the wolves savagely mangled, was now sitting on the steps to her house distraught. She watched as they picked up the remaining body parts of her husband and the woman, distinguishing each body part as they placed them in separate bags. A detective walked over to her.

Ma'am, I know this is really hard, but you said he was attacked by a pack of wolves?"

"Yes, wolves! They came from everywhere! My husband ran out on the lawn, fired a few shots and they did nothing. The wolves kept coming! I've never seen anything like it! I can't believe this is happening! What am I going to do?"

"I'm so sorry! Do you need to go to the hospital or something?" the detective asked, as he thought she might be distressed.

"No..." she sniffled.

Siege of Darkness/Robert Taylor

"I can't imagine your pain. It's a bloodbath out here! Hopefully, after some of its tested we can determine exactly what type of wolves they were. I'm deeply sorry for your loss." He walked away and headed to a black unmarked unit.

***

Friday afternoon, Jason sat watching the news. The news anchor spoke of the hurricane and the damage it caused, as well as the people attacked by wolves.

"Yesterday, as a tropical storm battered Florida, parts of the Carolina's, Virginia and scattered parts of the east coast, a man and a woman were savagely attacked, maimed, and killed. The man's wife, an eyewitness to it all is now undergoing psychiatric evaluation. This hurricane, which was reduced to a tropical storm by the time it hit the United States, caused major flooding in some areas along with minor damage here and there," the anchor reported.

Right away, after hearing the news anchor talk of wolves, Jason ran to get his notebooks. Flipping to an empty page, he eagerly scripted the imagery the reporter planted in his head moments before.

That night under the stars, the hellhounds were in the graveyard howling. They toppled a few headstones and disappeared beneath the surface. As they galloped through tunnels that passed millions of decayed coffins, maggots and snakes, heat that would make your skin boil met them. Dropping into the devil's realm, they transformed into humanlike creatures.

***

Siege of Darkness/Robert Taylor

A week later, the detective met with the phlebotomist to check on the blood samples. After testing, they couldn't find a match to any kind of wolf, any creature on earth for that matter. They were baffled. Also the blood specimen was hard to contain.

"When we went to test the blood sample, it moved around, making it hard to examine. So, when we finally did, one of the lab technicians mysteriously got sick and died." said the phlebotomist.

"Do you have any idea how that happened? I mean how he died?"

" Where doing a autopsy later on today. Hopefully, by then we'll have the answers to all our questions."

"So, what is this blood from?"

"We just don't know. We've never seen anything like this. The cellular make-up has a nucleus that in itself is a life force.

"Can yo explain that to me in terms I can understand?"

"Basically, what I'm saying to you is; the sample that was collected and tested is a living and breathing organism, with superior strands of DNA, one that is unknown to the medical profession.

"You're kidding me, right?"

"I wish I was. Here let me show you something." The doctor told the detective as he went in a freezer and grabbed two test-tube with blood samples in them.

"Now this one,which is normal blood, sit in the bottom of the tube motionless, while this blood here, seems to be moving about. You do see the difference, don't you?" the detective looked at them and saw exactly what the doctor had pointed out.

Siege of Darkness/Robert Taylor

***

As two days passed within the prison, smiles were heavy in the visiting hall. Sherrod's mother and father came to see him. Sherrod, who was equally happy, hugged and kissed them both.

"I sure hope you learned your lesson this time! You lucky they didn't put you away for the rest of your life!" Sherrod's father pointed out, as he got comfortable.

"Yeah...believe that! I wouldn't wish this on nobody! This is hell...literally!" Sherrod replied as he felt a sharp pain run through his head.

"Baby, you got to get God into your life and you'll see, things will change." his mother advised.

"Yes, Mom, I love you too." He closed his eyes briefly from the pain and not wanting to debate with her.

"Look at you...you look well-rested and clean!" she also added, causing Sherrod to blush slightly.

"When I get out of here, I was wondering, could I stay with you'll until I get a place of my own? It won't be long, I promise."

"Now boy, we love you, so don't bring none of that nonsense with you, or out you go!"

"I promise you...and thanks!" Sherrod smiled and hugged them to show his gratitude.

After his parents left, Sherrod sat in his cell deep in thought. At that moment, Pierre and two others stood in his doorway.

"Hey, what up my friend?" Pierre greeted. Sherrod stood up, walked over to him, and shook his hand. The other two introduced themselves.

"I'm Jackson,"

Siege of Darkness/Robert Taylor

"...and I'm Keith, but in here they call me Smoke." Sherrod shook their hands and they walked away, leaving Sherrod to himself.

***

That next morning, as the sun mounted its throne in the sky, Jason rubbed his eyes and smiled as he embraced the new day.

Twenty minutes later, as he was up and about, he peeked out of his room and saw his father's closed bedroom door. He knocked and called out to him, but there was no response. From down the hall his Uncle Jimmy yelled,

"He left for work a while ago!" Jason eased into his father's room and closed the door. Seeing everything in disarray, he stepped over clothes, as drawers sat open, and looked in the closet, which had boxes strewn all over. *He had to be looking for something*, Jason thought. Easing out of the room, he looked to see if either of his uncles were anywhere around and raced back into his own room. He grabbed his towel and headed to the bathroom to prepare for school.

Later that day, after Chris came home from work, he could be heard turning things over and moving things around. Jason's curiosity was driving him crazy, so he put down the book he was reading and decided to be nosey. Over to his father's room he headed and as he reached the door, he pushed it open.

"Boy, don't you know how to knock?" he yelled, as he rushed over, tripping as he did, and closed the door in his face. Jason could hear him shouting and turning over things. He wondered what had him so angry? What did he misplace that was so important? Suddenly there was a loud yell of relief.

Siege of Darkness/Robert Taylor

"Thank God!" came afterwards. Whatever he was looking for, he must have found.

Chris sighed, as he held a two-carat marquis diamond ring in his hand. He placed it in his nightstand draw.

The next afternoon, young Jason was on the phone with his mother and she was overjoyed.

"Hey, baby, how's my favorite man doing?" she asked.

"I'm okay, Mom. When's the next time you're coming to see me?"

"I'll be there on Friday and I've got a huge surprise for you!"

"You do? What is it? Tell me!" Jason carried on, wanting to know.

"I love you and I'll see you soon!" she told him, avoiding answering as she ended the call.

****

That Friday, as the sun shined through Jason's open window, he woke up rubbing his eyes. Hearing his mother's voice, he jumped out of bed and raced through the house, into the kitchen. She was sitting at the table, sipping coffee and talking to Chris.

"Mom!" Jason yelled as he ran to hug her. Equally happy, she kissed him several times.

"I was telling your father, we all should go out later. First, I need to go back to my hotel to shower and rest. Around six o'clock this evening I should be ready. Is that okay with you two?" she asked.

"That's fine, "Jason stated as he looked over at his father, who was smiling and nodding in agreement.

Siege of Darkness/Robert Taylor

"Now, boy, go get dressed before you're late for school," Chris told Jason, chasing him out the kitchen.

Later that evening, inside a small family style restaurant, Chris, Jason, and Tessa enjoyed each other's company.

"So, Mom, is it official, you're moving back here?" Chris with a painted smiled sat awaiting her answer also.

"I...I just have to give my job notice. They do have an opening near here, so I have to put in the necessary paperwork and if they okay it, I have to prepare for the transition. But, the answer to your question, is yes!"

"My second question is, are you and Dad getting back together?" Jason giggled slightly. Tessa looked over into Chris's eyes and all she could see was how overjoyed he seemed.

"We're working on it. We'll see what happens. Now pick up your menu and figure out what you want to eat, I'm starved!"

Hours later, as the restaurant was preparing to shut down, Chris was babysitting a glass of red wine, while they talked and laughed about quite a few things. The waiter sat the bill on the table and walked away.

For the next month or so, Tessa flew back and forth, visiting and preparing things. She and Chris were coupled up and spending a lot of time together. They were going to church and revivals together. One of the nights, while they were out, Chris stared into her eyes. She gazed back and sighed.

"You know, I really missed you spoiling me! I'm so happy we were able to work things out." she told him.

Siege of Darkness/Robert Taylor

"Me, too," Chris told her, as he extended a familiar ring box in front of her.

"...Oh, my God, I thought you sold it! I can't believe you kept it!" she shouted, covering her face with her hands.

"It was all I had left to remember our love! And, I never gave up hope. I love you. Will you remarry me?"

"Baby," she sighed, "of course I will. You are so sweet!" She marveled over her familiar gleamer.

Back at the house, the two giggled as they slammed the bedroom door behind them. Tessa with a seductive look in her eyes, pushed Chris up against the wall, and gave him a sloppy, wet kiss. Surprised, he froze momentarily, closed his eyes, and started kissing her back. Falling out across the bed, the two shedded their clothes, and bathed each other with their tongues. A red face appeared on the ceiling.

Across the hall, a smiling Jason lay in bed, as he could hear them moaning and giggling behind the closed door. He was happy things were working out in his favor.

***

Down in hell, Lucifer was furious. He paced as he thunderously pounded his fist into his webbed lengthy hand.

"I gave you all that you ask me for and you turn your back to me? When there was no one to hear your cry, it was I that answered you! No one...no one must mistake my generosity for weakness!"

7

Mid-October

Sherrod slumped over on his small, unmade bunk, deep in thought. He stared at a pale gray wall that separated him from a talkative, annoying younger man. While listening to him babble about nothing, Sherrod jumped down, put on his khaki-colored gear, and awaited the guards to announce breakfast.

As the sunlight paraded through the small caged window, in whisked a subtle breeze and, like clockwork, his skin hardened, as his pores closed. He still didn't know what to make of it, but was living with what the overlord had told him.

"Chow time!" a guard yelled, as the heavy iron doors slowly and noisily slid open. Like herded cattle, the inmates flocked together, rushing to move toward a large open room. As assorted scents flooded the air, all the hungry souls, Sherrod included, stood in line with empty trays, awaiting their turn to be served.

As Sherrod sat at a table with his group of new friends, he scarfed down his meal as Haitian Pierre looked across the table and asked him a question.

"Ay', Sherrod, what up with them dark patches around your eyes? You not getting enough sleep or what?" Not realizing how he looked, he ran the palms of his hands lightly across his face, feeling his scaly, solid flesh.

Siege of Darkness/Robert Taylor

"Yeah, can't sleep! I'll get it together, got a lot on my mind," Sherrod answered flowing with the question, as he knew what was taking place.

"You look like shit! You need to sleep for a month straight or better!" he told Sherrod, who laughed it off.

"You look like that and you get plenty of sleep, so how does that work for you?" Sherrod rebutted. The laughter continued as they joked.

Shortly after, a short stubby guy, with a small afro, sauntered past staring at the back of Sherrod's head. Smoke took notice.

"Sherrod, why is that guy looking over here at you like that?" Sherrod looked to see whom he was talking about and turned back as if it was nothing.

"Is there a problem?" the guy asked, as he walked over with confidence to stand with three others.

"Only if you want one," Sherrod pointed out, never turning to face them. The guy laughed, as he and his entourage approached the table. Sherrod paid them little attention, so little, one of them stood next to him and he never flinched, paused, or even thought to look in his direction.

"I heard about you. You need to get down with us, man! Forget these suckers!" the guy spat as his tart breath had more of Sherrod's attention than he did.

"Nah, I like the friends I have."

"Shit happens in here, you gotta know dat. I'm just looking out for you and your well-being!"
Sherrod to burst with laughter.

"You're right, shit does happen!" Sherrod added, staring them down. The guy and his boys walked off somewhat angry. The buzzer sounded and the inmates began to shuffle, making their way back to their cells.

Siege of Darkness/Robert Taylor

As Sherrod was walking back, another inmate came out of nowhere and stepped in his path. He smiled and refused to move. Sherrod looked into his eyes, nodded, while biting down on his bottom lip. Beginning to perspire, Sherrod's eyes grew red. His fist got tight as he fought to keep his cool.

"My brother, could you please move? I need to get to my cell!" The man continued to smile, as he shook his head. Two guards watched from afar, as if they had front row seats to a title fight. Angered by the man's continuous disobedience, Sherrod's attempted to walk away, but before he could, the man grabbed him. Without realizing what he had done, Sherrod turned and punched him clean off his feet, knocking him out. The guards jumped up from where they sat, yelling for Sherrod to back up, as they prepared to enter the secured area. Sherrod seemed to cool down as his eyes cleared up and he relaxed. Guards cautioned a crowd of inmates to back up, as a few angry ones looked on as if they wanted to get at Sherrod too.

"Take him to lock up! Everybody else, get back to your cells!" shouted the sergeant of the group.

"What? He attacked me!" Sherrod yelled out in his defense as his blood boiled, setting him afire.

The guards grabbed him and he tossed them around as if they were paperweights. Two others pulled out batons and ran toward him. He grabbed them up and pinned them to the wall. The prison alarm sounded and within seconds the riot squad stormed in, geared up. Sherrod released the guards, watching them drop to the floor, and raised his hands in the air, surrendering. They rushed him and beat him down as he curled up. He took the beating, never yelled or flinched, as his eyes took on a demonic stare.

Siege of Darkness/Robert Taylor

***

That same afternoon, while at work, Chris seemed distant. His eyes glued to the computer screen, he was lost in the happening of yesterday. He conjured an old vision, one of a killing, a beast-looking creature running through the woods with a limp female body dangling in its arms.

It moved through the trees and bushes so swiftly it was hard for Chris to keep up. He followed until it disappeared. Where did it go, he thought. Out of breath, he rushed over to the area, it jumped out and swung its huge tree-trunk-like arm at Chris's head. Filled with fright, Chris ducked and took off running like a bat out of hell! Stumbling and falling along the way, he couldn't hear a thing over his heavy breathing, as he dared to look behind him. Stumbling out onto a road, a speeding car swerved to avoid hitting him. Hysterically, Chris threw his hands in the air, yelling for the driver to come back. The car stopped, sat for a moment, and as the reverse lights lit up, Chris sighed. As the car backedup, the driver stopped in front of Chris, and he took a deep breath.

"Please help me, there's some sort of beast somewhere around here! Can you please take me into town?" he asked, as his head bounced around, side to side like a bobble head. The man scanned the area. With hesitancy, he agreed, "Sure, hop in!" After glancing over his shoulder one last time, Chris pulled the door open and jumped in, locking it before the man pulled off.

Chris was quiet until the driver looked over and struck up a conversation, his shotgun on the seat between them. He moved it, placing it just under the seat, beneath his legs.

"So, what did you say happened back there?"

Siege of Darkness/Robert Taylor

"Woo! Some type of creature was racing through the woods, carrying a female. I tried to see where he was taking her. He came after me and I took off running, scared for my life!"

"Are you sure of what you saw, a beast? You sure it wasn't a bear or something?"

"Look, I know what a bear looks like! I'm sure of what I saw! You don't have to believe me, go see for yourself!" Chris looked at him.

After a mental picture, the man expressed, "You need to go to the police and report this!"

"I would, but they'll think I'm some nut job trying to get publicity or something."

"Yeah, probably so…" The man paused.

"How did you get out here anyway?"

"I drove, but after I was chased, I didn't dare run to my car on the other side of the woods." With confusion written all over his face, the man looked at him, not knowing what to believe.

That evening at home, Chris sat in his room replaying the vision in his head. He jumped up, went down stairs into the kitchen, where he retrieved a bottle of moonshine from the refrigerator, to calm his nerves. Every little noise around the house spooked him. He guzzled a quarter of the jug.

"God bless that woman…God bless us all!" Chris recited, remembering that frightful night. He turned the jug up again.

Two days later, as the paper boy shouted from his bicycle, "Extra, extra, read all about it; *Woman found dismembered and mutilated in nearby woods.*" People rushed to purchase one paper after another. He sold out in just about a half an hour. Everyone was curious about the incident and farmers,

Siege of Darkness/Robert Taylor

business men and regular folks were buying guns, locking doors and traveling in packs wherever they went. The entire town and neighboring ones were shook.

Pressure to come up with answers, three days later the sheriff appeared at Chris' door, along with three stone-faced deputies. They barged in on him as he was having breakfast, and wasted no time questioning him.

"Why were you in the woods that day?" the sheriff asked.

"Well, I was out there fishing, but by that time I was finished and walking through the woods to get to my car. That's when I heard a scream and I looked to see where it was coming from. I saw a giant beast racing through the woods. This thing was huge! I couldn't believe my eyes, so I followed it and I almost got my head taken off!"

"That's when you supposedly ran out in the road, stopped a car and road into town. It's funny how we found a napsack near the body and it had your ID and things in it."

"You don't think I had something to do with this, do you? I know how this looks, but my knapsack was on the back seat of my car. How it got near the body…I don't know."

"So when you ran, why didn't you run to your car? Why out to the road? Wouldn't it have been smarter to run in the direction of your car?" the sherriff pointed out.

"I was scared and trying to get away! I…wasn't thinking about,"

"Okay, so you say! Stand up and put your hands behind your back." the sheriff shouted, as he stood up and had heard enough.

"What?" Chris was puzzled, as he jumped to his feet also, putting his hands behind his back. The officer handcuffed him, escorted out of his home and to jail. The charge was murder.

Siege of Darkness/Robert Taylor

He recalled sitting in a cell until three other murders happened around those same woods and they cornered the beast. Twelve officers died that day and the monstrous figure fled, and was never seen again. Out of thought, Chris picked up his head, rose to his feet and headed down the hall to the bathroom. Thinking of Tessa, he smiled; things were starting to get steamy again.

****

Two weeks later, after getting out of lock up, Sherrod was summoned from his cell to the institution's nurse. As a guard escorted him, he struck up a conversation wth Sherrod.

"You know, I was one of those guards you whipped on? What the hell you got in those mitts of yours? I mean, I can box, but you were throwing us around like rag dolls. Shutting dudes down with one punch! All the other guards still want to whip your ass! Not only that, you better watch yourself, because Oswald, the one you mashed out, is the head of one of the major gangs in here. Word is, they're plotting to kill you!" Sherrod looked at him but said nothing.

"What? Oh, you a tough guy, huh? Look, man, I've been working here ten years and if they want you dead, you're dead!" Sherrod's eyes changed from normal to black, causing the guard to back up.

"Please, leave me alone!" Sherrod demanded in a deepened voice.

"What the hell? How did you do that?" The guard was speechless and stayed that way until they reached the nurses office.

Inside, she asked him to disrobe so she could examine him. When she turned to face him, she looked him up and down.

Siege of Darkness/Robert Taylor

"How long have you been here? I've never seen you before." She placed her stethoscope against his chest. He didn't reply. She pulled out her pressure kit and wrapped the arm cuff around his bicep. She looked up into his eyes. After a brief trance, she felt weary, but shook it off.

"Mr. Tillman, something not right!" The reading was scrambled and it erred. She tried it again, and again it errored. Confused, assuming the apparatus was malfunctioning; she decided to try it another time and told him to get dressed.

In the midst of him putting on his clothes, another inmate walked in. She started testing him and decided to try the pressure-cup again and it worked! She turned, looking for Sherrod, who was gone, escorted back to his cell.

Throughout the remainder of October, the guy he fought and his boys were giving Sherrod dirty looks. He paid them no attention, as he went about his daily routine.

Days later, there was a big commotion as Sherrod sat on his bunk reading. He got up to see what was going on. The buzzer sounded and the inmates were scattering as guards advised them to get in their cells. As everyone was preparing to lock in, Sherrod noticed Pierre stretched out on a lower tier, face down in a pool of blood. Four guards stood over his still body. Angered by this, Sherrod walked into his cell, smacked the wall and it crumbled before him. Amazed, he bent down and picked up small bits of concrete.

The next day, as soon as Sherrod entered the cafeteria for breakfast, after briefly talking to Smoke and a few others, he approached his haters and called them out.

"Y'all want me? Here I am! Let's get this over with!" he hollered angrily. The entire table of twenty, stood up. Sherrod took a deep breath, as his eyes turned colors right before them. His skin tightened, as his eyes became fiery and he prepared

Siege of Darkness/Robert Taylor

himself for battle. Stepping into Sherrod's face, the leader Oswald smiled. Sherrod snatched him up, with his right hand clutched around his neck, and tossed him across the room. Three others rushed him and with the swing of that same arm, he knocked them over the table, onto the floor, and out cold. Everyone else stood in shock, as Sherrod's breathing was heavy. The buzzer sounded and guards were all over the place. A guard marched Sherrod out of the room, and down into lock-up, once again. This time he didn't resist. He smiled as he looked around at the destruction he caused.

***

On November 1st, Chris, happier than he had been in a long while, was preparing for Jason's surprise birthday party. His brother, Willie, took Jason to an indoor amusement park, where the two of them played for hours until Willie looked at his watch and realized it was time for them to get back.

On the ride home, Jason smiling because he had so much fun.

"Thanks, uncle, I really enjoyed myself!" He told Willie as he smiled uncontrollably. Saying nothing, Willie grinned and drove.

"Uncle Willie, my father seems a lot happier these days, doesn't he? I was praying that they'd get back together! My prayers were answered." Jason smiled.

"Anyway, why is my father so scared to talk about the things we talk about?"

"You mean all that supernatural stuff?"

"Yeah. Did something happen when y'all were young?"

Siege of Darkness/Robert Taylor

"No, boy, you're reading into things. Your father was just scared of his own shadow. He wasn't no punk, though, just scary as all outdoors!" Taking in what his uncle told him, Jason sat back and enjoyed the remainder of the ride.

***

In the devil's realm, he laughed loudly, surrounded by dancing rings of fire.

"There is a lesson in what I must do. In this lesson, I will gain the trust of one by bringing about the demise of another. I will birth anger in thy heart undistinguishable!"

***

Forty minutes later, Willie unlocked the front door to the house. Once inside, it was pitch black. No lights. Within seconds, the lights came on.

"Surprise!" yelled family and friends, as they gathered around Jason, hollering and bearing gifts. Willie led Jason, as he smiled from one ear to the other, to a colorful ribbon draped table. A large white cake awaited him, with the number 13 wax candle burning in the center. While Jason took it all in, Chris walked over, hugged him, and handed him several big boxes with bows around them.

"Happy birthday son, from me and your mother!" he announced loudly. Jason tore the ribbon from the first box and after digging in it, he emerged with another box with a train set enclosed. He yelled out in joy and grabbed the next.

***

Siege of Darkness/Robert Taylor

That evening, Tessa slept on a flight from Chicago to North Carolina. The smile on her face was evident of whom she was dreaming of, as Chris had been so romantic the last few months. Suddenly, turbulences jolted her back awake, she looked around as the stewardess cautioned passengers to fasten their seatbelts.

"Hello, this is your pilot," came over the intercom. "We are experiencing some minor problems and will be making a temporary stopover in Columbus Ohio. Sorry for any inconvenience this may have caused."

A half hour later, as the plane descended, approached the runway, a strong gust of wind caused it to shift during landing. Its left wing hit the ground, sending the plane into a spin in which it tumbled and burst into a ball of fire. Rescue crews and fire engines raced to the site and began the task of extinguishing the flames. Charred bodies, baggage, and plane parts were sprawled within a one-half-mile circumference of the crash. The airport shut down as emergency crews were dispatched and racing to the wreckage.

***

That same evening, Sherrod lay in his bunk, on his stomach, reading. The ghostly image of his friend, Pierre, appeared and walked into his cell. Sherrod dropped the book, sat upon the edge of his bunk, and stared at Pierre, who wore his usual grin.

"What up, bruh?" he spoke to Sherrod's amazement. "Yeah, they got me! Oswald stabbed me in the neck! A few of the guards were in on it, too! They watched it go down and let me bleed out." He disappeared seconds later. Sherrod turned over onto his back and closed his eyes.

Siege of Darkness/Robert Taylor

The following day, while Chris was preparing for work, he paged Tessa several times. Sensing something was wrong, he called her job in Chicago. They informed him that her transfer was final and she should be starting that day at the partnering office in Raleigh, North Carolina. Confused, Chris paged her again and that's when the visual of the plane's wreckage on the news caught his attention. In total disbelief, he dropped down on the side of the bed and listened. The reporter read off the names of the one hundred two possible passengers. When Chris heard Tessa Milosky, he cried out like a wounded animal. Hearing him, Jason rushed into his bedroom.

"Dad, what's wrong?" His father didn't reply, he just got up and walked over to the window and stared out.

"What is it, Dad?" Jason looked at the television in which the weatherman was talking about the temperatures for the week. Willie and Jimmy awakened by their voices, entered the room also.

"Hey, what going on? Are you guys all right in here?" Willie asked, as Jimmy stood next to him rubbing his eyes. Chris just stared out the window as tears glazed his cheeks. Jason looked around at them all, wishing someone would say something. Jimmy walked over and placed his arm around Chris to console him.

"She's gone! She gone!" Chris cried out softly.

"Who?" Jimmy asked.

"Tessa, man! She's dead!" Chris mumbled breaking down. Hearing this, Jason froze, Willie looked stunned and Chris softly bounced his head against the window.

"Your mother gone, son. She was in a plane crash!" Chris turned to Jason glossy eyed, lips quivering as he sniffled. Jason started screaming until his face turned red, ran out the

Siege of Darkness/Robert Taylor

room swelling in tears. Willie ran behind him, while Jimmy stayed with Chris.

Racing through the house, Willie looking for Jason, but he was nowhere in sight. He went out in the backyard and saw him running down the dirt road, that led to the old abandoned home. Willie ran after him.

Once he caught up to Jason, the two were in the cabin weeping together.

"Why, Uncle Willie? Why did God take my mother?" Jason begged him to answer the question.

"I can't answer that one, Jason. All I know is, if God got her, she's in good hands!"

"I hate God! I hate Him!" Jason yelled, as he cried even louder.

"No you don't, Jason, no you don't! It's going to be okay! We're going to be okay! Come on let's go back to the house." The two headed back up the road together.

"My birthday will never be the same! I'll never trust God, ever!" Jason tearfully added.

***

In his realm, joy filled the devil, as a bloody and zombielike Tessa stood before him.

"Your disobedience has prompted me to show my strength and for my troubles, I've gained two for one! he laughed, carrying on and dismissing her soul along with about ten others into a fiery hole.

***

Siege of Darkness/Robert Taylor

That next day in the cafeteria, Sherrod ate while looking around the room, from guard to guard, inmate to inmate. He knew who the culprits were that killed his friend and was desperate to avenge him. He entertained a handful of scenarios, all of which left a lot of people dead. Breaking up that onslaught of evil acts, a guard walked past, yelling at a prisoner, who was angry with another.

8

December 3, 1980

"Tillman, the nurse wants to see you tomorrow at one o'clock sharp," a guard told him, as he stood in front of his cell.

"Okay." He spoke lightly, as he never looked up. The guard walked away whistling. At that moment, Sherrod's body got warm and his hands started to glow. Amazed by the occurrence, he stared into his palms, that turned bright orange, as they continued to heat up.

"What the hell?" He was in a state of confused amazement. A voice shattered the moment.

You are experiencing cellular reconstruction. Your body is completing the transformation from its human state into somewhat of a super human. You will not be immortal, but you will possess certain characteristic.

Sherrod said nothing. He just listened. The voice disappeared, leaving him staring through the emptiness of the cold grey cell.

***

That evening, Chris stood in the window, daydreaming and depressed, rehashing the image of the burning plane, and that's when O'Conner appeared again. The two began to talk.

Siege of Darkness/Robert Taylor

I can't express how deeply sorry I am for your loss, but you must know that there are forces at work here. At work to prohibit love and fill your heart with ill intent and evil! As beautiful as she was, you must find beauty even in her death! Celebrate her life, for now you must cherish her within the very confides of your heart.

"But why? Why her, of all the people on this earth? Why my only reason for living and believing? Why?" Chris cried.

I know not why, but I am told that she had made a deal with Lucifer the devil."

"That's a lie! She would never do such a thing! She was a God-fearing person, and loved everyone!"

Some of God's loyalists give into him. People make deals with the devil for youth, knowledge, fame, or power. A deal with him is a dangerous one! Most try to outsmart him, but he is far too cunning and unscrupulous.

"The lies you tell! I need her, you hear me? I need her!" Chris cried out as he fell to the floor, displeased with the angel's explanation.

Rise, bare the armor God has given thee. You can conquer all that's before you with the strength He gives. Be strong in thy Lord and His mighty power!" After those words of empowerment, Chris rose from the floor and hung in mid-air.

Right now, I must prepare you for the life before you. There is much to know and much to be aware of! I, along with the Lord thy God, will fight alongside you to help you win this battle.

"I have nothing left. I'm exhausted! Yet you still ask me to fight Are you crazy? Plus, I am a mortal soul, how can I fight alongside you and God?"

You carry the word and a righteous aura. With that, together we can seek out and destroy all that steps into our path!" O'Conner went on while Chris sat glossy eyed, listening, but seemed confused.

"You must believe!" O'Conner added as he drifted.

"You must believe! He continued, and disappeared.

***

The following day within the nurse's office, Sherrod was sitting on a table with his shirt off. As she moved around the room, he picked up on her scent and closed his eyes, as to capture and enjoy it for that moment. Finally, she placed her stethoscope against his chest to check his heart. A few minutes later, she prepped to get his blood pressure and the pressure pump erred once again. Puzzled, she tried again and got the same results.

"What's wrong?" Sherrod asked.

"I don't know…it's odd. I've been using this thing for weeks and now it's not working properly." As she moved her lips, he watched her tongue dance around in her mouth. Aroused, he smiled while grabbing her wrist and looking her in the eyes. She resisted slightly and started to feel a little light headed as she made eye contact. He leaned in and tried to kiss her.

She pulled away. "What are you doing?" she shouted out of shocked.

"I'm so sorry. I just couldn't resist. You're so beautiful!" He hoping that would calm her down.

"Put your clothes on and please leave! Hurry, before I call the guard and have you written up!" Disgusted, she grabbed a paper towel and alcohol. She wiped her lips, while staring at him angrily. After getting dressed, Sherrod walked out. She watched him leave and was very much annoyed.

***

On December 23, the winds were harsh and cold, as the air was truly unfriendly. In the livingroom, dressing the Christmas tree, Chris stopped, as Jason entered.

"Come here, boy, help me with this tree." Chris was trying to get Jason out of his funk.

"Nah, Dad, it just doesn't feel like Christmas. I don't want to celebrate nothing that has to do with God!" He walked out the livingroom and to his bedroom, closing the door behind him. Chris continued dressing the tree, as he placed a golden angel on the top.

That evening, as the house was lit up with lights and frosted with snow, the one thing that was absent was the holiday spirit. While Jason lay curled up in his bed, Chris stood staring out the window, thinking of Tessa, thinking of what his guardian angel told him. He envisioned what he and Tessa would be doing if she were still alive. The spirit of O'Conner appeared before his eyes again.

God has Himself; informed me that Lucifer was definitely responsible for the tragedy that took your wife's life. He has taken her only to project and show his strength amongst the living. You must not wallow in guilt and pain or he will eventually find a way to retire you as well.

"I am sorry, but my heart burns."

"I understand what it is you are going through, but yet you must not let him win." Chris turned away from the window,

not wanting to hear any more. O'Conner watched and then vanished.

***

On Christmas day, in the devil's realm, he had new souls coming in by the minute. Lucifer cried with laughter as he watched.

This is what I'm talking about! Bring me more! My army must be of great size! I will conquer all!" he yelled, as those around pledged their allegiances.

I am God! Am I not? he added as he stood exalted above them. They all agreed spellbound.

***

Four days later, as the snow still blanketed everything, the nurse sent for Sherrod. While he sat in her office, they talked.

"Happy Holidays!" she greeted with a half a smile.

"I know a lot of you guys haven't been in the company of a woman in a long time, so I didn't report you. Please, don't try that again! As long as you don't disrespect me, you and I won't have any problems. Now…you're the talk of the prison. You're causing a lot of problems in here." She told him as she prepared for him.

"Look, I don't start this stuff, but I'm one hell of a finisher!" he explained in his defense, with an air of cockiness.

"Well, anyway, I called you down here to try to get your pressure amongst other things for my files. I don't understand what's going on. Every damn time I try to take your pressure it errors out. I know the pump works, because I never have a problem with anyone else. This whole thing isn't making sense at all!"

Siege of Darkness/Robert Taylor

"Well, I know I've been feeling kinda funny lately. Hot and cold, stomach cramps and all. What would make it do that?"

"I'm not sure," she paused, "and I don't want to guess. It's crazy, even the blood sample I've taken seemed to have disappeared. The jars were empty." Sherrod was just as baffled as she was.

"I tell you what, I'm going to need another sample," she told him, unwrapping a fresh needle.

As she stepped close to Sherrod, her scent began to excite him. He grabbed her, pulling her, pressed her against him. Just by his contact, for some reason, she didn't resist this time. He kissed her and her soft lips woke every hormone in his body. Grabbing her up, he sat her on the table while she was removing her lab coat. He hiked up her skirt, revealing her tight, white panties. She started kissing his chest. He pulled his pants down a few inches, revealing his manhood. As he pushed her panties to the side, at that exact moment, the alarm in the prison sounded. Shocked, he backed away as he wondered what was going on. Out of his grasp, she was suddenly free of his spell. She looked down at her open blouse and hiked up skirt with confusion. Seeing his thick rod, she hopped from the table and turned her back to him. The two of them without pause, fixed their clothes. Just as they finished, a guard banged at the door with a sense of urgency.

***

Within O'Brien's hotel room, his eyes rolled back in his head as he grabbed his genitals. He smiled at this erection. Within minutes, his face went blank and his arousal was no longer. He seemed disappointed as he pounded the bed with his fist.

Siege of Darkness/Robert Taylor

***

In school, while the teacher had stepped out of the classroom to talk with an administrator, Jason was drawing on a sheet of paper. The kid sitting in front of him turned around and began to watch.

"What kind of monster is that?"

"It's not a monster, it's a werewolf!" Jason pointed out. The kid snatched the paper and held it up to show the entire class.

"Look everybody, crazy Jason thinks they really exist! He believes monsters really exist!" he shouted and laughed, as the class joined in.

"Give me back my paper! Gimme!" Jason yelled as he reached over and grabbed it, ripping it in half. Jason got mad, got up, breathing heavy and balled up his fist. The teacher walked back in and called out to him.

"Jason, why are you up? Have a seat young man!" she told him, as she began erasing the chalkboard to write a new lesson. Jason sat down and slammed his fist on the desk, capturing the attention of his classmates.

Back in the prison twenty minutes later, while Sherrod was being marched out of the facility by a guard, a fire in the wood shop had the alarms throughout the place raging. As prisoners gathered outside in the yard, firemen stormed through the facility, led by two guards.

Minutes later, Sherrod would be amongst the others and all he could think about was the feeling he was consumed with when he held nurse Brown. Her image stained his thoughts the entire time he stood in the yard. Once everyone was heading back in, Oswald bumped him, and when their eyes met,

Siege of Darkness/Robert Taylor

Oswald laughed and kept moving. Sherrod thought nothing of it, as he was continued on in deep thought.

In South Carolina, walking home from school, Jason tossed stones into the woods as he thought. Haunted by images of his mother, he instantly got angry. Lucifer watched him from the clouds, recognizing how displeased he was with God.

"I don't know why people believe in God!" Jason shouted as he picked up a huge rock and threw it across the road. Lucifer laughed from the joy this was giving him.

***

Leaving the prison that night, Nurse Brown smiled, while walking in a daze to her car. She was picturing Sherrod's ripped body pressed against hers, which caused her nipples to sit up beneath her smock. Her mind shuffled perversions for her entire journey home.

In her driveway, she sat in her car, smiling until her phone rang.

"Hey, baby, what'sgoing on?" she greeted.

"Honey, I'll be home in a little while. I miss you!" the male on the other end told her in a happy tone. Though that brought a smile to her face, she couldn't help but daydreaming about Sherrod.

That night in his cell, he sat on his bunk thinking about Nurse Brown also. One of the overlords' joined him and spoke out.

Part of your hormonal transformation makes women surrender upon your touch! With each day, your magnetism will get stronger! In time, once you make eye contact with them and touch or hold them, they become slaves to your passion. Once the transformation is complete, we will talk further! There is more to it...

Two days later, on her day off, Nurse Brown was home, whistling while preparing dinner in her kitchen. She had a huge smile as she thought about Sherrod. Her husband walked in, grabbed her from behind, and gently kissed her on the neck.

"What the hell? she yelled, as she jumped, caught by surprise.

"It's me, baby. Who did you think it was?" She turned around and looked at him as if he were a total stranger.

"You caught me off guard. I didn't even hear you come in!" she explained, wide-eyed.

"You been around them prisoners too long!" he stated, somewhat agitated.

"What's that supposed to mean?"

"Nothing. Why are you so uptight? Did one of them try something?"

"Hell no…" She turned the flame off under the pot, drained the noodles, took off her apron and went to set the table. Her husband stood frozen with a confused look on his face.

That night, in her bed with her husband, he tried cuddling with her. Rejecting him, she turned on her stomach and planted her face in the pillow. Angered, he turned away and shut his eyes.

****

The next few weeks, numerous inmates had been placed in the infirmary with some type of sickness. A stomach virus of some sort was circulating heavily. As fast as they came in, the

Siege of Darkness/Robert Taylor

nurse shot them up with antibiotics, vitamins and so forth to no avail. Eventually a lot of them went into seizures, had strokes and died. The prison was immediately quarantined and each prisoner was subjected to a full examination. A few were diagnosed with an unknown sickness and separated as the quarantine was lifted a month later.

As days passed, after the sun went down within a well-lit bedroom, there was tension. Nurse Brown and her husband, both in their nightclothes, were arguing. With tears in her eyes, she held her battered face.

"I can't believe you're sleeping with one of those damn …degenerates! You have disgraced me! I love you and this is how you repay me!" Outraged, he was breaking up everything in sight.

"I can't believe you hit me! Oh, my God! It's not what you think! I never did anything. I swear to you!" she cried out.

"So what's this, huh? What's this? It's in your handwriting!" He waved a handwritten letter in her face, found earlier.

"It's not what you think! I never did anything. I swear to you!" He pulled out his gun and placed it to his own temple. She yelled and backed away.

"No, please no…" she screamed.

"I hate you for this! I dedicated my life to you and this is how you repay me? What were you thinking? I can't do this anymore! I can't," he yelled, frustrated and confused, as tears flooded from his glossy eyes.

Hours later, police cars canvased the street on which they resided. Yellow caution tape sealed off the area around their house. Officers kept bystanders at bay, as neighbors were curious to know what happened.

Siege of Darkness/Robert Taylor

***

That same night in the prison infirmary, four quarantined inmates lay dead in their beds, eyes wide open, with dried streaks of blood around their noses.

After work, Chris was preparing to go to an evening service at his church. With his brother not around, he told Jason he had to go with him.

"I'm not going, Dad!" Jason pouted.

"You are going! So go in there and get ready!" Chris demanded. Defiant, Jason ran out the house and down the road. Chris attempted to follow him, but stopped when he realized he couldn't catch him.

"That's quite all right! You're grounded!" Chris shouted, as he watched with anger. He turned, and headed back toward the house.

In the old cabin now, Jason propped a small wooden chair against the door and turned on the old oil lamp for light. At an dated wooden table, he sat breathing heavily as anger consumed him. He stared at the wall, as he mumbled to himself.

"You can't make me go! I'm not going! That's your God!" He relaxed and closed his eyes.

****

On February 8, a guard escorted Sherrod to the nurse's office. As he entered, he smiled as he strutted confidently, only to get the shock of his life. A male nurse was standing near a file cabinet, looking through paperwork and handling the routine check-ups.

"Sorry to be a bother, Mr. Tillman, but there's a few discrepancies in your medical history. I don't see a blood sample, nor do I see that you've been tested for STDs, among other things."

"I don't know. You should have all that. I've been down here a million times. You should have all that somewhere in here," Sherrod assured him, not wanting to be there, after seeing that Nurse Brown wasn't around.

"Well, unfortunately, Nurse Brown 'is no longer with us' and I have no clue to how she kept her records. Plus, due to…" Interrupting him, Sherrod blurted out, "What do you mean she's 'no longer with us'?" Dropping his hands to his side, the nurse looked at Sherrod and sighed. "She was murdered last month." In complete shock, and disregarding everything these, Sherrod exclaimed, "You're kidding, right? What happened to her?"

"Her husband killed her, and himself. It was all over the news! He thought she was messing around, with one of you inmates in here." The nurse looked him in the eyes.

"Wow, that's crazy!" Sherrod looked around in disbelief.

"Yes, well, as I was saying, due to all the deaths around here, I think it's better to be safe than sorry! Do you agree?"

***

In room 211 of the asylum, Jason's great grandfather stood commandingly as he talked to an empty room.

"Ain't nothing funny! Why are you all laughing? I'm telling you guys these stories for a reason. Byron Malic still exists! Father Bauser thought he put him to rest, but he didn't! His spirit is transferrable. Sit down and listen, you fools, and shut up! You think you know, but you don't! You don't know shit! I hope you're the first people he kills!" Johnathan angered that his invisible subject were disobedient.

9
EVIL DOESN'T SLEEP

March came in breezy and warm. Amidst the rain showers and fresh greenery, a priest looked through some old artifacts hidden in a secret room inside the church. He stumbled upon a nine-foot scroll. He stretched it out across a long table, and read it. *The war between the Sons of Light and the Sons of Darkness. The Sons of Darkness shall fall with no one to come to their aid, and that supremacy shall cease that wickedness be overcome with remnants. There shall be no survivors of the Sons of Darkness, and the Sons of Righteousness shall shine to all ends of the world, continuing to shine until all the appointed seasons of darkness are done. Then, at the time appointed by God, His great excellence shall shine for all the time of eternity, for peace, blessing, glory, joy, and long life for all the Sons of Light.*

After reading a few more documents, he placed them back neatly and exited the room.

***

A few days later in the prison gym, Sherrod was pressing two hundred fifty pounds repeatedly. When he had pumped out fifty repetitions, he placed it back on the rack. Amazed, he put four hundred sixty five pounds on the bar and pushed out sixty repetitions. After re-racking the weights, he laughed out loud. The other inmates looked on astonished. Suddenly the pain ensued and he fell to the ground. Inmates yelled out to the guards, who came running. Others stood around to see if he was going to be alright, up until they carried him away.

That evening, while Sherrod lay up with a thermometer stuck in his mouth, his body temperature was on the rise. His hands illuminated a bright orange, his eyes solid red, and his face hung with a look of mystery. The thermometer exploded into pieces. The male nurse looked on in disbelief.

Walking over to Sherrod, he pulled the remainder of it from his mouth, and looked at it stunned.

A half an hour later, as he was resting in the infirmary, Sherrod's temperature returned to normal.

The overlord spoke to him. *The transformation is finally complete! You are now ready for what is to come.*

"And what might that be?" he questioned.

You must first be free of this place and amongst the female persuasion.

"What does that mean?"

What it means is there is a lot expected of you.

"Why are so many inmates in here dying all of a sudden?"

That sample of blood that the nurse extracted from your body is the life force that lives within you. If not securely contained, it wil find it's way into others, either killing them or transforming them."

"So, what you're telling me is, there may or may not be more just like me, or worst?"

That's exactly what I'm telling you! The only thing is, in order for the soul to be deemed a host, it must possess a rare blood type and the linkage of an evil and destructive past! It must have tainted DNA also!

Siege of Darkness/Robert Taylor

"You're kidding me right?"
I wish I were. The overlord disappeared. Sherrod lay there pondering the overlord's words.

***

That evening, Marie Childs, a light skinned woman sat in her bedroom arguing with Aaron her boyfriend. As his voice elevated over hers, the argument seeped through the walls and outside into the streets.

"I'm so…so tired of you! All you do is constantly complain! You want me to screw you, cook for you and except all the bullshit you dish out too? You are a special type of fool!" she yelled in anger.

"I work all day, so when I come home, I should at least get a home-cooked meal!" he screamed back.

"I work, too! So, does it ever cross your mind that I may be just as tired as you sometimes?"

"You sit behind a desk, are you serious? That's not real work. Try working on the docks. Try offloading freight all damn day! Come home with your legs and back sore all the time! All I want is a woman who cares enough to fix me a meal every now and then."

"Really? I do occasionally fix dinner. I try my damndest to make this relationship work!"

"Whatever," Aaron finished as he turned and headed toward the door. Marie watched him as he walked out and locked it behind him.

****

Siege of Darkness/Robert Taylor

On March 27, in the dayroom, Sherrod sat watching television. He noticed four men moving around. As Dean Oswald, the one he fought, pounded his fist in his hand, Sherrod tried to pay him little attention. He stared at Sherrod with anger and headed in his direction. Sherrod paused from watching the popular comedic sitcom, *All in the Family* to get up and take on Dean's intentions. The closer he got the more evident it was things were about to get ugly. Sherrod clenched his fist tight as he smiled and his eyes turned black. Before he knew it, the man dove across a table and tackled him. Trying to get free and avoid the barrage of hooks and jabs, Sherrod found himself overpowered. After getting his face bashed a few minutes, he let out a roar and every vein in his body surfaced. Fighting and pushing, he kicked the man off of him, where he landed across the room. Sherrod jumped back to his feet. Everybody in the room stood on tables, watching and chanting. Three others rushed Sherrod, kicking and punching as well as they took. Overwhelmed, bruised and bloody, Sherrod realized they weren't the same inmates he fought before. As they all prepped to continue, guards burst in wearing full armor and clutching their batons. Sherrod froze where he stood, the others turned to take them on. They leaped into action and the guard's attempted to beat them. Other guards tossed in tear gas canisters, as more guards rushed in wearing full riot gear and gas masks. As fast as they entered, they landed against walls and glass petitions. They screamed for more help. On the floor, a few angry inmates' skin began to burn. They squealed loudly as they jumped around the room wildly. All the others were lying on the floor, coughing and choking. Eventually, the cloud of gas was so thick, the guards in the control room couldn't make out who was who and what was going on. When everything seemed calm and quiet, more

Siege of Darkness/Robert Taylor

guards cautiously opened the gate and slowly entered. Ambushed, inmates attacked them, overpowering and disarming them, beating them with their own batons and shields. After they were bloody and unconscious, inmates raced through the prison hall, ripping down gates and doors until they were outside the facility. The yard and surrounding areas all lit simultaneously. Warning shots echoed and the alarms screamed from all areas. The escapees headed for the walls, where they leaped up, scaled and crossed over. Bullets pierced the towering concrete security structure as the guard in the watchtower released round after round. Additional officers raced through the yard to the outside, but the escapees were long gone.

An hour later, back in the prison, guards escorted Sherrod and the others back to their cells. As prisoners screamed and yelled, the guards rushed to re-establish order. Seeing all the damage and torn out bars, inmates and guards alike couldn't believe all the destruction. It looked like a wrecking ball went through the place. Many inmates asked to go see the nurse, because of either their eyes and or throats were burning. The angry guards ignored their requests and locked them all in their cells.

The next day it was all over the news, from television to the radio.

Last night, three inmates escaped from New Jersey's maximum-security prison. They somehow ripped out bars and walls to make this daring escape. Three guards were killed and fifteen were injured in the process. These are some of New Jersey's notorious killers! Please do not try to apprehend! Call your local authorities!

The next few days, officers from different states around the country came to help recapture these desperados. They combed the woods, streets, yards, and parks, but came up empty. When all seemed lost, a call came in about a siting and truckloads of officials raced to the location.

Twenty minutes later, law enforcement cornered two inmates in a field. Closing in, police vehicles plowed through cornstalks. The men ran as a helicopter hovered closely overhead. Refusing to surrender, the two inmates met their fate, as bullets rained down on them. When the officers reached the site of the bodies, they were bewildered, as they looked around astonished.

"Where are they?"

Another officer bent down and looked at the pair of orange jumpsuits. "They're gone."

Confused, the officers looked around as one of them picked up a suit. White dust poured out.

An officer radioed up to the one in the helicopter.

"This is Sergeant Hill, we somehow lost sight of the inmates. Which direction did you see them go in?"

"They fell out right where you're standing!" the pilot announced. "I saw their bodies lying there! There's nowhere they could have gone, I've been hovering right here the whole time." After that bit of information they searched the area, but came up empty. One of the officers picked up the jumpers, placed them in clear plastic bags and carried them away.

***

Still angry at the world, Jason ripped pages out of the Bible and cried out loud.

"Oh God...Mama! Please come back, I need you!"

His mother's face appeared and she spoke.

Siege of Darkness/Robert Taylor

Baby, don't cry, I'm okay! You must be strong and become the man I know you can be. Stunned, Jason looked on in disbelief.

"Ma, I miss you! Why did you have to die? It's not fair!"

"Son, you must not lose yourself, I will always be with you!" she disappeared. Jason wiped his face and stood up, looking and waiting for her return. When she didn't, he got angry again.

***

On Monday, the 6th, the teacher introduced a nice looking young girl to Jason's class. She had a sparkle in her eyes, as her long blonde hair draped her round face and fell around her thin shoulders. She was new to the area and seemed a little out of place. The teacher led her to a empty seat behind Jason.

"Class, this is Linda Bukowski. She has moved down here from Richmond, Virginia. Let's all welcome her to Charlotte."

They all greeted her and smiled.

"Now, open your books up to page 17 and let's discuss tomorrow's assignment."

After school, Jason saw Linda standing on the school steps. Out of concern, he walked over.

"You waiting on somebody?" he asked.

"Yes, yes, I am. I'm waiting on my mother. She should be here any minute," she answered as their eyes met.

"Okay, well, I'm Jason. You sit behind me in English class." A blue Plymouth pulled up and the horn blew.

"I know…nice meeting you, Jason! I've got to go." She made her way down the steps toward the car.

Jason smiled and waved good-bye.

Siege of Darkness/Robert Taylor

Shortly after, Chris pulled up and Jason hopped in, tossing his books to the backseat.

"How was school today?" Chris asked, noticing a difference in him.

"It was okay. We got a new girl in our class." Jason grinned.

"I haven't seen you smile like that in a while. Since your mother passed! Does that grin mean you like this girl?" Chris looked in his face.

"No, it doesn't! She kinda reminds me of Ma though."

"How so?"

"She just does, it's weird!"

Chris got quiet and drove, while Jason sat thinking. Neither of the two knew the other was picturing the plane crash.

"Dad, what if I told you Mom comes to see me some nights?"

"Jason, you have to let go! I know it hurts, because it hurts me, too! We both have to let go! I cry every night, while I'm praying, but our tears aren't going to bring her back!" Chris' eyes got glossy, causing him to pull over to the side of the road.

"Dad, what would make God take her from us? You pray all the time, you got Bibles and stuff all around the house. Why would he do this to us?"

Chris hugged him and they sobbed together.

Chris closed his eyes. "We're gonna be alright." He uttered.

"I felt the same way when my parents died. We have to know that God's plan is much bigger than ours!"

"Dad, how can you put all your faith in a God that would take something you love so much?"

Siege of Darkness/Robert Taylor

"That was not God's work! That was the work of the devil!"

"You've always taught me that God was responsible for all death. Death was the ending of one journey and the start of another."

"This is true..."

"So God killed Mom!"

"Son," Chris sighed, "you must understand that Satan kills, deceives and destroys in God's name. God, teaches us to live and let live and multiply abundantly. God also said the last enemy he will destroy is, death! And, He that speaks it and has the power of it, is Lucifer!"

"All I know is, I can't love a God that took my mother's life! That's your God! Let him keep pulling wool over your eyes!" Jason jumped out the car when his father pulled up in front of their home.

Chris opened his mouth to say something, but instead shook his head. He looked in the rearview mirror to see Willie pull up in his rig. He watched as his brothers, Willie and Jimmy, climbed down from it.

On a windy but warm Thursday morning at school, Jason sat at his desk lost in thought. Linda tapped him on the shoulder, startling him. He turned around to face her.

"Jason, can you help me with my homework? I like to have a study partner; it makes it easier and much more fun."

"Sure, but I'm sure you're much smarter than I am!"

"Why do you think that?"

She stared at him awaiting an answer.

"You just look smart."

She blushed and twirled her pencil between her fingers.

That next afternoon, amidst a warm breeze, Jason couldn't stop smiling while he sat on his porch.

"What did you tell your mother?" Jason's heart pounded.

"I told her, I was going to a friend's house to study. I need to call her and let her know where I am."

"Okay, I'll get the phone for you. I'll be right back!" Jason got up and walked inside the house. Seconds later, he returned dragging a small phone, the cord dangled behind him.

After the call, he took the phone back inside and when he returned, he dropped down beside her.

Twenty minutes later, he offered her to go with him down a long dirt road to the abandoned cabin. Once inside, he lit the old oil lantern that sat in the center of the table. Linda looked around, taking in the old dreary place.

"How old is this place?" she asked.

"I really don't know. It used to belong to my great-grandparents, who gave it to my grandparents. My grandparents died in here mysteriously."

"Wow, I've never seen nothing like this! It's amazing!"

"My dad and his brothers decided to keep it, because of all the old memories," Jason stared into her eyes. He wondered, if she was thinking what he was thinking. He leaned in to kiss her, she puckered up to receive.

After smooching for a while, Jason sat down, smiling and talking.

"Linda, do you believe in God?"

"Of course, silly, who doesn't?"

"I don't, I can't believe in Him. If there was a God, why do so many bad things happen? My father's always telling me, all this stuff about His will and so forth. It seems to me like Lucifer has more power than God! Look at all the evil things that are happening. I hate God for taking my mother! Even if

Siege of Darkness/Robert Taylor

He didn't do it, He's God, He should have been able to save her."

"Jason, don't blame God for that. You have to know there had to be a reason," Linda told him and got off the subject by opening up her book.

That night, while Jason slept, a red face appeared on his ceiling, staring down at him. A voice spoke from within the darkness.

You have every right to hate God! He has betrayed you as he has me long before! Who better than I to know this! He has no loyalty! Show me your loyalty and I will repay you abundantly, in any way you so wish.

Never awakening, Jason's subconscious absorbed every word, as he turned over on his stomach. Grabbing and embracing his pillow, he mumbled,

"Tell me what I must do! Tell me what I must do…"

That evening in a dark alley, behind a restaurant, crouched down and hidden by a full, smelly dumpster, was Oswald, now a beast-like man. In a dingy jumper, he sat on his knees, tearing at a leftover steak dinner he fetched from the garbage. A glaring cat pranced over and when the beast growled, the shook animal darted out the alley. Resting against the wall, still chewing on a rigid piece of meat, the beast had a flashback. He saw himself, as he leapt from a tree onto a couple kissing, leaving them mangled and bleeding in the street. Taking his last bite, he thought of the man he chased down in a parking garage and tore into his flesh, devouring it for hours. The final thought was busting out of a prison and running for miles.

10 NOWHERE TO RUN

April 16th of 1981

    Sleeping in the back of an empty trailer, Oswald, the escapee, had flesh and blood under his fingernails. His teeth were red and yellow; his thick and wooly beard caked with dried blood and matted to his protruding face. As he heard noises, he sprung to his feet, walked the length of the container, and pushed the doors open slowly. Scanning the lot, he initially saw nothing, but more containers and unoccupied vehicles. Seconds later, loud barking captured his attention, as a big, black Rottweiler leaped up, startling him. His quick reflexes smacked it to te ground and out cold. Swiftly, he jumped down on it, listening to it howl, while its bones snapped and rib cage collapsed. He stayed there until its eyes sat still and was completely motionless. Oswald's face and arms grew tight as he closed his fist and absorbed yet another life.

    That same morning while Chris was getting dressed for work, the small radio played, *Pat Benatar's; "Hit Me With Your Best Shot."* He whistled in tune, while he moved about the house with urgency. He was running late because he was up all night and had overslept. With his spirits high, he pushed Jason's door open and yelled to him to get up.

Siege of Darkness/Robert Taylor

Rubbing his eyes, Jason sat up and fell back onto his pillow. When Chris didn't see him emerge from his room, he called out to Jason again.

With his eyes damn near shut, Jason dragged himself out of his bedroom and into the bathroom. While he leaned over the tub and turned the water on, he mumbled to himself.

"I will wander in this wilderness, until there come word from you to certify me!" Back into a nod he went. Chris pounded on the bathroom door. Jason's eyes jumped open, as he fell backwards into the water.

"Are you all right?" Chris asked, as he pushed the door open and saw water everywhere and Jason completely soaked and submerged in the tub still clothed in his pajamas.

"I'm okay," Jason told him as he climbed out dripping wet.

"I'm gone, got to get to work. Stop staying up all night and you won't be so tired! See you later." Chris marched through the house and out the front door, slamming it behind him.

In Manhattan, New York, within the Roman Catholic Church, an elder priest sat with three others, moments after afternoon mass. They were discussing world affairs and the events at hand.

"These beasts' sightings are proof that the end is upon us."

"Do not get caught up in all that's before you! As it says in the Bible; Jesus comes not to damn the world, but to save it! The devil has risen and along with him so has chaos!"

"We all acknowledge that Lucifer's thousand years imprisonment has all but ran its course. Can you not see that the people are blinded by him? He has become to so many... the Messiah!"

"Hold your tongue! He does not deserve such a title. Be patient, for God will come down from the heavens like it is written. He will then cast the devil into the lake of fire for him to be tormented forever and ever! After that, there will be no death, not for God's children."

"I do not doubt or dispute the word of our Lord. As His servant, I entrust in all that He is. Still, I can't help but be astonished by all the destruction and murder!"

After that they all shared a prayer.

Our father in Heaven, hallowed be your name. Your kingdom come, thy will be done, on earth, as it is in heaven...

For the next month, from Georgia to Virginia, corpses were turning up. The bloody massacre had people frightened as they didn't know what to make of it. One eyewitness sat down with the local police in Virginia and gave his account of a night of horror.

"I tell you, this was nothing normal, it was a beast! Something out of a movie! It came out of nowhere and those two poor girls it attacked didn't stand a chance!" the man dramatically carried on.

"Can you describe the man?" the officer asked.

"That was no man; I keep telling you…that was a beast! Y'all should have seen it! I've never seen anything like it!"

"Okay, we get that! What did it look like?"

"It was ugly! Bushy hair and smelled like raw damn sewage! You would know if you saw it, trust me!"

The officers looked at him as if he were a crazed nut job, as he continued dramatically telling the story.

"That thing was like nothing I ever saw before! There was one other thing I noticed, he had on a orange-colored jail suit with NJSP on the back."

The officers looked at each other and one of them got on the phone immediately and made a call.

Siege of Darkness/Robert Taylor

***

During one of those afternoons, Jason, who was grounded and unable to leave the house, sat in the livingroom watching television. Bored out of his mind, he jumped up and walked over to the window. Peering out, he spotted something strange. A shadow of something huge raced passed. Jason ran out onto the porch to try to get a glimpse, but it had disappeared into the woods. He eased through the grassy yard, wide eyed and alert, but the anger stricken sound of his father's screaming voice, stopped him in his tracks.
"Jason, get in this house, now!"
"Oh boy," Jason mumbled as he trotted backwards. The creature snarled after seeing this, as its hairy body sat between two large branches. Realizing his prey had slipped away, it leaped down onto all fours, and hurried off.

***

The same afternoon, while walking along a dusty back road in Charlotte, a young white girl sang as she plucked petals from a flower. Seeing a huge, ugly creature race through the towering corn stalks, she froze. When the stalks stopped moving, she dropped her flower and ran as fast as she could. When she reached the small, grey and white house she resided in, she lost it. She began screaming as she banged on the door repeatedly in her panic. Her father appeared from around back to see what the ruckus was about, as her mother opened the front door to do the same.

Siege of Darkness/Robert Taylor

"What is it baby?" her mother asked, seeing the fright in her face. The girl screamed and pointed, causing her parents to stare down the road. Her mother grabbed her and consoled her.

Minutes later, the father was pushing his tractor up the road, with his rifle locked under his arm. Scouring the path and field on both sides, he didn't flinch because he didn't know what to expect. Reaching an old condemned barn, he turned off the tractor's engine and dismounted. With his rifle clutched tightly at his side, he approached the large door. Slowly pulling it open, he anchored the rifle to eye level. Cautiously, he stepped in; the stench alarmed him way before he noticed blood, feces, bones, and bloody bits of flesh. Fearing he might encounter something beyond his comprehension, he turned and eased back out. Jumping back on his tractor, he started it up and rode off. He looked back as he did, but there was no movement. Whatever was there must have left the area, he thought.

During that weekend, as rain poured down and the sun shined, Sherrod lay in his bunk, staring at the ceiling. He thought of all he wanted to do once he got out of prison. He envisioned college and different jobs, but seemed truly unsure. Jumping from his bunk, he stared through the bars trying to see where the guards were. After spotting one walking on a lower tier, Sherrod walked back toward his bunk and started shadow boxing. As he did, his hands got faster and faster, his feet danced swifter and swifter and he grinned sinisterly. He was beginning to like what he had become, all the strength, power, and the ability to interact with the spirit world. His energy was unbelievable, as he dripped in sweat and continued on throughout the night. An overlords appeared and watched.

Siege of Darkness/Robert Taylor

With great power comes even greater responsibility! I see you are becoming one with all that you are. I am pleased to see this.

The overlord disappeared, as Sherrod stopped and grabbed a nearby towel. While wiping his face, he took a deep breath and lay back down. He grinned, as he stared up at the ceiling, and closed his fist tightly.

During that time, law enforcement had tracked down the remaining fugitive, who somehow found his way into the Carolinas. As patrol cars pursued the stolen red, pick-up, he weaved in and out of traffic, recklessly challenging the driving skills of everyone on the road, including law enforcement. As a officer in one of the cruisers smashed into the driver's side, he lost control and ran off the road. Swerving to avoid cars and a guard rail, his dodging left him speeding toward a tree. Crashing head on, he knocked his head against the windshield, smashing it. Dazed, he jumped out, hobbling on foot, continuing to avoid capture. Nearby, the officers stopped their cruisers at the shoulder of the highway. They released the dogs minutes later to pick up his scent. He ran like a cheetah, leaping and climbing, where even most dogs couldn't keep up or follow. Helicopters flew over and circled the area, but they, too had problems locating him. Finally, after hours of searching, he was spotted climbing from a trench alongside a huge, fallen oak tree. As helicopters hovered, the officers on foot closed in and the dogs barked as they led the way. Angry and done running, Oswald roared, stopped and prepared for battle. In a small clearing, surrounded by trees, the dogs charged at him on command. He grabbed them as quickly as they sprang into action, breaking a few of their necks, while tossing others into trees and slamming a few to the ground.

Siege of Darkness/Robert Taylor

Astounded by what was taking place before them, the officers made no attempt to approach; they pulled their guns and yelled.

"Freeze!"

Oswald took off running and the three officers bullets showered and littered the path behind him, a few of them striking him in the process. He howled as his squealing voice echoed. In seconds, his swift run turned into a weakened stagger as he collapsed to the ground, bleeding from the mouth and bullet wounds.

Standing over him, four of the officers began to have a discussion.

"We're going to have to airlift him to a hospital!" one of them stated not too happy.

"Man, this son of a bitch killed officers, civilians, police dogs, and God knows what else. All them bullets in his body right now and he's still breathing? I'm not traveling with that thing! He's something else, he's not human!"

At that moment, gunshots rang out, as one of the officers put two bullets right through Oswald's heart and another in his skull.

"Problem solved!" he spat, kneeling to make sure breath no longer resided in him.

The other officers in the area turned as they heard them, but said nothing.

Thirty minutes later, the coroner was on the scene, placing Oswald's body inside a body bag. Within seconds of zipping up the bag, the corpse disintegrated, catching the bag afire, causing it to melt. All that remained was a small pile of white dust and film. The entire team of officers came over to look and was amazed. A few of them looked around, wondering if he somehow got out.

Siege of Darkness/Robert Taylor

***

Inside the prison walls, the inmates were in the dayroom watching the news. Quietly, they viewed the footage of the police tracking and chasing Oswald into the woods. The newscaster told the story from a helicopter.

"This has been one of the largest manhunts in American history. Prisoner Dean Oswald and two others escaped from New Jersey State Prison on March 27, It's not the fact that they escaped, it's how they did it that was unbelievable! They ripped out bars and demolished walls, after causing a major prison riot. They baffled the police, prison guards, and the world alike! But now it looks like it's come to an end near Mecklenburg County Park in Charlotte, North Carolina."

***

Back at the scene, the coroner was curious about the white dust. He picked up a handful of it and sifted it through his fingers, but there was nothing that he could detect from it. He gathered as much as he could, placed it in a jar and carried it away.

***

Chris and his brothers were watching the news, Jason walked in and stopped in his tracks. He sat down as what he heard was unbelievable. Glued to the television, he realized how close it was to home.

***

Siege of Darkness/Robert Taylor

At home, Elijah sat writing and listening to his radio program. He dropped his pencil when *breaking news* interrupted with the capture of Oswald.

***

Later that evening, the officers returned to the abandoned barn where they initially spotted Oswald. During their search, they found bones from different animals, the head of a pig, squirrel flesh, and human remains. Hidden in a corner was a makeshift bed, which smelled uncivilized. Everything was gathered, tagged, bagged, and carried out. The family that lived on the land watched from afar, as all types of special police forces scoured the twenty acres on which it all sat.

***

Sitting out on his porch, Jason stared out as the sun descended. He envisioned the scene that was on the news. He wished he could have seen it firsthand. Then his mother's face appeared right before him, breaking up that vision.

"Jason, my love, I am here as always! I will never leave you. You must trust me and everything will turn out fine."

"I hear you mother, I hear you." Jason looked up into the sky.

"I know how painful all of this must be, yet it is for a reason. I am in a better place. A place where there is no death, no pain, nothing but beauty and absolute paradise!"

"Mother, please explain God's reason for taking you! Please, so I can better deal with it."

Siege of Darkness/Robert Taylor

"He wanted me to be an angel, an angel to watch over you. We must not question his actions. I love you, son."

Jason sat paralyzed in thought, then jumped to his feet and marched in the house. As he entered, his father and uncles were still sitting in the living room watching television, but turned their attention toward him.

"What's up, boy? You look like you seen a ghost!" Willie pointed out. Chris and Jimmy looked over at him also.

"What wrong, boy?" Chris asked, looking him square in the eyes.

"…Nothing." Jason rushed past them and headed upstairs to his bedroom.

In his room, he walked over to the window where he looked out, amongst the clouds and blue sky. Confused, he wondered if what he was seeing, was real. A knock at his door brought him out of thought.

"Jason, I'm coming in!" Chris announced before he pushed the door open. Seeing Jason staring out the window, Chris walked over to join him.

"The world's going to hell in a handbasket, huh?" Chris started up.

"Yeah, it definitely is," Jason responded.

Chris grabbed him by the shoulder and looked him in the eyes. "I just came to make sure you're okay." He hugged him.

***

Deep in the devil's realm, Lucifer's laughter was loud and strong. The soul of Tessa was there before him again, still and ready to do whatever he asked of her.

Siege of Darkness/Robert Taylor

Your soul is mine, to do as I please with! You cannot ask for my hand in marriage and walk out on me...I am God! You called upon me, when you were in need and I was there for you! Now your soul is mine to keep...forever!" Satan spoke, announcing his dominance over her.

***

In his prison cell that evening, Sherrod was deep in thought. He wondered if there were more of them that had been infected and are they just lying and waiting for the right moment. He was glad they caught the others, because they would have killed so many, while causing mass-hysteria and destruction. Closing his eyes, he got comfortable and drifted off.

11 NEW BEGINNINGS

Friday, September 21th 1984

The years breezed by quickly and sixteen year old Jason was in high school. He frequented the local library, researching the supernatural, from vampires, to gargoyles, to werewolves, to freaks of nature. Intrigued by the so- called myths, he was determined to bring forth the truth. In the midst of his research, he came upon a book *Byron Malic's Reign of Terror*. Staring at the symbol on the front cover, he took it to memory. Sitting on the floor, he pried it open. He was so captivated that he lost track of time and an hour had passed. With his forehead wrinkled, he flipped through the pages with anticipation. As others walked by, he barely flinched, or stopped to look up. Suddenly, he turned back to the opening passage, which read: *"From the least to the greatest of them, everyone is greedy for unjust gain; and from prophet to priest, everyone deals falsely,"* **Jeremiah 6:13.** Thereafter it read: *A scholarly priest roamed the Catholic halls with godly aspirations and unforeseen treachery. He sought out Satan in his quest for power and immortality. Through his weakness, he became one of Satan's most prized warriors.*

Closing the book, he sighed, taking in all the new information. Wanting to get home in a hurry, he rose and tucked the book under his arm. Striding quickly, he marched to the counter to rent the book and headed out the library, organizing the imagery in his head.

Siege of Darkness/Robert Taylor

In his second year of college, Elijah, a history major, sat in a park taking in the scenery. He was becoming more and more obsessed with the study of the human mind and body, which caused him to change his major. He ended up taking courses in biochemistry and cultural science. While studying, he worked as an intern under Professor Jenkins, a tall, distinguished, grey haired, Black man, who was fascinated with historic events, personalities, and supernatural life forces. Elijah became his understudy because he was overwhelmed with his level of intellect. There was much he could learn and he was up for the task.

***

That following Monday after school let out, Jason walked through the heavy breeze. His companion, Linda, strolled alongside him. He was burning her ears about the stories his uncles told him, always animated when he did so.

"Linda, I know you won't believe this, but I think what my uncles were telling me is true! I found this book here and it's almost word for word what my family's been telling me all these years. Can you believe this? I knew it, I knew it!" he rambled excitingly as he jumped around and she looked at him strangely.

"Jason, you are so crazy! Why do you believe in stuff like that? You are so weird! Even if it's true, who the hell cares?" She smiled, as she was tired of hearing it herself.

"I do! I'm not weird. I'm telling you, I can tell by the way they told me those stories that it had to exist. Why would people write books on it, if it didn't? Come on, I'm serious!"

She giggle softly.

Siege of Darkness/Robert Taylor

"People like Walter Hemmingway write all types of fictional stories and garbage to make money. That's how he makes his living." she chuckled.

"Who is Walter Hemmingway?' he asked, as he saw nothing funny.

"You don't even know the author of the book you're reading? He's the author of that book you're holding, idiot! And the author of five other murder mysteries and Sci-Fi's," she explained in detail.

"Okay, so he wrote it. I see you're a non-believer, too! I'm telling you this stuff is real! You watch, once I figure out where the ritual took place, I'm going to prove it to the world!"

The two of them crossed the street and walked into a small family style restaurant.

"You really aren't getting it. All this is just one man's answer to a world thirsty for a great read!"

Jason just looked at her as he pulled open and held the door.

"It's more than that…I'm telling you!" he spat lightly as he walked in behind her.

At one of the booths, shortly after ordering, Jason opened the book and began to show Linda pictures, as he read different passages from it.

"Listen…Linda, right here! Byron Malic was once a high priest of the Roman Catholic Church. He made a deal with Lucifer, the devil himself, for eternal life! Can you believe this stuff? You can't make this kinda stuff up! You can't make up stuff like this! Listen to this one right here, he was said to have been responsible for over two hundred murders! Wow…can you believe this?" he ranted, as she slurped on a chocolate milk shake the waitress placed in front of her.

Siege of Darkness/Robert Taylor

Linda's eyes danced around the room, as she really didn't want to hear what he was saying.

He dug deeper into the book, flipping the pages quickly.

She stared across at him like she wanted to slap some sense into him.

That evening, while he sat on his bedroom floor engulfed again, he embraced the supernatural world painted on every page. Chapter after chapter, he could see and feel the power of the beings as if they were actually in the room with him. He could smell their tart and unsavory scents, as his fingers thumbed the pages. Shadows moved about the walls, as his voice rose, bringing them to life with his very pitch.

***

Up north, a few days later, on September 24, beneath the heavy rain, a pregnant Marie Childs was sitting in her livingroom watching television, while knitting a pair of blue booties for her unborn baby. She smiled and hummed to herself, as her phone rang.

"Hello," she greeted.

"Hey baby," the voice of an older woman greeted.

"Hey Ma, what's going on?"

"Just, checking on my daughter and my unborn grandchild! Just making sure y'all all right in this weather."

"We're fine, just fine!" Marie rubbed her stomach.

"That's good, girl! You need anything?"

"No Ma, I'm okay, thanks anyway."

Suddenly, a door opened and closed. Followed by heavy pounding of the staircase. By the loud thud that hit each step, she expected attitude.

Siege of Darkness/Robert Taylor

"Let me call you right back, Ma," She ended the conversation before her mother could say a word.

The door to her apartment swung open. Her big light-skinned boyfriend, Aaron, who had on black overalls, walked in dripping wet. Without warning, he slammed the door, as he was angry about something, and stormed past her without saying so much as a word.

"Hello to you, too, Aaron!" she blurted sarcastically, but he didn't reply. The bedroom door abruptly slammed, leaving a cold silence. Marie went back to knitting as if he wasn't there.

Twenty minutes later, he emerged from the bedroom, frowning, in his boxer shorts and a blue T-shirt. He walked straight into the livingroom where she sat.

"I hope you cooked me something to eat, I'm starving!" he ranted commandingly in an angry tone, as he planted himself just over her.

"There's some left-over chicken and rice in the bottom of the fridge and sandwich meat in the drawer," she told him, while she never looked up and continued to knit.

"Get up and fix me a plate, I'm hungry!" He snatched her knitting needles and yarn from her. She looked up at him, folded her arms and held a defiant posture.

"Dumb ass! I hope my child don't act nothing like you!" he barked. Turning to walk away, he reached back, grabbed her by the arm and pulled her up out of the chair.

"Stop pulling on me!" she shouted, as she yanked away and looked at him astonished.

"You gon get in this kitchen and get me something to eat!" He forcibly escorted her. Pulling the refrigerator door open, he clutched her by the back of her neck and bent her over in front of it.

Siege of Darkness/Robert Taylor

"Would you stop!" she yelled, as the pressure from his tightly clinched hand pierced her neck.

"You reach in there and get me what you want me to eat! Warm it up, and bring it to me in the living room. I ain't playing with you! Am I making myself clear?" He let go of her neck and stared her down, as she remained silent. Looking at him in disbelief, her eyes rolling around in her head.

In the livingroom, he kicked her knitting needles and yarn across the floor, under the television stand. Holding the remote, he changed the channel.

In tears, Marie extended her trembling right hand outward, grabbing a bowl that held a few pieces of chicken. She carried it over to the microwave, put it in, set the timer, and stood there in front of it with her arms folded.

"Hurry the hell up!" he yelled from the living room. Suddenly, she felt sharp pains and dropped to her knees. Falling over on the floor, she lay in a fetal position, cradling her stomach. Hearing her cry out, Aaron got up and walked into the kitchen, where he stood over her.

"What's wrong with you? Come on now, get up off the floor," he shouted, as the microwaved sounded off, causing him to reach over her to get his food.

"Baby, I think something's wrong! Please call me an ambulance.," she mumbled softly, as tears ran against her nose and across her mouth.

"Stop faking, get up, and come sit ya ass down!" He walked away leaving her curled up. She started shouting, as the pain got worst. Realizing she wasn't faking, he placed the bowl on the coffee table and hurried to help her up off the floor. As she yelled and screamed, he carried her over to the sofa. She screamed louder, causing him to get on the phone to call 911.

Siege of Darkness/Robert Taylor

Two hours later, Marie lay in a hospital bed, glossy eyed, staring up at the ceiling after the loss of her unborn child. Aaron walked in with a bouquet of roses, smiling and confident as he approached her bedside. Seeing him only made her angrier. She turned her back to him and smothered her face in the pillow.

He sat down on the edge of bed.

"I'm so sorry, I was so mean to you. I'll make it up to you when you get out, I promise. I love you! We'll try again!" He expressed, with what seemed like sincerity, as he lay down behind her. Wrapping his arms around her, he cradled her silent and trembling soul, as he closed his eyes. Marie softly said a prayer.

"God, all I ask for is a good man! Send me a man worthy of me, and remove this misguided fool from my life! Amen."

***

Two days later within Sherrod's cell, as he curled up under two wool quilts, an overlord visited him. He stood watching Sherrod as he maneuvered, trying to get comfortable. Feeling a presence, Sherrod woke up only to visually scan through the darkness.

Through your troubled soul shall the life of the forthcoming prophecy come to be! You, the chosen one at the right time, will help align what shall be the new world order,

Sherrod listened as always. He jumped down from his bunk and stared through the bars.

"What is this prophecy you speak of?" he asked.

It's Everything, all we've been preparing for! It is what this world needs...

Siege of Darkness/Robert Taylor

That Saturday, Marie's parents came to visit her in the hospital and Aaron sat in a chair to their right. He smiled and spoke, but neither parent uttered a single word as their expressions said it all.

"Marie, why is this sorry…Lord, bless my tongue…piece of sugar, honey, ice-tea sitting in here with you and he caused you to lose the baby"

Aaron stood up. "No disrespect, Mrs. Childs, I didn't do anything to her! She fell out in the floor and started bleeding!" He pleaded his case as compassion rang out in his words.

"You…I know you had something to do with it, because I was on the phone with her and she was knitting and happy! You get home and she suddenly miscarries? I hate you and if my daughter has the good senses God gave her, she'd leave you alone!"

Aaron looked at Marie as if she were supposed to defend him. She turned her head, giving him her back. He stormed out the room.

***

Sunday afternoon, after spending the morning in the park, Jason and Linda sat in an ice cream parlor licking away at ice cream cones. Jason stopped eating his ice cream and stared at her.

"Why do you put up with me?" he asked.

"Oh, so you know you are a little out there, don't you?" She giggled.

"Yeah, but I am who I am. You got to understand, in my house there's just something wrong. I just can't put my fingers on it. I feel like the books I'm reading and my families are connected in some weird way. I got to find out who this

Siege of Darkness/Robert Taylor

Walter Hemmingway is," he added, causing Linda to stare through him.

"Now you're planning to go on a witch hunt to find the author of a science fiction novel? Jason, you really amaze me, of how far you are willing to take this!"

"I don't care what no one thinks, my gut feeling is telling me it's true and that's all that matters!"

"Well, let me be the first to tell you, Walter Hemmingway is dead! He died in the late 1800s."

"How did he die?"

"I haven't a clue, I just read somewhere that he disappeared and is presumed dead. They never found a body."

Jason just stared at her, but his brain seemed to kick into overdrive.

In that instance, a few guys from their school walked in, and upon seeing Jason laughed and pointed. Jason looked at them, smirked, and mumbled,

"Jerks!"

"Hey, Jason, have you seen any monsters lately?" one of the boys asked as they all stood at the counter ordering.

"Yeah, your mother!" he answered, hoping to get a rise out of him. The boy rushed over, smacked the cone from Jason's hand, and pushed him out of his chair and onto the floor. Smiling, Jason jumped up and before they could get to each other, the owner of the parlor was standing between them.

"Outside with this madness! Not in my place!" he shouted as he held them apart.

"You lucky, fart boy! I was going to embarrass you!" the boy told Jason.

"You were going to get embarrassed!" Jason stated with confidence. Linda just watched.

Siege of Darkness/Robert Taylor

12 BLESSINGS AND CURSES

Saturday, October 6

That following weekend, Jason lay across his bed reading *Execution of the Undead*, an old tattered book. Hypnotically trapped in the aged and bonded pages, he came upon a section that read,

On a dark night, as the moon's shadow blocked the earth, all unclean spirits had to temporarily vacate the bodies they inhabited. Rendering them defenseless, four priests along with a sheriff and a few townsmen cornered Malic. They hunted and found him in a cave just outside Blacksburg. Knowing what they had to do and the fact that it had to be done in a few hours, they armed themselves with Holy water, shackles, crosses, and pump shotguns. They searched him out, found, and carted him into the woods. They lay him on a bed made of tree branches and leaves. They were prepping to perform a ritual to drain his tainted blood, and offer it to God to rid the earth of such an evil force.

"Oh Lord, the most high, as a testament of our love we give to thee...this soul whose greed has driven him to do thee unspeakable, thee unimaginable, and thee ungodly! We ask for your forgiveness and mercy, oh Lord, amen."

"Cast out from him, never to return, you unclean spirit! Let him be!"

Siege of Darkness/Robert Taylor

Leave me be, I have rights upon this soul! came a voice from the sky. Everyone turned, holding guns and crosses in the air.

You fools, you all can kill thy flesh, but I will be forever! Hear me...forever! It is prophesied that evil will inherit the earth.

"What book do you read from? It's prophesied that the meek shall inherit the earth! The humble and just of hearts!" Priest Bauser shouted in return.

Your scriptures are filled with lies as you will soon see in time; it's a paradox shielding its followers from the real truths. You speak like your heart knows of no evil, like you're pure like that of Adam before the bout with temptation.

"No, I speak the words of my Lord and Savior, Christ, who knows that I am not without flaw, and bears witness too. and I cast you out, out of this soul, off this earth, forever!" Bauser continued.

Bauser turned, armed with a solid silver four-foot spike, threw his hands high above his head as the others chanted loudly. With great force, he drove it through the chest, rode it through the heart and out his back. As blood poured and darkened the soil beneath, there was thunderous laughter. The priests stood in prayer as the townsmen looked on horrified.

Grabbing a highlighter, Jason marked up the book vigorously, while also noting that Walter Hemmingway wrote it. He thought back and remembered the fact that it was similar to the stories his uncles told him. It picked up right where *Reign of Terror* left off. Nowhere in the book did it insinuate it was the sequel, but it was evident by reading the two books. This Walter Hemmingway seemed to be the link and the key to Jason's mystery.

Siege of Darkness/Robert Taylor

Minutes later, in his father's bedroom, he found an old Bible in an armoire drawer. In the midst his searching, he spotted the book, *Noita Lever*. Remembering his father reading from it on several occasions, he pulled it down also. Then, he noticed a giant wooden crucifix just to the left, wrapped in a white cloth. Being the nosey kid, he opened the cloth to reveal a big *JESUS CHRIST* symbol and what could possibly be old dried up blood. Hearing the rustling of keys and someone coming through the front door, he hurriedly placed the crucifix back in the cloth, the books back in their place, closed the armoire door, and exited the bedroom quickly.

Entering his room, Chris sat on the edge of his bed and noticed the cloth hanging. He walked over, opened the armoire, and picked it up. He looked around just before unwrapping it, revealing the stained crucifix. He went into thought as he ran his right hand across it; the sky instantly became dark and he looked up and out the window.

"Oh my, Lord, let no danger find my doorstep, let not the devil find fulfillment in the lives of those around me. Bless me, for I humble myself in Your presence." Chris spoke as if he was expecting something, company maybe. Jason watched wide eyed with his room door slightly cracked. He wondered why his father was trembling and praying over the old bloodstained crucifix. Suddenly, the sky lit up and rumbled as Chris walked over to the window. Without warning O'Conner appeared, but this time he donned enormous wings and was garbed like a titan prepped to do battle. Chris stood still as the crucifix started to glow.

As I have told you, as the holder of that crucifix and the word of God, no harm shall come to thee! But, within your household there is one who seeks truth from falsehoods, who

Siege of Darkness/Robert Taylor

is fascinated by those of darkness. He has a hate for the Lord that stems from the death of his mother. You must bring his soul to a more righteous place, so he can be spared the misery of God's wrath!

Hearing this, Jason eased his door shut and climbed into his bed, where he closed his eyes. Suddenly, he heard footsteps nearing and entering his room.

"Jason, are you asleep?" Chris asked softly, but there was no response. He began to search through his room. Jason watched with his eyes slightly open and could see him going through his clothes, dresser, he even peeked under the bed. Back on his feet, he got ready to leave when he noticed two books sitting on the nightstand. He eased over and picked them up, *Byron Malic's Reign of Terror and The Execution of the Undead.* He tucked them under his arm and headed out and across the hall to his room, where he sat on the bed. Opening *Byron Malic's Reign of Terror*; he came upon a passage that read; *the devil lives amongst us*! He read further and his eyes widened as he could see areas highlighted by his son. Wondering why Jason was so adamant in his quest to unveil the truth about Byron Malic, Chris returned to his son's room.

"Jason! Jason! Wake up, boy!"

"Hmmm, what?" Jason responded groggy, pretending to be sleeping.

"Why are you reading this garbage? I told you Byron Malic was only an old folktale. A made up story! Just an old folk's tale told to us, to scare us. What you need to be doing is focusing on your school work, not this dumb stuff!"

"Okay, Dad, okay..."

"Don't 'okay' me! I mean it! Leave this stuff alone! This here is God's house and God's house only! Don't bring the devil in here, not now, not ever! He's not welcome!" Chris held the books, shaking them angrily. Feeling he made his point clear, he stormed out, slamming the door behind him.

"God killed my mother! Have you forgotten?" Jason yelled out of frustration just before he grunted and planted his face in his pillow. He closed his eyes and fought to calm down. The vision of his father talking to the angel appeared. Amazed by the interaction, he couldn't help but become even more curious.

Two days later, after school, Jason search through the house for the books his father had taken from him. He opened the armoire doors and saw that the crucifix and the books were gone. Moving things around, there was nothing. With nowhere left to check, he walked down stairs into the living room and over to the fireplace. He noticed pieces of burnt pages surrounded by ashes. There wasn't enough of it left to even waste time trying to salvage. Heartbroken, Jason stormed up to his room and flopped down across his bed.

"I'll just go to the library and get another copy, that's all! He can't stop me! I got to know!" he mumbled as the phone rang.

That afternoon, Jason rode his bike from one library to another, until he got lucky. Finally, he found one copy of each of the books that he was looking for. As he walked to the counter to rent the books, he just happened to look out the window. Noticing his father peeking in, he immediately got angry, realizing he'd been following him. Tossing the books on the counter, Jason apologized to the librarian for one of them hitting her about the hip.

Realizing Jason saw him, Chris raced back to his car, jumped in and sat waiting for Jason to exit.

Inside, Jason stood at the counter talking to the librarian.

Siege of Darkness/Robert Taylor

"Can you put these books aside for me? I'll be back to get them tomorrow."

"You have to leave a deposit, otherwise at the end of the night I have to put them back on the shelf."

"No problem, here's five dollars. Is that enough?" Jason kept looking around and at the windows.

Ten minutes passed and there was no sign of Jason, so Chris got out of his car and hustled back to the window again. Stunned that he didn't see Jason, he ran around to the front entrance and went inside.

At eight o'clock that evening in Newark, New Jersey, Marie and Aaron were arguing. She had his things packed when he came in from work. A patrol car sat outside at the curb, as two officers waited inside their apartments.

"I can't believe you're doing this?" Aaron looked at her, frustrated that she would put the police in their business.

"I'm tired of you! Go find you a woman that will put up with your mess! I'm done!" she yelled panting.

"I can't believe you're doing me like this! I love you!" He stared into her eyes.

"No, you love yourself! Leave…please." She walked to the door ahead of him. He picked up his bags and shook his head in disbelief. The officers followed him out.

***

The next morning at the breakfast table, Chris sat in deep thought. After a few minutes, he looked over at Jason and sighed.

Siege of Darkness/Robert Taylor

"Jason, I'll tell you what. If you graduate from high school with honors and leave this supernatural stuff behind, I'll buy you a vehicle of your choice!" Chris looked him in the eyes.

Pausing from his breakfast, Jason smiled. "For-real? You got that!"

Chris sat staring at him, hoping he meant what he said.

"I'm serious Jason, no more of this. No more blaming God for your mother's death…nothing! You hold up your end of the bargain and I'll hold up mine!"

Jason nodded in agreement after forking up bits of pancakes and eggs.

"I want a black Jeep Wrangler!" Jason told him with a huge smile on his face, which disappeared within seconds.

"Dad…I don't understand, why you aren't still mad at God for taking mom? I know it hurts you too! You still praise him, day and night, like it never happened! I can't forgive him for that!" Jason was tired of seeing his father sad.

"Look, and this is the last time I'm going to have this conversation. You hear me? God is the Almighty, unquestionably, the all-seeing. He didn't make the choice but, if He had made it, who are we to question it? Yes, I do miss her, but she's not coming back!" He got up and walked from the kitchen.

***

That afternoon, beneath the pouring rain, within his cell, Sherrod was counting down the months and days. He sat thinking of all that he was missing. He wanted nothing more than to do the normal things like; cuddle with a woman, eat normal food and have an occasional beer. As he sat there pondering, he couldn't help but think about the changes to his body, and the words the overlord had spoken upon him.

***

That next morning, Jason was up bright and early, eagerly reading and studying. He was racing through his homework and preparing for a quiz his teacher had planned. He seemed inspired by his father's offer and decided to give his other research a break, at least for the now.

***

A few hours later, Sherrod sat on his bunk, when the overlord appeared and began to speak out.

You are ready…ready to spearhead what is set before you! From the time you leave this place, your mission is of great importance! I hope that you are truly all that we hoped you'd be.

Sherrod looked in a mirror he had glued to the wall adjacent to his bunk. It seemed as if he was making sure he was still the same person, because he felt altogether different.

****

For the next three weeks, Sherrod's body felt like someone had tuned him up. There were no more hot flashes or fevers. No headaches. No painful transitions. Nothing but an overwhelming curiosity to know what was in store for him, once he regained his freedom.

Siege of Darkness/Robert Taylor

***

Month after month, Jason was in the library, on the back porch, or in the abandoned cabin studying relentlessly. He and Linda grew exceptionally close and his grades were back up. His teachers applauded his improvement and sent letters home, which brought a smile to Chris's face. He and Jason began to laugh, joke and talk more. Everything and everyone seemed to be moving toward a better place.

That early spring, Chris was standing over Tessa's grave.

"I thank God for every minute I spent with you! You were my happiness. I pray every day that God gives me the strength to get through this. You came back to me, just for me to lose you again. Life can be so unfair at times." He kneeled down and placed a bouquet of red roses in the ground, just out in-front of her tombstone. After walking away, he suddenly got dizzy and fell out. Another person in the cemetery saw this, and ran to his aid.

Hours later, resting in a hospital bed, Chris opening his eyes to his brother and Jason by his side, which brought an instant smile to his face.

"Ahh, it's so good to see all your faces," Chris mumbled.

"What happened?" Willie asked.

"I was at Tessa's grave site, talking to her. I kneeled down and placed the roses I had brought by her tombstone. When I stood back up, I felt lightheaded. I started walking and everything got blurry. Next thing I know, I was being placed in an ambulance."

"Dad, you scared us. I don't know what I would do if I lost you, too!"

Siege of Darkness/Robert Taylor

"I love you guys!" Chris hugged each of them.

The doctor walked in.

"Mr. Milosky, I'm Doctor Chang. Now, I've done x-rays, a cat scan and a brain scan. I've only noticed one thing. My conclusion is, you had a mild stroke."

"A stroke?" Willie questioned, somewhat surprised. He looked at Chris worriedly.

"I'm okay, you guys go home! I've got this." Chris assured them, but looked worried. Jason stared at him, not wanting to leave as Willie pulled at him. They left as visiting hours would end in twenty minutes..

***

That same afternoon, Elijah walked through the Newark Museum with Professor Jenkins as he schooled him on things from the past.

"You see this creature right here?" Professor Jenkin pointed at the grey wolf.

"They have been described in folklore negatively. Superstition has it, that throughout the south in the eighteen hundreds, people had great fear of the wolf. That's where the stories of the werewolf originated. The town's people that lived near the woods, began to find limbs and mangled bodies," he added. Elijah, absorbed the conversation like the sponge he was. They moved on, up a set of steps, into a huge room.

"Now this creature here…" the professor went on teaching as they made a day of it. From one room to the next, Elijah enjoyed himself.

***

Siege of Darkness/Robert Taylor

That weekend, a bored Jason sat in the abandoned cabin as he thought back to his uncles telling him the stories, his father talking to an angel, to voices speaking to him in his sleep and finally his mother's death. Coming out of thought, he stood up, walked to a broken window, and stared out.

"Sorry, Dad," he uttered. "I've got to finish this. I've got to finish what I started!"

He turned and headed out the door and back up the road to the house. He mentally battled with going against his word, but it only took seconds for him to convince himself that he was doing the right thing.

Later that day, carefully browsing through the racks of books within every library in the area, Jason got frustrated. He couldn't find anything that detailed the whereabouts of Byron Malic's burial site or where he died. He found story after story, giving what part of town, but nothing to pinpoint with exactness. Irritated, he jumped on his bike and pushed down the road.

On Sunday morning, Chris was preparing for church. He walked into Jason's room to ask him to come along. Jason ignored him and continued watching television. Annoyed and running late, Chris rushed out the house and to his car.

Moments later, Willie stood in Jason's doorway, shaking his head.

"What?" Jason parted his lips as he looked up.

"You know your father just got out of the hospital! You should have gone with him, just to make sure he was all right. Stop being such a selfish brat!" Willie snapped, somewhat angry. Jason didn't say a word; he just looked at him.

Siege of Darkness/Robert Taylor

An hour later at the church, Chris sat with his Bible open as the pastor preached.

"There is only one God. He has no brothers, sisters, cousins, uncles, or otherwise. He is a jealous God. Do not think because He is merciful, that He will keep allowing you to spit in His face, compare another to Him or even take Him for granted. Not my God, you won't! He may not be there when you want Him to be, but He's always there when you need Him. Praise the Lord! I said, praise the Lord!"

The church repeated him and applauded. The pastor's words comforted Chris as he thought about all that was going on in his life. As much as he was hurting, he didn't blame God for all that took place. He also thought if he had died, the comfort would be that he could be with the one he loved.

That Monday, while Jason was in school, Linda was out sick. Not seeing her in the classroom, he began to worry.

After the final bell and on his stroll home, Jason decided to stop by her place. When he got there, her mother was just getting out of her car.

"Jason, can you help me with these groceries?" she asked opening the trunk.

"Sure." He sat his books down on the porch and hurried over. Grabbing two bags, he followed her as she opened the door. Jason walked in behind her and placed the bags on the kitchen table. Linda came down the stairs, with a cup of hot tea in her hands, wrapped in a thick purple robe. She smiled and coughed.

"Hey, baby!" she greeted him, placing her cup on the table and gave Jason a hug. They looked into each other's eyes and smiled, as Linda's mother started putting away the groceries.

***

Siege of Darkness/Robert Taylor

Deep in the wooded forest of Cherokee Falls, seven young men were filming. As it got late, they began to hear noises. The director refused to stop shooting, so they wandered, take after take. As they set up for a shot, they looked around for their cameraman, who seemed to have disappeared. They yelled out his name to no avail. One of the others tried to call the police and there was no reception. When he turned, his entire crew was gone. Standing in the woods by himself now, he took off running, and stumbling, until he came to a wrought iron fence. He stopped to look back. Scared to death, he took off again, jumping over tombstones. A loud, growling roar vibrated his being. Screaming for his life, a force unknown to him, threw him against the wrought iron fence, pinning him to one of the rods, leaving him twitching and dangling.

Siege of Darkness/Robert Taylor

13 *HIGH SCHOOL*

Thursday, September 26th, 1985

In his senior year of high school, Jason was focused. Every time he thought things were getting too rough, he thought about the wager with his father. Through it all, he saw that hard work and diligence definitely had its rewards. To avoid his father's prying eyes, he hid all the literature on the supernatural, in his school locker, or he gave it to Linda to hold. As much as he wanted to place it aside, he couldn't. He yearned to know all there was.

Many days, he sat with Linda at her house and spent the entire time discussing what he was going to do once he finished high school.

"Once I graduate, I'm going to really figure this whole thing out. Every intimate detail, you watch! I don't care who thinks I'm crazy! I know I'm not, that's all that matters! The more I research, the realer it all seems."

Linda sat across the table, staring into his face, showcasing her boredom.

"And, you wonder why you don't have any friends? Jason, you rarely talk about anything other than that! I wish you would focus on something else, something relatable. You're obsessed! Look at you; you're practically drooling like you're some type of mad scientist or mad man!"

"Whatever you say, I'm not crazy though! I bet you that much!"

Siege of Darkness/Robert Taylor

Not wanting to agitate him further, Linda sat quiet watching him write in his notebook. After a short silence and feeling ignored, she couldn't take it any longer, so she got up and headed upstairs. Jason paused long enough to wave his hand and smirk.

***

That Friday, Elijah was in Professor Jenkins's home. The two were at the dining table finishing up a meal the professor's wife had cooked for them. The cool breeze wafting through the opened dining room windows set the stage as they started to talk.

"Sir, your wife put her foot in that meatloaf and that mac and cheese was to die for!" Elijah complimented.

"Yeah, she does her thing in the kitchen. I can't complain. I've got the whole package! God definitely blessed me." He bragged as his wife walked over smiling and kissed him on the temple.

An hour later, he was showing Elijah around his beautiful, lavish home, venturing from one room to the next. Amazed, Elijah marveled at all the furnishings and dark cherry wood finish that trimmed the walls and doors.

"Here's my favorite room, my library. I've read every book in here. I refuse to put a book in here that I haven't read from cover to cover," he stated proudly.

"Wow, you read all these books! That's amazing!" Elijah reveling at the floor to ceiling, built in bookshelves, filled with book. Walking closer to a shelf, he picked up a book and thumbed through the pages. The professor watched and smiled. At that moment his wife called out to him.

Siege of Darkness/Robert Taylor

"You go ahead and look through them; you might find something that interests you!" Professor Jenkins left the room to tend to him wife.

Forty minutes later, Elijah had made himself comfortable. He sat in a plush burgundy leather recliner with a stack of five books on the floor to his right. With one open, he seemed captivated. He read to himself.

"As the rain danced against the window pane, a woman's high pitched scream echoed from within a dreary and darkened ally. After her screams were muted, a creature was revealed by a lonely street light. This beast's elongated fingers dripped with her blood as it growled, revealing a horrific mouth that sheltered a corral of jagged teeth."

The professor walked back in.

"Did you find anything?" he asked as he sat down himself.

"Sure did, this book right here and those on the floor."

"Oh, so I see your interest, is in that of the supernatural world?"

"Not really, I just like a good read, something that's going to hold my interests."

"That particular book you're reading will definitely hold your interest! That's a collector's piece, dated back to the mid-1800s, back in the south when they were hunting a man-eating gray wolf. When they finally caught it, the townspeople burned it in front of the entire town, as a show that sorcery and abominations of any kind would not be tolerated. The Roman Catholic Church was instrumental in ridding the south of these witches and demons. Priests like Father James Bauser and others had been said to have encountered hundreds of spirits in their lifetimes."

"Do you have any books on the Roman Catholic Church and the abominations they faced?"

Siege of Darkness/Robert Taylor

"I got just what you need, right over here!" He got up and moved to a wall right behind him.

"I got the Dark War, Byron Malic's Reign of Terror, the Roman Catholic Book of Demons." He pulled them from a shelf. Elijah listened and right then the doorbell rang. Three minutes later, a beautiful light-skinned woman with long, black, shiny hair walked into the library.

"Hey, Daddy," she greeted the professor and gave him a kiss on the cheek.

"Mya, this is Elijah Cross, my student, and Elijah, this is my Daughter Mya."

She walked over and gladly shook Elijah's hand.

***

In school that following week, after leaving his homeroom, two football players targeted Jason. They saw him at his locker and one of them decided to bump him in passing. Hitting his head on the corner of the locker door, Jason got angry. After slamming the locker shut, he stood still as he thought about rushing the buff and blonde-haired White boy. The two locked eyes just before Jason shouted, "Watch where you're walking, next time!"

"Or what, you weirdo?" He grinned, not taking Jason seriously. Jason approached him, clinching his fist so tight a few knuckles cracked, which captured the attention of everyone congregating in the hall. The two stood face-to-face. Many began to yell in favor of the jock, as the principal rushed down the hall, hoping to reach them in time to defuse the situation. An overlord appeared in the crowd of loud, yelling students. In that instance, Jason pushed the principal out of the way and, without hesitation, punched the football player, who flew into a wall and crashed to the floor. The crowd silenced, as the jock's shocked friend helped him up and escorted him away. The stunned crowd dispersed immediately, before the angry principal got up and brushed himself off. Realizing what he had done, Jason pleaded to no avail. The principal grabbed him by his arm and led him to his office. Jason surprised but proud of what he had done, smiled the whole time.

In the living room that evening, Chris was scolding Jason about the incident. As Chris yelled, Jason sat silent, paralyzed in thought.

"Oh, now you want to be a tough guy? Shoving the principal and punching somebody in the face! Are you serious?" he shouted.

"Dad, if I had let him get away with that, it would have never stopped! He would have bothered me every time he saw me! That's why I did what I did!"

"You're on punishment, how's about that, for doing what you did?" Chris walked out of the living room, leaving Jason at a loss for words. Jason grinned as he raised his fists and marveled over them. With a large gaping smile, he was proud of himself. The fire in the fireplace jolted out at him and recoiled, causing him to jump away.

***

That same evening alone inside the prison shower, Sherrod smiled and closed his eyes. Suddenly he started singing *Stephanie Mills. "You stepped into my life. You stepped into my life and I'm oh...so happy!"* In that instance, the room began to fill up with steam. The hot scolding water hit his flesh, having no effect on him. He didn't so much as even

Siege of Darkness/Robert Taylor

flinch. As it torched his skin, he lathered up heavily. A few inmates entered the shower room. The steam wafting toward them, cause them to pause. Through the cloudy fog, Sherrod emerged, grabbed his towel, looked at them, spoke, and walked out. As he headed back to his cell, he whistled that same song and grinned. He was in great spirits.

***

At midnight in the graveyard in Cherokee Falls, the beast sat in a tree, watching as two men walked with a small map, a lamp, and hunting rifles. The men roamed, measured, and calculated. They grabbed shovels and sat against the trunk of a tree to relax.

After resting for a spell, with shovels handy, they were prepared to do some serious digging, when suddenly out of the tree leaped the giant beast. Horrified, the men hollered and took off running. With the beast breathing down their backs, the margin for error was next to none. The slower of the two and the one most likely to get caught took a chance as he was tiring, so he turned and swung his shovel at the beast's head. The beast caught it mid-swing, snatching it out of his hands and beat the man into a bloody unconsciousness, while his skull sat bashed open. After a loud, echoing growl, with his large foot, he stomped in the side of the man's head, dislodging his eyes, as his skull cracked while caving in.

Getting a partial glimpse, the other man ran for dear life, screaming for help along the way. After reaching his vehicle, he fumbled and rushed to start it up. As soon as it cranked, he put the car in gear and quickly turned it around. Heading back out to the road, he nervously looked both ways and locked his doors. Relieved, he sat back. Without warning, smashing though the front windshield was a large tree branch. It was thrown with great force from twenty feet away, striking the man in the chest, killing him instantly. The beast ran off through the woods and disappeared. For miles, his loud, snarling growl rolling with the breeze that cooled the landscape.

***

That October weekend, Elijah was driving through Manhattan, New York. As he cruised, he took in the sites, from the Empire State Building to 42nd Street. Wanting to get close up and personal, he hopped out of his car with his camera. He took picture after picture, as people bumped him in the elbow-to-elbow crowded streets.

Shortly after, he was heading up the Westside Highway on a quest to get to the Roman Catholic Church. Exiting on 82nd Street, he drove until he came upon the large structure. Pulling over and parking, he got out and started taking more pictures. Then he headed up the stairs of the church with a book tucked under his armpit.

Inside, a few people were scattered about on pews, their heads bowed in prayer. Elijah eased down on one of a pew in the rear. He opened the book, titled, *The Roman Catholic Church and Its Demons.* He plowed through the pages until he got to a section that read: *There was a demon known to the priesthood as Amon, who later was acknowledged to be Byron Malic. It was said that he was granted eternal life by Lucifer himself. He also gave him great power. Malic was a vicious killer and manipulator. Throughout the 1800s, he singlehandedly murdered villages, sparing no one!* Pausing, Elijah watched as a priest walked in and down the center aisle toward the front.

Siege of Darkness/Robert Taylor

Forty minutes later, he saw that same priest come back up the aisle and head back out the door. Curious, Elijah got up and followed. Once he reached the door and walked outside, he saw the priest heading across the street into another facility. Elijah crosssed the street, but when he reached the door, it was locked. He peeked inside through a small caged window, only to see another door, which was closed, so he headed back to his car.

***

A few days later, inside the school gym, Jason sat on the bleachers watching the girls volley ball game. The lights in the gym started flickering, eventually turning off. The students stopped playing to look around. One of the coaches ran over to the area where the switches were housed; they were all on. As he stood there, the gym illuminated. He shook his head as he headed back onto the court. Jason was suddenly surrounded by four dark hooded figures. No one could see them but him.

Jason, we are watching you, and have been watching you for some time! one stated.

Jason stared in amazement.

Your curiosity has more than warranted our attention! said another.

Believe it or not, if you stay true to what you are seeking, there will be a greater glory! another added.

Before Jason could respond, the lights flickered again and they were gone. Jason stood up and looked around in astonishment.

***

Siege of Darkness/Robert Taylor

Back at the Roman Catholic Church, the priest was searching through the old documents again. He stumbled upon some papers on the Roman Catholic Church during the late 1800s. He sat down and began to read, Before High Priest James Bauser died, he wrote; *"The devil walks the earth. I've seen him in the eyes of many. He has spread his seeds globally. He has even corrupted the priesthood. I was informed of a former priest by the name of Byron Malic, who gave in to such. My first years in the priesthood, I didn't take the stories serious. Once I encountered him, my prospective on the devil changed. The night we killed him, I watched his flesh burn and a voice spoke from the skies. I have been fortunate, if you can call it that, to have witnessed everything from vampires to werewolves to other supernatural phenomena. I, being the high priest James Bauser, can only imagine the destruction the devil will bring in the future. God, help us all!"* The priest finished reading aloud and thumbed through the rest of the old papers. Getting up from where he sat, he took them and a few books and left the room.

***

That evening the prison tiers were empty and the entire place was quiet. It was quiet enough to hear mice race across the floor as they were on their desperate nightly pursuit. Sherrod lay resting on his bunk, staring out through the bars, awaiting the arrival of the ghostly guardians. For nights, he watched, while making small talk and playing chess with the spirit of Pierre, as he had began to see more and more faces he recognized. They were the new recruits the devil collected daily. All of the people he saw either get killed or died naturally in there, eventually became part of this army. Only a

Siege of Darkness/Robert Taylor

few were given a pass to cross over. Finally, they started to appear and for some reason, there were a lot less of them. Sherrod curiously jumped down, walked to the bars, and looked in both directions. The numbers were down.

I see you are wondering where all of the spirits are. A lot of them have been summoned by Lucifer himself. They are standing before him as we speak. Because of their time in, they will now be put to work in the real world, some as Jinns, others as Alps and poltergeists etc. Only a few will remain spirits amongst the prison population.

Sherrod stood silent as he tried to grasp the concept placed before him.

There is nothing to be afraid of. As confusing as it may seem, there is order to it all! For Lucifer is as strict as he is powerful!

"I understand," Sherrod answered like a trance stricken mummy.

***

That weekend in the car, Uncle Willie and Jason took an early morning drive. Jason asked if he could go with him because Willie's plan was to go to breakfast and hang out in the mall. So, as Willie drove, Jason sat in the passenger seat, bursting with questions.

"Uncle Willie, do you know the spot where they drained the blood from Byron Malic?"

"There you go! You supposed to be focused on your schoolwork! Don't you and your father have some type of bet?"

Siege of Darkness/Robert Taylor

"Yeah, but, my father doesn't understand. He knows I'm not going to give up. But, you're right, I do need a vehicle. I'll just wait."

Willie smirked at him like he was stupid.

"Yeah, please wait. I really don't want to get in between you guys anymore!"

Willie pulled into a restaurant parking lot.

After breakfast, as Willie and Jason traveled a long hill-filled stretch of road, they were listening to *"And the Beat Goes On,"* on the radio, a classic by the whispers. As they cleared one of the hills, not even thirty feet away, a broken down truck sat in their path. Unable to stop, Willie plowed right into it. There he sat unconscious, bleeding from the head. Jason, who had hit his head on the windshield was barely conscious; but turned to check on his uncle. The owner of the truck came running.

"Are you guys all right?" he asked.

"I hope so. Uncle Willie! Uncle Willie!" Jason shouted, waiting for a response. The truck driver raced around to the driver side and placed his hand against Willie's chest.

"He's alive! We need to get him to a hospital!" the man added.

In that moment, a car came from the opposite direction and slowed down as it came upon the wreckage.

"Are you guys all right? Anybody hurt?" he asked, as he sat idling.

"My uncle…" Jason blurted out.

"Let me go into town and call you an ambulance," the man told Jason.

Siege of Darkness/Robert Taylor

Three hours later, as nurses rushed past, and a doctor was being paged, Chris, Jason and Jimmy stood around Willie's bed.

"Damn, the first thing I got to see when I open my eyes, is all y'alls ugly faces?" Willie joked as he forged a smile.

"You lucky to see anybody, you almost didn't make it!" Jimmy told him.

"You fractured your spine, broke your femur bone, your right arm, shattered your left knee and both your wrists!"

"Thank God!" Willie looked up to the ceiling.

"You all right?" Willie asked Jason as he looked him in the eyes.

"I'm okay. I was worried about you."

At that moment, a doctor walked in holding a clipboard. He smiled and looked around the room before he spoke.

"Are you guy family?"

"Yes." Chris spoke for everyone. The doctor looked at Willie before he continued.

"Other than a few broken bones and the spinal fracture, you have some internal bleeding. We need to go in and stop the bleeding right away, and

Three days later while Willie was being operated on, he went into cardiac arrest. Fortunately, they were able to revive him. As he lied in the critical care unit, Jason, Chris and Jimmy all looked from behind a large glass window.

"How did that happen, they said he would be fine?"

"Look, Jason, nothing is guaranteed when they operate on you. Let's just be thankful he survived."

"Yeah, you're right," Jason agreed as Uncle Jimmy put his arm around him and they all headed to the elevator.

An hour later, beside his bed, Chris sat on his knees, holding his crucifix. His Bible sat open as he locked his hands in prayer. As he began to speak, images clouded his head. Trying to shake himself free, he took a deep breath and continued.

"Father, guide my brother to safety and strip him of all that ails him. Bless this world and all those here. Bless my family and give me the strength to overcome all adversity, Amen!"

Out on the porch, Jason sat staring out into the woods. He got up and walked out past the old cabin into the dreary silence provided by nature. The further he walked, the more he started to take notice to what looked like human body parts. The stench stopped him in his tracks, as he stepped over the detached head of an elderly Black male. His eyes set in such a way, you could see he died horrified and from excruciating pain. A few paces more, he saw bodies everywhere, against trees, crushed, beaten, mangled, and half eaten. Seconds later, right before his eyes they disappeared. Bewildered, Jason spun around with the quickness, looking in all directions, wondering what happened to the horror show. Without warning wolves had surrounded him, mouths wide-open revealing blood- drenched teeth. With nowhere to run, he stood in fear of his very life. Without pause, they raced toward him and just as they lunged, he screamed, while wrapping his hands around his head and closing his eyes. Then there was silence. He open is eyes and saw nothing but the empty forest. "What in the hell's going on?" he mumbled, shaken from it all as he looked around.

Loud rumbling laughter came from behind him.

I've shown you some of the horrors that now possess your world and the power I have. What you saw was real, but yet perpetrated elsewhere! As long as you are willing to help me, I will protect you! Every weapon formed against you I shall destroy! Believe in me as I believe in you and we will become the greatest of allies. Lucifer recited, as the fear of God was in Jason, so much that he pissed in his pants.

***

That same evening, Elijah was reading, *Byron Malic's Reign of Terror.* He started connecting the dots. Flipping through the pages, he read everything from Malic's time in the priesthood, to his murderous rampage, to his demise at the hands of the Roman Catholic Church. Then he searched through boxes under his bed. Finding one that was labeled "school thesis," he pulled it out and began to sort through it. He pulled out a folder labeled; Is there such thing as supernatural life? Going through the pages, he stopped fifteen pages in.

There are definitely other forces on this earth. I'm not talking about ghosts or aliens. To believe in religion is to believe somewhat of the supernatural. There are so many things that cannot be explained such as; wouldn't the earth, the atmosphere and the universe be supernatural wonders? Why can dogs hear and smell things we can't? So as much as we know, isn't it safe to say there is equally as much we don't know? When we speak of vampires, gargoyles, monsters, and of the people who've said they encountered them, can we denounce these accounts? For years, people have been disappearing all over the globe, some found mangled and half eaten...

14

June 25, 1986

Graduation day came quickly and Jason was all smiles as he strutted across the stage. He yelled joyously as he threw his hands high in the air after receiving his diploma. Chris and his brothers became his personal cheering section as they stood up and applauded. They wore huge smiles in the midst of rows of other proud parents and family members. After the last of the graduates walked the stage, the room erupted as they tossed their caps in the air, while whistling and screaming.

An half an hour later, shortly after taking pictures, Jason proudly walked from the school with Chris, while Jimmy pushed Willie along in a wheelchair. Out a side entrance and into the parking lot they went. Chris stopped and pulled a set of car keys from his pants pocket. He smiled and dangled them in front of Jason's face. With a look of surprise, Jason took them, hugged his father and turned around scanning the lot for his new jeep.

"Where is it?" he asked overjoyed as he looked around trying to locate it.

"It's right over there, between that black car and that grey car." Willie chuckled and pointed.

After spotting it, Jason darted toward it, yelling, hopping and jumping in the air with excitement. Chris, Willie and Jimmy watched as they were equally happy for him.

Siege of Darkness/Robert Taylor

Minutes later, Linda came out the side door with her mother walking alongside her. Jason pulled up on them blowing his horn as he came to a stop and rolled down the window.

"You want to take a ride with me?" he asked Linda, grinning. Her mother stood at her side smiling.

"Go ahead, go have a little fun! You deserve it, baby!" she told Linda, urging her on. Without hesitation, Linda raced around the front of the truck, jumped in on the passenger side and they pulled off. Jason started blowing the horn again and continued his celebration.

As they drove, Linda just gazed at Jason lustfully. After which, she took off her shoes and relaxed her sore but freshly pedicured feet against the dash. Passing through his area, Jason continued to pound the horn as he yelled out the window. Everywhere he went, he showed off his new jeep and people congratulated him. He was beyond happy, he was ecstatic.

That evening, the two of them decided to get themselves a hotel room. They had a bottle of champagne chilling in a bucket of ice, as they lay across the bed, kissing and groping each other. Jason stopped, got up and grabbed the champagne and two glasses.

"Here's to us! School's out and the fun begins!" he shouted as he poured half a glass each for the two of them.

"Drink up, so you can get back to what you started." She grinned as she passed him her empty glass. Smiling while flipping off the lights, Jason crawled into the bed. She giggled as he slowly undressed and fondled her. She kissed him about the neck arousing him instantly. He paused to take off his shirt and pants. With both of them naked, she pushed him over on his back and took charge. Placing a condom over his erection, she massaged it, while closing her eyes. Seconds later, she slowly eased it into her wet and uncharted territory. He grabbed her hips, as she gingerly gyrated. Slowly opening her eyes, she took him in as her walls loosened up. She smiled from the pleasure. Jason raised his head so his tongue could meet her thick pink nipples. The two were enjoying themselves as they giggled and grunted together.

For the next few days, the two hung out. They took the time to visit and view different college campuses, sat in the parks picnicking and at times they were in the cabin just enjoying each other's company. They were becoming quite the couple and inseparable. When you saw one, you saw the other. Through it all, Jason never once stopped thinking about his quest.

***

June 28, that Saturday afternoon, Elijah was at the professor's house browsing through his library. He search shelf after shelf.

"Elijah, what are you looking for?" the professor asked.

"Something, that pertains to supernatural life on earth! Anything that can substantiate other life forces here!"

"What? Hold on, I got just what you're looking for." The professor reached up high and pulled down two books.

After giving them to Elijah, he looked at the titles. *The first Werewolf, and There's Danger in the Woods.*

Elijah sat in the professor's study reading the preface from, *There's danger in the Woods.*

It is believed that in most of the surrounded wooded area there is some form of demonic or supernatural force lurking.

Siege of Darkness/Robert Taylor

From as far back as man has been known to exist, there have been millions of mysterious and unexplained deaths. People have reported seeing all types of beasts, werewolves and creatures beyond comprehension. Is there any truth to it all? One has to wonder.

Elijah read on for hours and when he realized he wasn't home, he closed the book and jumped up. Walking from the study, he called out to the professor. Mya came out of her room and stood at the top of the stairs.

"He stepped out. He said to tell you he had to meet with some friends, and he'd call you later." She slowly walked down.

"Thanks. Could you lock the door?" Elijah asked as he eagerly rushed through the foyer. Out the door he went, never even looking back.

***

That evening as it cooled off, Jason was standing on the back porch talking to his Uncle Willie about a few things.

"Uncle, where do you think they got the story of Byron Malic from? Do you think they got it from a book or something? I'm confused, because if the family was chronicling it all, it makes sense to believe it really happened!"

"Your great, great grandfather shared them with your great granddad, my granddad, so I guess they were passed down through the generations. Now we're sharing them with you. Where they truly originated from, I honestly don't know!"

"I got this book from the library, *Byron Malic's Reign of Terror* written by Walter Hemmingway. It's word for word, everything you've told me! Do you think that's where they got it from?"

"Maybe, I don't know!" Willie was unsure.

"I would tell you to ask your great grandfather, but he's probably too medicated to even remember anything," Willie added.

"Could you take me to see him one day? I would love to meet him. Could you take me, please?"

"I'll think about it. Don't hold me to it. No promises!" he stressed.

"But, I do remember grandpa talking about how much his father hated his father, who would be your great, great, great grandfather. He said he never spoke of him, but when he did he never had anything nice to say."

"Why was that?"

"I couldn't tell you. He never even spoke his name. It was said that he had some deep-seated hate for the man.

"What was great, great Granddad's full name?"

"That's an easy one, his was Stephen Walsh."

"So where did Milosky come from?"

"That's our Father's families name and Walsh is Mother's."

Jason not having his notebook handy took all the information to memory. Getting no clarity from their conversation, he left confused.

Around that same time, Chris was sitting in the house at peace with himself, as he watched television and spoke out loud.

"Baby, we did it! The boy finished high school. He's becoming a man. A man…can you believe it? Our little boy is all grown up! I wish you were here to see all of this, but I know you're watching. He didn't turn out to be half bad. He got him a girlfriend that's good for him and who knows, maybe we'll have some grandkids one day." He smiled and drifted off to sleep.

Weeks later in Charleston, Jason went to their Hall of Records first, where he researched and located a few Roman Catholic churches and sacred burial sites in the area. After copying the addresses and getting directions from an employee, he hurried out to his jeep. Riding through town, he came upon a huge brick structure, which took up an entire city block.

Entering the church through the open front door, Jason took in everything from the dark mahogany wooden pews, to the large stained glass windows, to the pulpit, high ceiling and lighting.

As he reached the front, a priest came out smiling as he approached, garbed in his vestment robe.

"Hello, may I be of some help to you?"

"Yes, I'm doing some research on," he paused sighing. "Let me be honest. I heard that Byron Malic originated from this region. He was born and raised in South Carolina and a former priest of the cloth."

"…Your research has served you right, but that's a subject, neither I, nor the priesthood is at liberty to discuss."

"No…no, I don't want you to discuss him, I just want to know how I can get information on where he was buried."

"Oh my, God, forgive us of our sins, save us from the fires of Hell and lead all souls to Heaven, especially those in need of thy mercy. Lord…forgive him! Are you some crazy person? Are you sure you want to go there? No one in their right mind would want to visit such a place!"

"No, I just wanted to know that it really exists," Jason told the priest as he gave him a stare.

Siege of Darkness/Robert Taylor

"I don't know if you've heard any of the stories, but the last four groups of people that went out there, were never found. They were all assumed dead. They disappeared mysteriously; no one ever found any of their bodies. That particular burial site, those particular woods for that matter, we no longer use. No one goes there, no one that values their life!"

Not wanting to here that, Jason kept quiet.

"Okay, it's your funeral! Oh, Heavenly father, whose glory fills the whole creation and whose presence we find wherever we go, preserve this traveler and carry him in Your loving care. Protect him from danger and bring him in safely to his journey and to Jesus Christ our Lord. Amen," He looked at Jason.

"Now…if you must know, he was buried deep in the wooded area, far beyond the sacred Catholic burial grounds of Cherokee Falls. You must not go there, but if you chose to, you will encounter many evil spirits along the way!"

Jason smiled and took it in, but had his mind made up.

"Thanks for all your help! I truly appreciate it." Jason told him as he turned and headed out. The Priest shook his head as he knew his words fell on deaf ears.

With all his newly acquired information, Jason began to put the pieces of the puzzle together. He gave very little thought to any of the horrors that were spoken of. His undistinguishable desire to seek out the truth defied all reasoning.

That next morning as Chris held up the newspaper, an article grabbed his attention.

<u>Humans eating Humans</u>

Two men were sited in an alley eating away at a dead man, as blood soaked their clothes. This horrific scene baffled the police as they were called anonymously. The officers told our correspondent that; the men never looked up, not even after they were told to stop and put their hands in the air. The officers fired a warning shot, and when they saw the look in the men's eyes, they said they knew something wasn't right. They backed away to call for back up and were attacked. The two men were shot dead and their bodies turned to dust.

***

That next afternoon, while Elijah stared out his window, he called the professor's house. Mya answered the phone.

"Hello, is your father there?"

"He had to teach this morning and he hasn't gotten back in yet,"

"Well, could you let him know Elijah called?"

"…Elijah…I hope I'm not being too forward, but I need a companion to go with me to a school function."

"What kind of function?"

"I was invited to a rally,"

"What type of rally?"

"We're protesting sexual assaults on the college campuses,"

"Wow, that's a touchy subject! I'm…not sure if that's somewhere I should be." His response held an air of uncertainty.

"Why is that?"

"First of all, it's probably going to be all women! A bunch of angry women! Second, I really don't want…"

"I tell you what…if you come with me; I might let you take me to dinner afterwards."

Siege of Darkness/Robert Taylor

"Is that supposed to entice me? If so, it didn't work!"

"Just come, I'll treat you, how about that?"

"Now, how can I turn down a free meal? Are you sending a limo to pick me up?"

"Oh, you've got jokes, huh?" She laughed.

"Seriously, pick me up around seven," she told him chuckling. Elijah agreed and the two hung up shortly after.

At the rally, beneath the scorching rays of the sun, Mya and Elijah stood in the crowd listening as different people spoke. As she looked on, Elijah began to notice how breathtakingly beautiful she truly was. He was happy she asked him to come along as she looked over at him periodically.

A speaker carried on,

We must bring awareness to this problem. Women have not been put here to be disrespected, raped and humiliated. This is not a new problem and it's been in existence far too long! So, we're here to address it. One of the students here, was raped by a basketball player, who she trusted! He knows who he is! He told her no one would believe her, and she is embarrassed to come forth! She's not the only one, there's many more. Can you believe, how our institutions protect animals like this? We must speak for these women, who can't and won't speak for themselves!" The crowd yelled, whistled and rallied behind her.

That evening while sitting in a small steakhouse, Mya stared across the table at Elijah. He acted as if he weren't the least bit interested in her as he viewed the menu.

He broke the long silence between them.

"You know, Mya, I had a great time. The rally was a lot more interesting than I thought it would be. The speakers were dynamic!"

"Yeah, that poor girl, she's a freshmen and the guy's a senior. She really trusted him, because they grew up together."

"It's sad how some guys think of women, especially when alcohol becomes involved. They lose all self-control.

"Tell me about it! I went to one of those parties and almost had a similar incident. I went to the bathroom at a frat house and when I came out there were two guys standing out in the hall. I tried to squeeze by and they wouldn't move. They started feeling me up and I couldn't break free! I yelled, but the music was so loud no one heard me. Lucky for me, another girl came up the stairs and they let me go. I don't attend those parties anymore." She seemed saddened by the bad memory.

"Who did you go with?"

"A few of my girlfriends begged me to go. I didn't feel right about it, but of course, I went, because they're my girls! They wanted me to show them who the guys were, but I just wanted to get out of there!"

"Are they still at the school?"

"No, they graduated last year." She finished right before the waitress came to take their order. After which they started back up.

"Did you tell your father?"

"Of course not! He would have lost his mind. I could see him now, trying to find out who they were and he wouldn't have stop until he did!"

****

In mid-August, Linda and Jason were sitting in Linda's living room talking.

Siege of Darkness/Robert Taylor

"You're really going to go through with this, aren't you?" Linda questioned, but basically could tell by his conversation there was no doubt.

"Yes, I am. I've got all the information I need. All I need now is to know the exact spot where the ritual took place. I found the site, but it's a large area. I need a map or someone knowledgeable of it all, to help me. Everybody's so damn scary; they won't even go near the place! Can you believe that?" Jason rambled as he got long winded.

"I can believe it. Only a crazy person would go looking for something demonic! Nobody in their right mind would pursue this the way you do!" Linda expressed, trying to kill his momentum.

"So, I guess I'm crazy then? What, you're not going to help me no more?"

"I tell you what…you slow down a little with all this and I promise I'll help you. Let me get settled in college, get my associates degree and then it's whatever! What about you? Didn't you say you wanted to become a teacher or something?" Linda spoke reminding him.

"I did, but not right now, in a few years maybe. You don't understand, I dreamed of this day, the day I would find out the truth and unveil it to the world!"

Linda looked him in the eyes.

"But, what if what you find kills us all? What if you get killed in the process? Think about what you're doing, all in the name of proving a point!"

"You're always the pessimist, looking at the glass as half empty. I already got confirmation nothing's going to happen to me!"

"That's right, a spirit came to you and told you that you were chosen." She said with sarcasm. "What world do you live in? Do you listen to yourself at all? I love you, but come on, Jason. You don't have an ounce of common sense!" She got up and walked away, out the front door, where she stood on the porch shaking her head.

***

That evening Elijah pulled up to the professor's house and Mya came out the front door dressed in a nice black dinner dress. The professor came behind her and the two walked to the car together. Elijah got out and met them half way.

"You take care of my little princess," the professor told Elijah as he looked him in the eyes and shook his hand.

"I will sir, you can be sure of that!"

Elijah walked her to his car, where he opened and held the door for her. As she climbed in, her perfume had him lost in a fantasy.

"Elijah," she called out, bringing him back, causing him to close the door and race around to the driver side.

Ten minutes into the drive, Mya smiled as she spoke.

"You look nice!" she told him as she looked him up and down, from his nice black slacks, to his beige and brown sports jacket, to his black loafers that met the gas pedal.

"I didn't think it was possible for you to look even more gorgeous than you are, but I guess I was wrong!" Elijah flattered.

"Thank you, you're so sweet! Where are we going?"

"You'll see," he told her, smiling as he drove.

A half hour later, they were cruising near the waters of Weehawken, New Jersey, as boats small and large sat docked in the water. Pulling into a parking space nearby, Elijah got out, opened her door and led her to a packed, white cruiseliner. Once on it, they were lead into a dining area and seated. From across the table, Mya smiled blushingly.

"I didn't have you pegged to be such a romantic,"

"Why? Because I'm into my studies? Where you think I learned it from? I used to read a lot of romance novels before I got hooked on mythology, biblical studies, historic events and so forth."

"You have such a beautiful smile, almost boyishly cute!"

"It's my job to dish out complements! I'm flattered, but you're treating me like a piece of meat!" He blushed.

"You are so funny! Hilarious, almost!" She grabbed a slice of warm bread from a basket that sat in the center of the table.

***

That weekend, Jason and Willie were at the asylum. They were being led by a nurse down a long corridor, passing door after door and finally the nurse stopped.

"Here we are, room 211!" She pulled out a set of keys and opened a door.

Inside, strapped to a small bed, was a thin elderly white man staring up at the ceiling.

Willie approached slowly and cautiously. "Hey, Granddad, it's me, your grandson Willie, and I got your great grandson Jason with me."

"Boy, I know who you are! I'm old, not slow!" He turned to look in their faces. His eye were yellow filled with red streaks, and held an unsettling emptiness.

"Sorry, didn't know if you remembered me!"

"I read bedtime stories to you every night, how am I going to forget who you are? You know your grandmother's in the kitchen cooking, so go wash your hands and get ready for dinner. Tell your brothers to come in the house, it's getting late. I had a hard day out in the field, I got get some rest."

Confused, Willie and Jason could see he was delusional.

"Grandpa, how are you doing?" Willie asked, trying to bring him back to the present.

"Boy, don't play with me, I'm as healthy as a horse, as healthy as I've ever been! I'm just so tired of that son of a bitch…"

"Tired of whom?" Willie asked.

"Boy, you must be as dumb as a rock! You know that son of a bitch killed your father and mother. He told me he was going to do it! He told me and I didn't believe him. That evil son of a bitch!"

The more he would rant the angier he got. A nurse came through the door and immediately gave him a needle to relax him. As he calmed he spoke.

"The devil is a liar, murderer and a thief! Don't trust him! He will promise you everything, but he speaks with a forked tongue! Kill me then and stop talking about it! You can't do any more then you've already done! Liar, liar, liar!"

Realizing this was not a good time to talk to their grandfather, Jason and Willie headed out the door without uttering another word. The withering old man continued to argue and shout, while trying to free himself from the restraints.

15. THE WORLD AWAITS YOU

By the end of September, Jason had sought out and finally got his first paying job. He ended up working as a cashier at a local burger joint. After receiving his first check, he was happy to have his own money and independence. He started buying Linda small gifts and flowers regularly. Through all of this, every night he couldn't help but think about being in South Carolina, with a shovel tightly in his grasp, mounds of dirt piled everywhere, standing deep in a moist grave. He also pictured himself grinning as he pulled a rotted casket from that same hole he had dug. Shaking himself free of his thoughts, he came back to reality. He fought himself against getting in his truck and driving down the highway. The more he contemplated, the more he begged Linda.

"Come on, Linda, please! Let's go now! I can't wait any longer."

"Jason, I'm working and will be starting school in a few days. Plus, you just got a steady job. I told you I would go with you after I finish getting my degree. If you can't wait, find someone else!" she stated angrily.

"That's how it is, for real? Forget it. I'll go by myself! I don't need anyone to go with me! You're just like everyone else. You're jealous because I figured it all out! Not you! Not anyone, but me! Everybody's against me." Jason yelled.

At that point Linda just listened, because she knew when he got like that, there was no defusing him.

Siege of Darkness/Robert Taylor

***

Early the next morning, Elijah was thousands of miles away. Amidst the beautiful South African countryside, he was drenched in sweat as he and ten others had been driving, sightseeing and hiking for over three hours. As their African guide led them, Elijah was taking pictures of all the animals and scenery. They walked through beautiful streams of water, over exhausting hilled areas and came to rest, where the sunset was perfect and peaceful. As they relaxed their tired feet and legs and hydrated themselves, Elijah pulled a book, *South African Mythical Creatures*, from his backpack and found him a nice shaded spot under a Baobab tree.

In early African culture there was said to be several creatures that the native feared, one being the werewolf. Documented back as early as the mid-seventeen hundreds, the first part man-part wolf was seen as it chased down a wild buffalo. Sinking its sharp fanglike teeth into the neck of it, the wolf tackled it to the ground. There the buffalo moaned and fought until it bled out.

He read on for the entire time they lay resting. After a few hours, they were back up and moving on. Fascinated further, Elijah must have loaded his camera at least three to four times.

***

That afternoon, Willie was enduring physical therapy. As he fought to stand up out of the wheelchair, his caretaker cheered him on. It took every ounce of his strength and energy for him to stand on his feet. He held onto the parallel bars and took a step. That first step turned into two and two turned into three. As he paused, a tear rolled the length of his face. Pushing through the pain, he was determined to walk again. Within a half hour, he had expended all his energy and was dripping in sweat. The caretaker helped him back to his wheelchair as she congratulated him.

"You did very well! I am so proud of you!"

"I'm not spending the rest of my life as an invalid!"

"Don't let them doctors get under your skin. God makes the final determination. I have you in my prayers every night."

"Thank you, you're a sweetheart!" Willie said as she pushed him down a long corridor.

***

Sitting in her bedroom, Linda was lost in thought. With stacks of books on her dresser and a half packed open suitcase on her bed, she was prepping to go the college campus. Suddenly, Jason crossed her mind. She pictured him flying down the highway by himself eager to get to South Carolina, when a dark figure appeared in the sky. She saw him swerving off the road out of fear. The truck rammed full speed into an unforgiving tree, leaving him unconscious and bleeding from the head. At that moment, the phone rang and she got up and went downstairs to answer it.

"Hello, is Jason Milosky there?" the voice asked.

"Jason doesn't live here," Linda replied.

"This is the phone number he gave us."

"What's this in reference to?" she questioned wondering why he didn't give them his number.

Siege of Darkness/Robert Taylor

"I'm not at liberty to discuss that with no one but the party who it's meant for. I'm sorry; do you know what time he'll be in?"

"He doesn't live here. I can give him a message if you'd like."

"Okay, my name is Kenneth Barnes. My direct line is 1 555 431 7878. Thank you and have a nice day!"

Ten minutes later, Linda had called Jason several times and when no one answered, she started to worry. As she sat wondering where he could be, her mother came into the room.

"Hey, honey, what's wrong?" her mother asked as she could see something had Linda in a deep fog.

"Nothing, just worried about Jason. He refuses to give up this craziness! He's dead set on seeing it through!"

"Seeing what through? What are you talking about? You mean to tell me all that research you two been doing is actually?"

"Yes Mama, he believes it's all real!"

"That boy done lost his mind! I thought all that was a school project you two were working on."

"No Mama, no…" Linda engaged in a long stare with her. Her mother walked away shaking her head in disbelief. Through the entrance to the kitchen, she marched as Linda sat worried. Breaking the tension of the moment, the phone rang again. Linda quickly reached out and grabbed it.

"Hello," she greeted.

"Hey, Linda, this is Jason. Did anyone call there for me?"

"Yes,"

"What did you tell them?" he asked anxiously.

"What are you up to now?"

"Listen Linda, if they call back, please, tell them to call me back around four o'clock tomorrow and I'll be there."

Siege of Darkness/Robert Taylor

"Okay, but you're going to tell me what you're up too?"
"Honey, who is that?" her mother yelled from the kitchen.
"It's for me, Mama," she answered just as she hung up the phone.

In deep thought, Jason drove home from work. He smiled as he thought of the conversation he had with his co-worker.
My uncle was killed in the forest some years back. His friend, who had gotten away, said he was killed by some huge beast. Nobody believed him. In fact, he was evaluated and investigated for the murder. He was acquitted after they saw there was no way humanly possible another man could have done it. My uncle was a big man, six-foot-seven and two hundred sixty pounds. They said he tried to put up a fight. That was my favorite uncle. Jason pulled up in front of the house to see Chris sitting on the porch. He honked and his father waved.

That next day as Jason sat in Linda's livingroom, talk show host Phil Donavan was on television talking to an actor about his next movie project.

"Yes, it's based on a novel written by the late Walter Hemmingway, who himself mysteriously disappeared. It's called the Reign of Terror. It's about a colorful 19th Century character, which after joining the priesthood was later manipulated into becoming Satan's second in command!"

Trying to hear the interview clearly, he walked up on the television. In that moment, the phone started ringing, drawing his attention from the interview. Jason looked at Linda as he took a bite of the burger he was holding. She picked up the phone and after a brief greet, she passed it to him.

"Hello, is this Jason Milosky?"

Siege of Darkness/Robert Taylor

"Yes, yes it is!" he answered as he was still trying to hear the television.

"Mr. Milosky, I'm Kenneth Barnes, you reached out to us a few weeks ago. You were looking to find out who your great grandfather was. Now you told me, your father's name was Christopher Milosky and your mother's name was Tessa Spellman, right. Now your father's parents were Susan Smith and Peter Milosky. Your grandmother, your father's mother, Susan Smith, was the daughter of Johnathan Walsh and Maryann McCauley. Johnathan was the son of Stephen Walsh, who was the son of a former priest."

"Hold up, what did you say?" Jason took a deep breath and as he thought he missed something.

"What part?" the man asked.

"The part about my great, great grandfather's father being a priest?"

"Oh yeah…your great, great, great grandfather on your grandmother's side of the family, was a priest. My colleague is trying to get information on him as we speak."

"Please do. I need to know his name and about what year he died?"

"Okay, give me a few days and I'll get back to you."

Staring in Jason's face, Linda had heard the entire conversation. She had a look of curiosity about her.

"What? You want to know why I'm looking up my ancestry, don't you?" Jason questioned.

She nodded, but didn't utter a single word.

"Well, it's strange that my family seems to be one of the only families that are truly knowledgeable of this Byron Malic. Though the book, *Byron Malic's Reign of Terror,* was a best-seller and read worldwide, there is a certain attachment my family has to it! How could my great grandfather's stories be so detailed and similar to the ones in the books? I know what you're thinking, he read the book, but it's more than that. Now Hollywood's going to make a movie out of it? This is crazy! Anyway, I asked my father what my great grandfather's name was, and he told me Christopher. He was named after his great grandfather. It didn't dawn on me to ask about my grandmother side of the family," Jason explained as Linda was all ears.

"I've got to research this Walter Hemmingway. I need to know what or who inspired him to write *Reign of Terror!*" Jason thought out loud.

That following day, Jason was in the library reading the autobiography of Walter Hemmingway. Chapter after chapter, he breezed through the pages until he happened upon a paragraph that read: *I've always dreamed of being a great novelist with as many as ten best-sellers to my credit. My first book Diamond Head, a great read in its own right, did well and there are as many as one hundred thousand copies in print to date. My second novel, Byron Malic's Reign of Terror was the most sought after book of it time and continuously sold out worldwide. It catapulted me to instant stardom. It was second only to, Pride and Prejudice ,written by Jane Austen.*

Toward the end of the book, it talked of how he was so obsessed with the story of Byron Malic; he mentioned traveling to South Carolina to investigate. No one knows if he ever went, as he disappeared shortly after. A team of officers searched the wooded area of Cherokee Falls, South Carolina, and many were killed. After finishing the book that evening, Jason read the acknowledgements and spotted the name Johnathan Walsh. He flipped a few more pages and he noticed an entire three-pages dedication. Jason smiled as he read it.

Siege of Darkness/Robert Taylor

Special thanks goes out to Johnathan Walsh, because without his insight this novel would not have been possible. Thanks for having confidence enough to believe I could breathe life into such a profound tale.

After digesting that bit of information, he closed the book and stared into space.

That Friday, back at Linda's place, Jason was talking to Kenneth Barnes about his ancestry again.

"Your great, great, great grandfather was Harry O'Conner. He was struck by lightning as he sat beneath a tree on May nineteenth in the year of 1887. His body was laid to rest two days later in a Catholic cemetery in South Carolina."

"Wow, this is crazy! Harry O'Conner is my father's guardian angel and also my great, great, great grandfather! I saw it with my very own eyes, Linda!" Jason rambled until the investigator chimed back in.

"I hope I've been a great help! Thank you for your patronage. You have my number, if you need me."

After he hung up, Jason's mind was all over the place.

****

Two weeks later, on a plane returning from Africa, Elijah was flirting with the thought of making love to Mya. He smiled as he envisioned to two of them on a secluded beach, with nothing between them, but opportunity. With the sun tanning their backsides, he pictured her inviting him to share a blanket, while her eyes offered something more appetizing. Could she be the one, or was she just a temporary high to embrace to help pass the time.

At the airport, Mya awaited his arrival with a dozen roses lying across her lap. She too was fantasizing. Smiling while in thought, she too had thoughts of making love, until some kids bumped into her as they played in the area.

Fifteen minutes later, Elijah came bouncing out the chute from the plane into the airport. He paused to look about, as he had bags strapped and hanging from his shoulders. Glowing, he seemed well rested and happy. Mya raced up to him, still holding the roses and smiling. Blindsiding him, he jumped as she wrapped her arms around him.

"Hey, sweetie!" she greeted as they stood holding each other's. Elijah smiled, recognizing the fact that she truly missed him. That feeling seemed to be mutual. When she let go and handed him the roses, he leaned in and gave her a long, saliva swapping kiss.

***

That same morning, Linda's phone rang and rang, until she came barreling through the door in search of it. On her hands were dirty rubber gloves that she snatched off to grab the receiver from the wall in the kitchen.

"Hello, Jason Milosky?" the caller greeted.

"No, no it isn't."

"Well, could you have him call Kenneth Barnes. Tell him, I have information on his great granddad's death. Thank you and have a nice day." He hung up, leaving Linda wheezing as she slowly began to catch her breath. Right away, she called Jason and gave him the message.

Even though he was running late for work, he sat on the edge of his bed to make the call.

"Hello," Jason greeted as soon as someone picked up.

"Yes, Kenneth Barnes, may I help you?"

Siege of Darkness/Robert Taylor

"Yes, this is Jason Milosky. You called me back about my great grandfather."

"Okay, how are you, sir? Yes, now let me see. Where are my notes?" he rambled while he went through some papers.

"Yes, here we are! Now, you great, great grandfather, Stephen Walsh, was a laborer for Peter Winslow from 1865 to 1880. His father Harry O'Conner, worked in the mills years earlier. He and Mary Walsh, married in 1840. He left her to join the church in 1847, when Stephen was about six years old." As the investigator went on, Jason's mind raced out of control. After listening to him a short while longer, Jason interrupted, thanked him and hung up.

Getting to work a half hour late, Jason was called into the office by his boss.

"Jason, your tardiness is unacceptable. I've given you chance after chance and you just can't seem to get it right. I'm so sorry, but I have to let you go!"

"What? Aww man, come on. I need this job! You can't do this to me! I know I promised you I wouldn't be late anymore, but one more chance, please!"

"No, sorry, I can't do it no more. Come in Friday and I'll have your last check waiting for you. Have a nice day."

Angered by this, he marched out of the office, passed fellow employees, and out the door.

While driving home, he switched from thinking about losing his job, to going to South Carolina. Reaching into his pockets, he realized he hadn't enough money to cover the trip's expenses. He thought of asking Linda, but didn't want to hear her mouth. Thinking harder, he decided to wait until he got his last check and no one would be the wiser. With all that was running through his head, he could hardly keep his eyes focused on the road as he was swerving.

Siege of Darkness/Robert Taylor

***

That weekend, Elijah and Mya were sitting on his couch kissing. Elijah continued until she was flat on her back. Sliding his hands under her dress, he eased her out of her panties. A smile rose as she wasn't resisting. At that moment, she pushed him away and got up. Smiling herself, she pulled her dress over her head revealing her petite frame. Elijah glared at her like a deer caught in headlights. Unfastening her bra and allowing it to fall to the floor, Mya stood completely nude before him, her bite size breasts perked up, begging for attention. Elijah's temporary paralysis affected everything but the rise in his pants. Seeing that he was stunned, she leaned over and kiss him, while pulling his sweatshirt over his head. Pushing him down on his back, she drove her hot, wet tongue down his neck. With a since of urgency, he maneuvered his way out of his pants, as his body sensually became enslaved. They nibbled and tasted each other as their lust for one another had taken the driver's seat.

***

That same evening, Uncle Willie was brought home in an ambulance. As the driver helped him down from the van, he was put in a wheelchair and rolled over to where Chris and Jimmy sat on the porch. They help him as the van drove away. Willie waved them off. He slowly stood up, grabbed the banister and climbed the stairs. Cautiously, he walked toward the door and went in the house. Chris and Jimmy followed, screaming with joy as they watched.

Later that night, Jason was watching the sky as he saw something dark with enormous wings circling. Suddenly a high pitch squeal caused him to hurry onto his porch. He looked up again, but whatever it was had disappeared. Right away, he noticed an empty wheelchair. Sensing his uncle must be inside, he looked up in the sky one last time and burst in the house, where he immediately scanned the living room.

"Uncle Willie," he called out, waiting to hear him answer back. When no one answered, he rushed to his uncle's door and knocked impatiently.

"Uncle Willie, you in there?"

"Yeah, come in."

Jason walked in and his uncle slowly sat up and smiled.

"What's going on nephew?" Willie greeted. Jason walked over and hugged him.

"I saw your wheelchair outside, that's how I knew you were here. It's good to see you home and moving around again."

Siege of Darkness/Robert Taylor

16

Spring of 1987

After Friday's class, Elijah was reading while sitting in the grass in Central park. He was caught up in a book called, *The Urban Legends of South Carolina*. Captivated by the stories, he lay back and read for hours.

Everyplace has an underbelly, a place where darkness lives and light seems to have abandoned. These places can breathe life into the terrifying and unusual. In most cases, they become the storyboards for the supernatural, the daunting horrors that make up urban legends!

Shortly after going through the entire book, it had gotten dark and the park was empty. Elijah got up, grabbed his belongings and headed out himself. As he reached the exit, he sighed as he looked out into the traffic, waiting for the light to change. Crossing the street, he started to relish the thought of going to South Carolina. He made his way to a payphone and called Professor Jenkins.

"Hello Professor, this is Elijah. How are you?"
"What is it, Elijah?"
"I'm considering going to South Carolina and going into the sacred forest of Cherokee Falls. The story of Byron Malic has me super curious!"
"Now, Elijah, "He sighed heavily. "I knew this would happen. Now, I'm going to tell you a story, one that I haven't

Siege of Darkness/Robert Taylor

told anyone. Years ago, two of my buddies and I went on an expedition to that same area you're talking about. When we got there, police and rescue vehicles blocked the entrance and the roadway. I got out of the car to see what had happened and that's when I saw officers running from the woods screaming. A high-pitched piercing growl caught my attention. Not knowing what it was, I turned and ran back to my car and me and my team sat waiting to see what made such a sound. One of the officer's went in his trunk, grabbed his shotgun and if you could have seen the look in his eyes...it was frightening! Another jumped in his patrol car and sped away. I can remember it like it was yesterday! The big hairy son of a bitch appeared atop a hill with an officer anchored above his head. After which it tossed him out onto the road where he met the pavement with such an impact, you could hear his bones shattering! The screams I heard that day from beyond the trees made me start my car and get the hell out of dodge! The next day, as we lay up in a hotel, I got a newspaper to see what happened and I read the horrific story to my boys. At least twelve or more officers were killed that day. Even as I drove away, we heard gunshots. After that I left them woods and all forest areas around the country to the outdoorsmen, hunters, etc."

"Wow, that's a heck of a story!" Elijah was amazed. After that, it wasn't long before they hung up from one another.

****

Weeks later, Jason snuck off to South Carolina. There he searched through the library for books on old local burial grounds. He came across several, but only two stood out. He wrote them down and headed out to the town hall, to the

Siege of Darkness/Robert Taylor

records department. He pulled up maps for each of them and drove out to both sites. One, more than the other, had a chilling feel to it. Giving that one his full attention, he got out of his car. There he roamed around hoping to find some type of evidence, a clue to the whereabouts. Finding the entrance gate locked, he climbed over and continued on. As he walked, he stepped over broken statues of saints and angels, tombstones dated back to the late 1700's. The grass and weeds stood at least four feet high, making it difficult to view. Though the place could have stood some light maintenance, it was for the most part pretty well kept.

After walking three quarters through, he notice an area where the stones and tombs, were all of former priests and bishops. One of the tombs caught his attention upon sight. Over the doorway, the insignia *Harry O'Conner* was embossed. He couldn't believe his eyes. It was all coming together. Walking over to it, he pulled at the door hoping to find it ajar, but found it was locked. Pulling out his camera, he took a quick snapshot. Realizing he was losing daylight, he decided to move on. As he continued through a heavily treed area and over yet another wrought iron fence, things got dreary. After forty yards, thousands of old trees were as far as the eyes could see. Through this forest, he wandered until he spotted an empty patch. He spun around looking for something, but what, he had no idea. As the large oak trees eventually became the towering backdrop, Jason's gut was telling him this was it, so he took more pictures. There to his immediate east, he saw something that was mentioned in one of the books and his camera flashed several more times. His eyes widened as he slowly walked, approaching what he hoped was his landmark. The link to a world he had only heard stories about, a world that his father and others feared.

Siege of Darkness/Robert Taylor

The closer he got the more disturbing things became. Suddenly, an unfriendly wind introduced itself, followed by a choral of noises, animal and human alike. Frozen in fear, Jason raced to get a look at what he believed would open the door to what had for so long been forbidden and too many, forgotten. Seeing the symbol that was on the front of the book, *Reign of Terror*, Jason burst with laughter and it transcended for miles. Unaware of the dark forces that lurked, he continued to look around, continued to be amazed, continued to smile.

***

Chris at work that afternoon seemed to be in great spirits. Looking up at the clock, he was counting the minutes until it was time to go home. He just wanted to relax, drink a few beers and watch a little television. He had an exhausting week and he was looking forward to doing absolutely nothing.

***

Two hours later, on his journey home, Jason flirted with different visions, each leading him to become a super force. As he enjoyed the countryside, he found himself driving exceptionally fast and within minutes, a flock of dead birds started falling out of the sky. A few struck the jeep and the road around it. The hood and roof buckled from the thunderous impact. Jason swerved to avoid the majority and gassed up as the birds littered the road behind him. As he sped on, he caught the attention of a patrol car hidden by a few leafy trees, sitting in the cut. With its flashers blaring, it sped up behind him. Astounded by the chain of events, Jason nervously pulled over. As he looked in the rearview mirror, he saw the officer as he approached. With his window down, he awaited his first words.

"How are you this evening?" the officer greeted.

"I'm fine," Jason answered as he looked up and out.

"You do know you were going ninety miles per hour?"

"Sorry officer, a bunch of birds came falling out of the sky! It was crazy! I've never seen anything like it."

"I need to see your license, registration and insurance," the officer requested seeming unconcerned with Jason's reason for excessive speed. As the officer walked back to his car with Jason's paperwork, Jason sat thinking. He pictured the burial site and all the surrounding trees. In that instance the sky got dark, the officer got back out of his car and walked up to Jason's truck.

"That was truly original," the officer uttered lightly, but loud enough for Jason to hear him.

"Here's your paperwork, and I gave you a ticket for speeding. You have a nice day," the officer told him as he walked away. Jason started his jeep and at that moment, a strong gust of wind came through. The officer's hat took flight. He chased it across the road as a tractor-trailer sped from the opposite direction, with its driver beating the horn hysterically. As he slammed on the brakes, they screeched, locked up and smoked. The terrified officer hurried to get out the way, but he was struck as the truck driver swerved slightly to avoid him. Horrified, Jason jumped out of his jeep, the truck driver brought the truck to a screeching halt and there was blood everywhere. The officer's body lay out mangled with guts and brain matter scattered about the roadway. Sinister laughter caught Jason's attention, causing him to look around.

Siege of Darkness/Robert Taylor

"What the hell?" Jason yelled as he looked on. The truck driver stood in shock as he shouted, "He stepped out in front of my truck and I couldn't stop! What was he thinking? I blew my horn!" he stated hysterically as he paced holding his head.

An hour later, the road was barricaded off and flashing lights danced against the hillside. An officer was talking to Jason as the truck driver stood nearby in tears.

"You said the officer pulled you over and after he gave you a ticket, he started walking back to his car? That's when his hat flew off?" the officer questioned as he took notes.

"Yes, oh my God, it was crazy!" Jason emphasized.

"Why did he pull you over?" he asked.

"He said I was speeding. But like I explained to him, there was a bunch of birds that fell from the sky for some reason. I swerved to avoid them. I was scared to death, so I was driving to get away from this area," Jason pointed, explained more in-depth. The officer looked down the road, in the direction referenced.

"There were no birds in the road back there! I'm sure of it, because that's the route I came!" the officer added.

"I'm telling you that's what happened!" Jason expressed with sureness. The officer just stared at him. After which, he turned back to the driver and began to thoroughly interrogate him also.

About four hours later, after dropping the film off to be processed, Jason came through the door at home holding his ticket. Willie and Chris were sitting in the living room laughing about something. Seeing the unsettling look on Jason's face, they quickly diverted their attention to him.

"Jason, what happened?" Chris asked.

"Are you all right?" Willie added equally concerned.

Siege of Darkness/Robert Taylor

"I'm okay, just had a bad day, that's all," Jason answered and headed up the stairs. Willie and Chris looked at one another.

In his bedroom, Jason sat on the bed lost in thought. Chris knocked at the door. Jason got up and opened it to face him.

"What's up, Dad?"

"Is there something wrong?"

"No, I just want to be alone, if you don't mine." Jason slowly closed the door.

Chris walked across the hall into his own room, pondering heavily.

Lying across his bed the following day, Jason's mind was in turmoil. He envisioned the sight; from the eerie forest to the markings on the tree to the police officer getting splattered across the highway. But what stood out the most was the abrupt echoing laughter. Spreading the pictures out across the bed in front of him, he looked from one to the other. Pulling his worn old notebook from between his mattress, he flipped to the back and began to jot down notes. Afterward, he placed the pictures inside the pages, closed it and put it back where he got it from.

****

That May, Sherrod sat in his cell reading an old newspaper. The article was dated and titled: January 20, 1981, The end of Iran Hostage Crisis. Sixty American diplomats and citizens were taken hostage by a group of Iranian students. They were held for a total 444 days.

After reading through the article, Sherrod placed the paper on the bed, got up and walked out of his cell. Through all the noise, his mind danced in and out of reality. He knew he could break out anytime he got ready, but also knew he would be hunted like a dog. Being that his time was getting shorter by the day, he practiced patience.

***

That evening as Jason sat on his bedroom floor, he was sketching out the cemetery and forest as he saw it. Thinking momentarily, he jumped up and went in his dresser drawer. There he reached up under a stack of folded shirts and pulled out the book, Byron Malic's *Reign of Terror*. The visions of it all plagued his conscience while he did so. Flipping through the pages, he stopped at a chapter that read: *There will stand an oak branded with the mark of the beast. Northeast of that, twenty yards, just beyond a dreary slope, evil will surround you. There amongst the foggy air you'll come to find naked land, the area beholding to the grave of Byron Malic*. After reading that information, he sat laughing. He couldn't believe it was in his face the entire time. He got crazed and jumped around like he struck gold.

Twenty minutes later after he had calmed down, he grinned. The fact that he wanted to reveal the truth overrode all rational boundaries as he fought to suppress those bad images from his earlier trip. Knowing that he would face even more challenges and supernatural forces, he wanted to be prepared when he went again. He packed his hunting knife and his Uncle Jimmy's shotguns.

That evening Chris caught himself daydreaming while looking out the window. O'Conner appeared in this normal blinding way.

Siege of Darkness/Robert Taylor

You must beware for your son has not given up. He still seeks to uncage an evil that will change the very existence of man on this planet!

"No, he has promised me he would not do so! I refuse to believe he'd defy me."

"Why not? He has always defied you! Do not let your love for your child be your demise. Why do you not see the truth? He has been researching this forever! Did you think by promising him material gifts, you could undertake what it is he truly wants? Is a leopard not still a leopard, if you remove his spots?"

"I can't believe this!"

Seeing that you are blinded by all that's before you, I must inform you of God's reason for placing me at your disposal. I am more than just a random angel. I am your late great, great, grandfather.

"How is that so?"

You see, your great, grandfather, my only son, was born and raised outside of the priesthood. His mother refused to let him spend time with me. She feared I'd try to bring him in to join me. As he got older, he came around on his own. He became great friends with most of the priests and bishops.

"So, you two did have some type of relationship?" Chris asked.

"We were working toward a healthy one, but he started dredging up the past. That caused us to fall out and we never spoke again."

"Wow," Chris stressed.

The worst of our arguments was maybe a week before I died. I told him; do not speak my name in life or in death! Let me be dead to you!

Chris nodded.

"What was the argument about?" Chris questioned.

I explained my reason for abandoning him and my wife. I told him I needed to find my sense of purpose. I expressed that I loved his mother, but we began to have problems. I never wanted to leave my family, but we were miserable together. He told me I could have worked it out; she was still in love with me. He told me my reason for leaving was unacceptable and I was a coward! I, over time tried to make it right with him as God would have it, and it seemed to be working out fine. But one morning, he came to see me enraged and unforgiving! He blamed me for his mother's unhappiness and her becoming sick. There at the church, he blasted me for all my past transgressions! A few of the priests tried to calm him, but he stormed out and I never saw him again." O'Conner paused.

Chris was dumbfounded that he was conversing with his great, great grandfather.

"Question not...God's deeds or his word, for no one is more trustworthy than he! He is the best of all planners!"

Talk to your son, it is of great urgency! O'Conner faded. Chris sat in a trance, trying to grasp the depth of their conversation.

Late that evening in her apartment alone, Marie lay in her bed weeping. Her phone rang again and again. Letting it go to voicemail, she listened as the caller was leaving a message.

"Marie, this is Missy! I haven't heard from you. Call me to let me know you're all right. Talk to you later. I love you, sis!"

Marie turned over, buried her head between two pillows and wallowed in tears.

***

At school the following day, Elijah had posted a notice. It was to solicit a team of five, strong and eager young men to travel with him to South Carolina. He wanted to investigate the forest at Cherokee Falls. From all that he had read, all the urban legends and supernatural occurrences, this journey was destined.

Later that evening, he and Mya were at his place sitting on the couch talking.

"This Byron Malic has definitely grabbed my attention. How the Roman Catholic Church sought him out and killed him. According to all the books on the subject, he may not be dead!" Elijah blurted.

"What makes you think he's not dead?"

"Because in the book, *The Execution of the Undead*, it said that during a sacrificial ceremony, the spirit of Malic spoke out from beyond the clouds. So when they killed the soul he possessed, he had to find another host, but whom?"

"Are you serious?" Mya grinned.

"I'm dead serious, why are you smiling?"

"I don't know. It's like your brain is on steroids. Your quest for knowledge is un-extinguishable!" She stared into his eyes.

***

Two days later, Jason and Linda were in a hotel naked beneath the sheets. As they kissed each other, Jason couldn't help but keep picturing the burial grounds. Rolling onto his back, he stared up at the ceiling.

"Jason, what's wrong? Why did you stop?" she asked somewhat frustrated, but curious.

"I'm not going to lie to you. I went down to South Carolina to the find the burial site of Byron Malic."

"You couldn't wait, could you? I knew you were going to go eventually. I told you I would go after I got out of school."

Siege of Darkness/Robert Taylor

"I can't wait that long! I got to know now! I'm sorry, but that's how it is!"

"Since you want to be hard headed, I should let you go by yourself, but I don't want anything bad to happen to you! Wait until next weekend, and I'll take the ride with you, okay?"

"That's why I love you!" he told her happy and grinning. Suddenly, the need to please her arose and he rolled back over on top of her.

17 THE ALIGNMENT OF A NEW ERA

Saturday, October 10, 1987

It was a cold and windy day, Jason Milosky feverishly searched through a bush-filled area of the woods. Nineteen years old now, he longed to have possession and control of the Black Sabbath Scrolls, and he wasn't going to let anything or anyone stop him. To possess such items would place him in a key position to bring forth the will of the four dark overlords, Satan's most prized and evil demons. Their responsibility was to spread evil to all four corners of the earth and to ignite the dark forces, including empowering the dead that had possessed evil spirits, so they could roam the earth and subdue human life.

"If I can only find the exact spot where the Roman Catholic Church held the ritual, find the place where they drained the blood from the prince of the living dead, Byron. It's got to be here somewhere! I've followed all the instructions!" Jason mumbled lightly as he had dug a few small holes.

"Didn't you say we would be cursed if we bothered this burial site? What the hell are we doing?" asked Linda, who after months of Jason's begging, finally agreed to go with him.

"I don't believe none of that shit! People just said those things to keep others away. I'll prove it to you, you'll see."

"Okay, but God, I hope you're right! Birds falling out the sky and everything! God help us!" She started digging in another area.

"Please lord, let him be right!" she continued.

"Baby, remember when I told you about Byron Malic, who was a high priest of the cloth and was turned into a servant of Satan? Well, the reason why was never known. When he became more than they could handle, they set out to find and kill him."

"Why on earth would someone do that?"

"It was horrible! He was persuaded by Satan himself. The priest was greedy for power, so he struck a deal with the devil,"

The two continued to dig up the grounds that surrounded them. It seemed as if they wouldn't find the altar.

"It has to be here, somewhere. I'm sure of it!" Jason seemed baffled. He stopped and rubbed his hands together to warm them up.

"Maybe you're wrong about the exact location?" she added as her nose started running.

"No, I'm not wrong!"

***

At that same moment, the angel of Harry O'Conner abruptly appeared in Chris's bedroom. A cool but soothing breeze followed as it came through a partially opened window. As soon as his angry voice spoke, the television went black and exploded.

You must stop your son; he has no idea to what havoc he will bring! He is at the old burial site in Blacksburg, South Carolina.

"How am I supposed to do that? It'll take at least half a day for me to get there."

Siege of Darkness/Robert Taylor

Reach out to him. It is imperative that you somehow prevent him from carrying out the ritual that will bring total damnation.

Chris raced to the kitchen and grabbed the phone from the wall.

Not even a minute later, Jason's pager started ringing. He looked at the screen and ignored it. Again, it rang and again he paid it no mind. All the while seeming to search harder, Linda would not leave his side, no matter how crazy it all seemed. To Jason, she had become his trusted and most loyal friend. As weird as others thought he was, she thought he was heaven sent, so she stayed by his side.

"Look! What is this here? I think I found something!" she stated as she dug around and dropped down in the dirt. There she used her hands to push aside more and more dirt, so she could view her findings more clearly.

"Where? Where?" Jason anxiously asked as his pager beeped again causing him to turn it completely off.

"Let me see. Here, let me see!" He motioned for her to move aside, so he could get a better look. He was excited. He laughed from the joy it was giving him. They found it! They could see its decayed wooden structure. The two started digging up the area, because they believed the Sabbath Scrolls to be in the vicinity. The hard dirt made the task difficult, but Jason's adrenaline was flowing. After a few hours of digging, the altar was plain to see. Jason dug further and bingo, he found a rusted black case. Upon opening it, he felt something whisk upward as his hair was blown out of his face. Stunned temporarily, he dropped the case and looked around. Reaching into it seconds later, he cautiously picked up a few of the documents and the top one read: Byron Malic's Rampage.

Sitting in the dirt now, the two of them began to go through old articles. They read some of the gruesome and horrifying details to one another.

THE MASON PLANTATION

Stephen Mason, one of the largest crop producers in South Carolina, took his own life after being infected with an unknown virus. His wife and staff were all found dead also. Several plantations were quarantined because of all the death and destruction. They were all later burned to the ground in the night.

THREE WOMAN MURDERED

The vicious murders of three have the local police baffled. The three were killed as they slept. Each of their mouths were covered with tape, as they were tied down and stabbed three times each. They also had puncture marks on each of their necks. Their bodies were drained of all its blood, as it could be seen dripping from walls and dried in the sheets. No clues, no witnesses, no nothing. The only noticeable thing was that one of the windows was wide open, but it was two stories up.

This article was dated 3/17/1827. Jason eagerly flipped through the articles, which were mostly dated back to the early eighteen hundreds.

Byron Malic Welcomed

At thirty-five, Byron Malic is accepted into the priesthood. 2/22/1801 Realizing things didn't add up, Jason stopped to think.

"Jason, this guy was dangerous! Are you reading some of these articles? He savagely murdered, raped and destroyed everything in his path! I've never heard of anything like this."

Siege of Darkness/Robert Taylor

"Crazy, right? He was promised eternal life. He'd still be alive today, if they didn't perform the ritual," Jason answered gleaming.

"...No one is sure if he is truly dead, though!" he added after he thought momentarily.

"You're scaring me. Let's get out of here!"

"There's nothing to be frightened about, trust me!"

"So, why are we digging all this stuff up? Haven't you ever heard you're not supposed to mess with the dead?" Her face exposing how she was beginning to feel.

"You don't understand, for years my family told me stories about Malic and his reign and now I know it's true! I have proof! Now, I want to know the rest of it. I got to know the rest of it! Having bloody crosses and crucifixes all around the house, my father always...always praying!"

"Okay, but what now?" she asked as she began noticing leaves and dirt began to fly about. A heavy breeze engulfed them. There was definitely something strange going on. Scared, Jason grabbed the scrolls and altar, and with Linda's help, they threw everything into the jeep. Upon racing away, a loud sinister laugh echoed amongst the trees. Thinking he heard something, but scared to pause due to the stories, he hurried on.

"Jason, I'm really scared! I don't think you need to be tampering with this stuff. What are you planning to do?"

"I don't know yet. I just wanted to see if the stories were true. My uncles used to love scaring me, but this one used to really shake them up. That's why I needed to find out the truth."

"Okay, now what?"

"I don't know," Jason softly stated as he conjured a vision of the overlords in the gym telling him no harm will come to

Siege of Darkness/Robert Taylor

him. Scared to death, Linda folded her arms and looked at him. He stared straight ahead as he drove, until Linda screamed, the jeep struck an animal and it squealed as it raced away. Jason swerved into a ditch, where the jeep stalled.

"Damn, are you all right? Jason reached over to check. She turned, half frightened.

"You hit a deer! You hit a deer!" she shouted after getting over the initial shock, and dropped her head back onto the headrest. Jason, on the other hand trembling, grabbed and turned the key. The jeep started up once again. Back up on the road, he jumped out and upon looking around, he was confused. Noticing that there was no deer, no blood, not even a scratch on his jeep, he turned around looking in every direction. Hopping back in the jeep, he shook his head in disbelief.

"What? Why do you look so puzzled?" she asked.

"There's no deer, no blood and my jeep looks like nothing ever happened!" More shook up now, he put the pedal to the floor and raced away. His mind started shuffling memories; it ran through all the stories as he thought of what his next move would be. Linda stared at the side of his head as if it was transparent, watching the wheels as they turned, wondering what he was thinking.

"I'm going to prove to the world and all those that thought I was crazy, it's true. I'm not crazy, not one little bit!"

"Jason, you are crazy! I really don't think you need to be messing around with this. It's something about it that frightens me!"

"Linda, please, if you want I'll take you home. I'm not going to stop now, especially now that I'm so close." Linda just stared at him. A bolt of lightning lit up the sky and crashed thunderously causing the two to look up and around.

Siege of Darkness/Robert Taylor

Pacing and looking at his watch, Chris looked worried as he repeatedly called Jason's pager.

"Jason, where are you? Please call me and let me know you're all right! Please son!" he spoke out loud.

A loud cry of laughter caught Chris's attention. He looked around and ran to get his crucifix.

On the highway, a nervous Jason swerved through the sudden fog. He turned on his windshield wipers and they flew from the car. Unable to see, he pulled over to the shoulder of the road. A tractor-trailer and a car ripped passed shaking the jeep. Linda yelled out,

"Jason, get me off this bridge before one of these trucks hit us." At that moment, emerging from the fog was an angel. When completely visible it spoke;

There is great evil in what you have sought out. You mustn't attempt to contact those spirits. They must not be let onto the earth!

Stunned, Jason and Linda both stared up into the sky in disbelief. In the next few minutes, the fog left, Jason started the truck and pulled back onto the road.

Thirty minutes later, pulling into a Motel Six, Jason and Linda jumped out the truck and headed into the office to get a room. A light snow began to blanket everything outdoors.

Once in the room, Linda turned on the television as Jason headed into the bathroom, where he closed the door. As he stood over the toilet with his eyes closed relieving himself, he felt a breeze.

Hello Jason. Thank you for your undying spirit. You have survived only because your eagerness to see this through. With your help, together we will accomplish all that is necessary. I look forward to our alliance."

Siege of Darkness/Robert Taylor

Coming out of the bathroom in a daze, Linda immediately asked;

"What's wrong? What happened?"

"Nothing…nothing at all." He walked over to the window and looked out.

***

That next morning, Elijah and his team were out in that same wooded area of South Carolina. He was curious about the sightings of the monstrous figures. As he and his team trend slowly and cautiously, carrying rifles and backpacks, they were ready to shoot anything that didn't look right. After hours of walking, they stopped to rest, and that's when Elijah noticed a huge old bone. Curious, he picked it up assuming it was that of an ancient reptile of some sort. It was an actual shinbone of a mammal or something of great size. It was riddled with bullet like holes. Searching the area further, they found the skull and various other bones also riddled. After laying them out, Elijah took pictures. Seeing this, he knew of no animal whose bone structure they resembled. Gathering them, they hiked back to place them in his pick-up.

Less than an hour later, he stumbled upon the dug up area where Jason and Linda found the scroll and altar. Elijah searched the small graves, but they were clean.

"I wonder what was here?" he questioned as his team looked on. Walking over to another, he noticed a casket. He had one of his men climb down to open it. As he slowly and cautiously pulled back the lid, inside there was nothing but white dust. Trying to figure things out, Elijah walked in circles. Suddenly, the wind started to shift, as it got fierce and forceful. The trees began to swing as branches started falling and crashing to the ground. Elijah and his team raced through the woods trying to get somewhere safe. It was as if they made the forest angry. Without further warning, a large tree came crashing down and landed on three of the men, crushing them. Elijah stopped and ran back, attempting to help, but saw it was no use. There was blood everywhere as the men lay lifeless. Also, to block his path, two more large trees fell and thunderously struck the ground, changing his thought pattern.

Twenty minutes later, the winds stopped and there was calm. Elijah and the two remaining members of his crew, frightened beyond belief, ended up standing on an old bridge. There a ghost of a white male on a horse followed by several slaves passed them. Slaves hanging from trees crying out were everywhere.

"Help me," the slaves each yelled sporadically.

"What in the hell?" Elijah questioned.

"Let's get the hell out of here!" one of his crewmembers shouted. No one questioned why, they moved on quickly.

***

That evening as Jason and Linda drove passed his home, his father and uncles were sitting on the porch. His father yelled to him as they passed, but Jason continued on. He turned down a bumpy winding road and headed to Linda's place, which was on the other side of the hill.

After pulling up in front of the small home, a weary Linda kissed Jason on the cheek, forged a smile and jumped out of the jeep.

"That was the scariest road trip I've ever been on!" Linda pointed out.

Siege of Darkness/Robert Taylor

"Yeah...for sure. I need to get home and get some rest." He got ready to leave but remembered something;

"Linda, you have the scrolls in the backpack, I need them." Jason reminded her.

"Let me run in the house and make you some copies; that way you'll have two sets just in case. I would hate for your father to get a hold of these! I'll be right back, okay?

"Good idea," Jason agreed. She hurried on and within minutes, she came back out with the documents and passed them to him through the jeep's window.

Sitting on the porch when Jason arrived home, his father Chris and his uncles stared him down.

"Boy, something crazy happened last night and today, which makes me believe you're still chasing that myth!" Chris immediately addressed.

"If it's such a myth then, let me find out for myself. What could it hurt?" Jason shouted out of anger.

"I can't believe you come from my balls boy! You amaze me with how stupid you can be! Damn boy, please listen for once in your life!"

"Dad, you're always preaching; tell the truth. You have been lying to me all my life!" Jason carried on as he stood angry.

"Jason, your father and us didn't know whether or not the stories were true. We didn't care! Our grandfather, your great granddad told them to us out of fun," Willie jumped in, placed his beer on the wooden banister. Chris stood lost in memories of yesterday; from his uncle arguing with Satan to the many nights hiding under the bed and so forth.

"Jason, please tell me you didn't go and dig up that burial site?" Chris asked.

Siege of Darkness/Robert Taylor

"How did you know where I went? Dad, how did you know?" Jason asked baffled because he told no one.

"I find out everything!" he yelled as he stepped into Jason's face.

"Whatever, I'm grown!" Jason shouted as he tried to walk away. Chris angered, punched Jason off his feet. As he lay out, he just looked up at his father and held his jaw.

"Since you so grown, you need to be getting out my house! I don't take care of grown people! And leave the keys to the truck when you go, since you can't keep your word!" Chris walked away mumbling.

"I did keep my word! I finished high school!" Jason yelled, while his uncles stood over him stunned at the entire incident.

Sitting in his living room an hour later, Chris watched television and drank a beer. He rubbed his forehead as he thought.

"What has this damn boy done?" he questioned. "Oh Lord, help him, for if he has done what I think he's done, we all need prayer!"

I have spoken with this son of yours and he refuses to listen. He is hell bent on following through with this demonic revival. If he succeeds, the world as you know it will be far worse, as the evil in it will be magnified. You must reach him! O'Conner spoke from beyond.

The very next day at five that morning, Jason woke up and eased out of his room, peeking into his father's to make sure he was asleep. What he saw was a man drooling on his pillow, knocked out with a beer bottle just out of the reach of his fingertips, as his arm hung over the side of the bed. Walking softly to avoid waking him, Jason headed down the hall to a rear door and out to his truck that sat in the driveway. He opened the hatch, retrieved the black box, and headed back inside.

Back in his bedroom, he sat on the floor with the copies of the scrolls and newspaper clippings resting between his outstretched legs. After thumbing through them, he came upon one that looked like it came from a holy book of some sort; the page was stained and jagged. The scripture read, *The earth will becometh thee inhabitance of those that art the followers of the truth, and that truth being thee undisputed word of thy God. Your pomp and magnificence have been brought down to the grave, along with the music of your harps; Maggots [which prey on the dead] are spread out under you [as a bed] and worms are your covering.*
How you have fallen from heaven, O star of the morning [light-bringer], son of the dawn! You have been cut down to the ground, you who have weakened the nations!
But you said in your heart, I will ascend to heaven;
I will raise my throne above the stars of God; I will sit on the mount of assembly in the remote parts of the north.

After reading that amongst the other documents, he paused in thought, long enough to hear a woman's scream. Racing over to his bedroom window, wide eyed, he scanned his immediate surroundings, but visually there was nothing. Six gunshots echoed thereafter, bringing Chris stumbling out of his room into Jason's room.

"What was that, and what the hell is this on the floor?" Chris stood awaiting answers.

"…Just some things I found."
Chris dropped to one knee and picked up what looked like a copy of an old scripture and began to read it.

Siege of Darkness/Robert Taylor

"What is this? And where did you get this from? You got this from that burial site, didn't you? You refuse to listen. What do you hope to accomplish? You need God in your life!" he scolded almost tearing.

"You really went out and dug this stuff up! What in the world is wrong with you?" Chris shouted, picking up a few of the pages and stood angry.

"Dad, listen, I know you told me not to pursue this, but you have to understand I had to know the truth. All these documents and scriptures represent the fact that there is supernatural life. Malic existed back then and probably still exists today! Please don't be mad at me."

"Boy, you don't understand what you're doing, you're bringing the devil to our doorstep and I can't have that! I will not have this!" Chris grabbed up the documents and walked out the room.

"Dad, there's something happening as we speak! You taking those documents won't stop a thing. He's here!"

"Shut up, boy, I'm tired of this silly shit!" Chris yelled as he made his way downstair into the living room, where he started up the fireplace. As the flames rose, he put one document after the other in and sat there staring as they burned and turned to ashes.

Minutes behind him, Jason came running into the living room. Briefly, he was captivated by the documents crumbling to ashes.

"Dad, you have to hear me out! I know about the angel that comes to see you! I know about him being the spirit of my great, great, great granddad! I know why you're scared, I get it!"

Siege of Darkness/Robert Taylor

"No you don't, because if you did, you would not have done what you've done!"

"Dad, don't you see? All that's taking place was inevitable! It's Lucifer's time, he has risen with great power over the living and those who do not accept him as thy true God, he will slaughter!" Jason ran on, as if he was possessed.

"Boy, what in God's name is wrong with you?" Chris felt a bad energy in the room. Suddenly, beams of blinding light came through the walls.

"Dad, you must see that times have changed. Lucifer rules!" Chris was overwhelmed as he stared at Jason. He walked out the front door, slamming it behind him.

18

October 19th, 1992

Finally, being released from prison, Sherrod was being picked up by Walt, who sat on the hood of his black Camaro smiling. As the big iron gates opened, Sherrod stepped out with a black satchel sitting over his right shoulder. His muscles, now rippling were easy to see beneath his bright white t-shirt, while he was looking around amidst the glare. Spotting his friend, he made his way to him. After the two embraced, they both addressed each other.

"Good to see you."

"You, too," Sherrod returned. They jumped in the car and hightailed out of the parking lot.

"Damn man, you look really good!" Walt told him as he glanced over and shifted gears simultaneously.

"Don't get sweet on me," Sherrod cautioned jokingly.

"You been in jail too long, I'm not pushing up on you! I'm just complimenting you! If I was gay, you wouldn't be my type, anyway!" Walt stressed also jokingly.

"Funny! Anyway, how's everybody doing?" Sherrod asked changing subjects.

"Well, Ray-Ray died last year; I thought I told you he got shot stealing somebody's car. J.J. started getting high and if you saw him, you wouldn't recognize him. He looks really bad!"

"You're kidding right?" Sherrod asked.

Siege of Darkness/Robert Taylor

"No, I'm dead serious," Walt told him and they began sharing stories for the entire half hour ride.

Arriving at Sherrod's parents' home, Sherrod hugged Walt once again and climbed out the car. After ringing the doorbell several times, the door opened and his father smiled and invited him in.

"Ha, ha, boy, look at you! Looking like somebody's damn superhero, all muscular! Baby, look who's home! Come look at your boy!" his father hollered overjoyed. Sherrod's mother came into the room, moving a lot slower than usual, but bearing a huge smile. Sherrod noticing right away, walked to meet her.

"She had a small stroke. We didn't want to bother you and have you worried in there," his father announced. Holding his mother in his arms, Sherrod whispered in her ear.

"Ahh..mom, I love you!" and kissed her on the cheek. She smiled and rested her head against his chest.

"I love you, too, son," she stated softly while patting him on his back. After that, they all sat down in the living room, where they did some catching up. His mother rocked and smiled as she stared over at him. Sherrod stared back smiling as he was sort of uncomfortable with her condition.

"Son, your mother's going to be all right! So you can relax," his father assured him as he read through his expression.

"I know, I know." Sherrod quickly chose to switch subjects. "I couldn't wait to get out of there and see you guys. Ahhh, I miss being home! Now I can get me a home- cooked meal. It seemed like I was in there forever!" Sherrod carried on happily. His mother just continued to stare and smile. Regardless of what his father told him, his mother not being her usual perky self, had him worried.

Siege of Darkness/Robert Taylor

***

  That afternoon, Jason and Chris were at odds. Chris could barely stand the sight of his own flesh and blood. They walked past each other in the house without saying hello, good morning or even good night. They wouldn't even sit in the same room together. Willie and Jimmy saw this and tried talking to both of them, but to no avail. Willie sat Jason down more so on several occasions, but Jason was dead set on moving forward. With the house in turmoil, there was little conversation amongst any of them. All day long doors opened and shut, as they all stayed in their rooms. Frustrated with it all, Willie got up off the edge of his bed, grabbed his cane and headed out and into Jason's room.

  "Jason, you got to stop this, you're driving your father crazy! He loves you and you know he does! Give this witch hunt up!" Willie pleaded.

  "You know it's not a witch hunt, that's why you want me to give it up! Don't you get it? Don't you want to know the truth? You said you loved those stories just like I do, so I know you're just as curious as I am. Come with me Uncle Willie!" Jason went on playing on him.

  "Cut it out Jason. I'm definitely not going down there! Stop making this about the stories; this doesn't have anything to do with those stories anymore. It has to do with right and wrong! Good and evil! God and Satan!" Jimmy interrupted as he came to stand in the doorway. At that moment, Jason got quiet and looked at the two of them.

  "This is how it's gonna be, y'all ganging up on me? I'm moving out!" Jason blurted and walked passed them, down the stairs and out the front door. Willie and Jimmy both looked at each other and shook their heads.

"He won't listen. He just won't listen!" Willie spoke in disbelief.

"We tried. Chris was right; we shouldn't have told him those stories," Jimmy said, taking part of the blame.

"Who knew he would go to this extreme? Digging up burial sites and having conversations with the dead!" Willie added.

"At that moment, Chris walked into the room and sat down next to Willie and got comfortable.

"I can't understand why he is so dead set on going against God! I've taken him to church, I've groomed him to know right from wrong, I just can't understand why?" Chris carried on worriedly.

"If we had known he would take it this far, we wouldn't have," Willie spoke somberly before he was interrupted.

"It's not y'all's fault, it's my son's unwillingness to let go. He wants to fight with God! He is out for revenge!" Chris explained.

"I'll go try to talk some sense in him," Willie added as he walked from the room.

***

Elijah, after spending countless hours searching through books on mammals past and present, drew a blank for an anatomical match. After which he made quite a few calls to see if within the last thirty years were there any sightings of an eight-foot beast.

Siege of Darkness/Robert Taylor

After about an hour of phone calls, he finally found an elder news reporter that recalled an old incident. They began to talk candidly about it all.

"Yeah, I remember it like it was yesterday! I was out in the woods, me and my crew and oh yeah…most of Charleston, Cherokee Falls, and Blacksburg's police officers were out there too. We all were out there hours before it surfaced. Whew…boy, when it did, bullets came from everywhere and that beast let out a roar that would have made your hair stand on your head! In its rage, it killed quite a few officers as they ran for their lives! The creature ran and was never found.

"Well, I think I found it!" Elijah told him.

"Wow, that's something I'd love to see! You got a piece of history there! A part of history no one will ever believe!" The old reporter rambled excitedly.

"I'm sorry to be a bother," Elijah expressed sympathetically.

"A bother, boy you gave me something to do! I sit around this house staring at the walls. You know I'm retired now, just waiting around until the Lord calls my number!

"I thank you for all your help and time. I'll keep your number and will call you if I need you again. Bless you!" Elijah went back to writing in his journal.

***

That Friday evening as Chris was driving home listening to his radio and singing along, a force took control of his car. As he fought to keep it on the road, it was skidding left toward an embankment. Terrified, he gripped the steering wheel, but the force was just too powerful. Suddenly when O'Conner appeared it all stopped, and he straightened up the wheel and

Siege of Darkness/Robert Taylor

avoided a near tragedy. Taking several deep breaths, as he continued to hold the wheel tightly, he pulled into the next clearing. O'Conner disappeared as Chris brought the car to a complete stop and turned off the engine. At that exact moment, a sinister laugh floated passed and drifted away.

"What the hell!" Chris shouted as he looked around totally confused. He grabbed the cross hanging around his neck and kissed it. Just as he got ready to pull back onto the road, a tractor-trailer came barreling around the curve. Chris hit the brakes as he sighed and took yet another deep breath.

***

That evening with books stacked all around him, Elijah was exhausted. Suddenly his phone rang. He picked it up.

"Hello," he greeted.

"Hello, is this Elijah Cross?" the voice questioned.

"Yes, this is he."

"I'm the guy you spoke with from the Carolina Times." Waking from his stupor, Elijah sat straight up and became energized.

"I think I may have some pictures around here somewhere, maybe somewhere in my basement or attic. As a matter of fact, I know I do! Give me your address and a few days. I'll locate them and send them to you!"

"Thank you, and I truly appreciate this. Right now, I'm staying at the Charleston Inn. Just call me and I'll come meet you somewhere," Elijah suggested.

"Okay, sounds good," the guy agreed.

"You have a great day!" The two hung up.
Excited now, Elijah sat imagining what the creature might look like.

Siege of Darkness/Robert Taylor

***

The next morning Jason rode around town filling out applications, everywhere from the pancake house to local car dealerships and stores. He needed a decent paying job, because he wanted to move, his truck needed some minor repairs and he couldn't even afford to fix or put gas in it.

Frustrated that evening, he pulled up to Linda's place with all his clothes piled in the back. She came out as he blew his horn and jumped into the passenger seat.

"My mom said you could stay with us for a few months, until you find a place. Jason, don't you think you need to stop being so pig-headed and at least talk to your father?"

"He don't want to talk, he wants to yell! I'm going to finish what I started, cut and dry!"

"Even if it tears your family apart?"

"Even if so!"

She stared at him and shook her head. After which, she jumped out the truck and headed back toward the house.

"Grab your things and come on, with your stubborn ass!" she walked away shaking her head.

***

Early that next morning, Elijah, realizing he hadn't been home to spend time with Mya, picked up the phone to call her.

"Sorry to wake you, but I wanted to hear your voice," Elijah told her.

"At one-thirty in the morning you call me when I haven't heard from you in days? Talking about you wanted to hear my voice. I wanted to hear yours, but you couldn't even answer the phone." She flat out rained on his parade.

"I'm sorry, so much has happened out here that I didn't expect, that I plum forgot."

"Damn, I must not be that important if you can forget me as soon as you go away!"

"I'm so sorry, I'll make it up to you when I get back, I promise," he told her. "Oh yeah, I promise!" he emphasized. "Get your sleep and I'll call again tomorrow," he added. Still somewhat angry, she hung up and dosed off.

After hanging up from Mya, Elijah sat up thinking. Picking up the shinbone of the creature, which laid on the nightstand, he looked it over thoroughly. Recognizing the massiveness of the monstrosity, he held it up in admiration. After which, he looked over at the skull on the dresser and then the few other various pieces.

That evening, within the tower of the Roman Catholic Church, one could see two bald, semi-muscular Black men looking out. Their flesh began to harden and become reptilian. They grew tails and took on the look of gargoyles. Leaping from the tower, they took flight and in mid-air, they were joined by ten others. They greeted each other with ear-busting squeals and headed north into the darkness.

Three days later, Elijah reached out to the news reporter and didn't get an answer. He called, again and again, there was no answer. Sitting for a second in thought, suddenly the phone rang.

"Yes, may I help you?" the reporter answered.

"Hello, this is Elijah Cross. I spoke to you and you were supposed to be sending me some pictures."

"Okay, I remember, I just located them and I'm duplicating them as we speak. Are you still staying at the hotel?"

Siege of Darkness/Robert Taylor

"No I'm not. I'm going to be back down there in a maybe a month or so. Can I meet with you when I get there?" Elijah told him.

"Sure, just call me when you get into town and I'll make arrangements from there," the reporter spoke in return. On that note the two had very little to say and ended the call seconds later.

By mid-December, Elijah was driving down Interstate 95 south heading to South Carolina. With Mya riding along, they sang and laughed the entire time. Once they had finally reached Charleston, Elijah found a nice hotel for them to stay in. After the bellhop gathered their luggage, they registered and headed to an open elevator.

Fifteen minutes later, as the two lay resting on the bed, Elijah picked up the house phone and called his reporter friend.

"I just got into town. I'm going to rest up today and we'll make arrangements to meet tomorrow," Elijah told him as he was exhausted from the fifteen-hour drive.

That next afternoon, Elijah and the reporter met, shook hands, and sat within a small, out of the way restaurant. The reporter passed Elijah an envelope and he opened it immediately. Pulling out five photos from the envelope, he started looking through them.

"This thing is huge, man, look at its hands! Wow, it's hard to believe something like this existed!

"Yeah, if I wasn't there, I would have never believed it myself," the reporter agreed. The two ate, got acquainted, talked for just about an hour and then said their good-byes. They promised to stay in touch.

****

For the next six months, Jason worked and helped Linda and her mother out around the house. If one didn't know any better, you would think he had forgotten about Byron Malic and his quest to unveil the hidden truth. He and Linda often went out to the movies and sat in the park enjoying each other's company. One day while they sat on a blanket in a heavily shaded area, Linda gave him a soft kiss on the lips, while staring him in the eyes.

"You can be so wonderful! I wish you were this way all the time!" Linda expressed.

"You bring the best out of me! I don't know where I'd be without you! After my mother died, I hated the world and wanted to kill myself!" Jason told her.

"Jason, what's wrong?" she asked seeing him get sad almost immediately.

"Nothing, nothing at all."

After that, he sat quietly, looked her in the eyes and said, "Let's get out of here!" They packed up and jumped in the truck, Jason began to talk again.

"You know, Linda, I wanted to give up on all my research and just get married and make a family. I know I love you, but all this anger that's built up in me, is driving me crazy!"

"Why can't you let it go? God is showing you a way out. He's showing you how to love again. You just have to be willing to give it a chance!"

"Stop with all that God stuff!" he yelled as he suddenly lost it. She looked at him sympathetically, reached out and massaged his shoulder.

At Chris's home, he and his two brothers were sitting out on the porch conversing with an old friend they hadn't seen in

Siege of Darkness/Robert Taylor

years. Laughter spilled from their tongues and tears slid down their faces.

"Ah, man, I haven't laughed this hard in a long time."

"It's so good to see you guys. So many of us are dead and gone, it's crazy."

"Well, he's gonna call all of us home sooner or later. From dust we come and to dust we'll return. When it's your time, it's your time!" Chris added as he kissed his cross.

"What up with that son of yours?" the friend asked.

"That's a long story. He moved out after high school. He's living with his girlfriend. You know how they get once they think they're grown. They start smelling themselves!" The guy went on and the four talked and had a few beers until the sunlight started to fade.

***

A few days later, as rain dampened the soil and the spirits of many, Elijah sat with the professor discussing a few things.

"Professor, why have they not told the world what's going on? The people have a right to know!" Elijah stated baffled.

"You can't just put something like that out there and have people hysterically running around. Years back when the news got wind of something similar, everybody and their mothers, aunts, uncles, and cousins were buying guns and ammunition. People became savages and there were more accidental murders than ever!" the professor pointed out.

"But professor, the people have every right to know what's going on around them, don't you think?" Elijah added.

"They do, but you have to look at things from a broader perspective; do you alarm the people and cause mass-hysteria or do you send the troop in and eliminate the problem altogether?" the professor put out there for Elijah to reason with and come to his own conclusion. He didn't respond as he understood the professor's point.

***

That weekend, a naked Linda bounced up and down as she straddled Jason. The two moaned loudly as the bed squeaked and knocked on the floor. Downstairs, entering the house, unaware of what was going on, Linda's mother was stopped in her tracks. She walked to the steps and listened closely. After hearing enough, she called out,

"Linda...Linda," and waited for her to answer.

In the bedroom caught up in the moment and about to climax, she and Jason couldn't help but finish and collapse.

"Ahhh, yes Mama?" she pushed out exhausted.

"Can you put something on and come here?"

Coming out of the room in a pair of gray shorts and a white tee, she looked drained, but happy.

"Yes Mama?"

"You and Jason are going to have to find your own place! You two aren't going to sit up in my house and screw, or worse make a baby!"

"Mama, I understand. I'm sorry!"

"I knew this was a bad idea from the start! I don't know how I let you talk me into it. Isn't he supposed to be at work today?" She walked into the kitchen.

"He took the day off," Linda answered, as she followed, smiling from ear to ear.

19

November 2nd, 1998

Up north in the heart of Newark, Sherrod who had been home from prison six years now, had adjusted and was living a normal life. On this Friday after cashing his check, he ran across a few women in short dresses and heels, patrolling Broad Street. He made eye contact with a beautiful Spanish woman in yellow; her sexy long legs had his undivided attention, while her wavy blonde hair danced in the wind and about her shoulders. She blew Sherrod a flirtatious kiss, as her bright red lipstick made her gesture that much more enticing. He looked around to see if it was for someone else, but everyone was doing their own thing. She smiled and gestured for him to come over. He walked toward her like a well-trained poodle.

"Hi, how are you?" he greeted.

"I'm fine," she answered as her beautiful smile stopped his next sentence from tumbling off his tongue.

"Is there a problem?" she asked.

"Excuse me, you're just so sexy I can't help but stare at you and wonder if you're single."

"I'm whatever you want me to be, your wife, your mistress, your fantasy, you call it!"

"Let's go somewhere and talk," he suggested.

"First off, are you police?" She looked into his eyes.

His face held a look of surprise. He grinned.

"No, but why?"

"That's good, let's go talk."

Ten minutes later, sitting at a bar in the hotel, the two of them were having a conversation. With a beer in hand, the woman continued to smile as her lipstick canvassed the top of the bottle.

"You are gorgeous!" Sherrod told her.

"Thank you; now let's get down to business! A blow job is forty, one nut is two-hundred and a night is five!"

"What? Your a prostitute?" he questioned stunned.

"I prefer the title; call girl. What did you think I was?"

"Not that!"

She got up and walk away. He raced behind her and grabbed her by her left wrist. She instantly became cooperative.

"Look, a brother don't get much action, between working and trying to put my life back together."

"That's not my problem! I'm not a social worker!" She yanked away from him and folded her arms across her chest.

"Look, I got a hundred dollars and that's all I got!"

"How do I always get all you charity cases?" She sighed.

"Come on," she walked away and toward an area that housed three elevators.

A half hour later, as the headboard pounded and cracked the wall, Sherrod held her pecan colored limbs in the air, as he drove his glistening solid rod deep into her sea of moisture. Excited, a large vein appeared on his forehead as his body stiffened and suddenly she began to holler.

"Oh, oh my fuckin' God! Shit, oh yes!" She moaned as she forged a smile and grabbed the sheets tightly, then him about the waist. She began sinking her nails into his skin and like a maniac, he turned and flipped her, picked her up and carried her about the room sliding her up and down on his pole.

Siege of Darkness/Robert Taylor

Finally, on the floor with her ass in the air, he picked up the pace as her soft round cheeks bounced against his pelvic area. One orgasm after another, she seemed to be in sheer heaven. Her mouth sat open as she squealed and thrust backward anticipating every pump. He pulled her hair like the reins of a horse, yanking it like a madman. His eyes got dark, his body hardened and he started shaking. She squinted from the pain then yelled, echoing throughout the hotel and into the midnight air. People throughout the place looked up and around wondering what and who. Her body began to feel funny as it started to tingle all over. Trying to break free of his grasp because of the otherwise intense pain, she fell off the bed and finally, to safety.

***

Simultaneously, O'Brien who was watching television, smiled as he closed his eyes and fell back onto his bed. Aroused, he began to shout,

"Oh...you feel so damn good! Oh baby...I'm going to fuck you until the sun come up! Damn...you're so soft." He went on tossing and humping, but there was no one visible.

Around that same time while lounging around his very own place now, Jason was listening to the news. He was captivated by the slaying of a couple in their home.

In the early morning hours, a couple was stabbed and shot to death as their apartment was trashed. Robbery was not believed to be the motive. The man was holding a crucifix tightly in his right hand! The couple was in their late sixties. Anyone with information pertaining to this killing, please call us at 1888 654 -1600

Jason slid on his sneakers and headed out to his jeep. Linda got up from the table, walked to the window and watched as he pulled off. She wondered where he was heading too.

***

Daydreaming while at work the next day, Sherrod hammered in some nails as he couldn't stop thinking about the prostitute. How explosive the sex was and how his body seemed so alive! The look on her face and the anger she expressed as she lay on the floor.

"What the hell are you trying to do, rip out my insides? Give me my money and get out!" she shouted as she jumped at the movement of her stomach.

"I'm sorry, I got carried away! It won't happen again," Sherrod promised as he sat on the bed butt naked. She continued holding her stomach as she stared at it.

"Is there something wrong?" Sherrod asked.

"It's weird, something moving around in my stomach. It's weird, like something swimming inside of me, as if …that's impossible!" She looked up at Sherrod mystified. Out of thought, he got up and went to get a few two-by-fours from a pile near a wall.

Later that evening, his friend Walt took him to a bar called the Last stop on 14th Street and Madison. As the two entered, they could feel the energy, as they noticed quite a few young guys hanging out or playing pool. Sitting down at the bar, they looked around, as the bartender came to stand just out in front of them.

"May I help you?" he asked.

Siege of Darkness/Robert Taylor

"Could we get a couple of beers?" Walt requested. The bartender walked off and went into a freezer, grabbed two cold ones and headed back in their direction. After he placed them on the bar, Walt paid him and he went on his way.

"Sherrod, you don't seem like that same dude I used to know."

"Am I supposed to be the same after twelve years in prison, let me know?"

"I'm just saying, most guys go to jail and come out and do the same ol' shit!"

"Man, you can't find anything better to talk about, all these fine women in here?" Sherrod responded annoyed. He looked over at Sherrod, smiled and went back to looking around as he started nodding his head to the music.

"Yeah, you're right, but one day soon we gone have a heart to heart, know that!" Walt finished as he got up and headed over toward the pool table. Sherrod sat still watching all the young ladies as they passed. He missed this scene and it showed as he grabbed one of the lady's arms. Pulling her toward him, she immediately got angry.

"What the hell are you doing? Get off of me!" she shouted, and as soon as she made eye contact that all changed. She smiled and started kissing him. Walt, who was watching from afar, was amazed. He was happy for his boy and had a painted smile until he saw an angry, black six-footer heading in Sherrod's direction. Propping his pool stick against a nearby wall, he rushed to Sherrod's aid. Before he could get there, the guy pushed his girl to the floor and grabbed Sherrod around the collar. Sherrod's eyes flipped colors and before anyone could flinch, he hit the man three times, leaving him planted against a wall and out cold. Sherrod turned looking for the woman, but she was long gone and so were half the patrons.

Siege of Darkness/Robert Taylor

That Sunday after resting in the bed most of the morning, Sherrod's father knocked at the door and yelled,

"Are you alive in there?" he asked.

"Yeah Dad, I'm just tired," Sherrod replied barely awake.

"You want some dinner? It's ready!" his father told him. Sherrod sat up, looked out the window and noticed that it was dark outside. He had slept the day away. Remembering pieces of the night before, he looked at his fist.

After eating dinner, he sat talking to his father, who had retired to his recliner and was smoking a pipe. As the two shared a stare, a conversation ensued.

"Dad, I'm so sorry for what I took you and Mom through. I'm going to do a lot better, I promise you this time, for real. Jail's no place for me."

"I heard it all before! I hope so boy…we love you, but if you can't do right, we'd rather you stay as far away as possible. I can't see your Mom heartbroken anymore! You hear me? She's everything to me and I don't want to lose her!" his father pointed out as he stopped to pull on his tobacco pipe.

"Yeah Dad, I understand. I'm a show you I'm a changed man. Trust me!" Sherrod told him as the two stood up, locked eyes and embraced.

The following weekend on Veteran's Day, Sherrod was in the hotel again with the prostitute. They talked after having sex, as they sat naked wrapped in the sheets.

"You need to take a break! Look at you! Are you pregnant?" Sherrod asked her.

"Please, I can't get pregnant! Plus, I don't ever have unprotected sex!"

"So explain your stomach and why it feels so hard," Sherrod carried on.

Siege of Darkness/Robert Taylor

"I can't, I'm going to the doctor next week to find out why I'm swelling up like this. Sometimes the pain is unbearable!" she pointed out while Sherrod lay there and rolled over on top of her.

"You gotta put money in the jukebox to get it to play your tune!" she explained jokingly. Sherrod laughed as he pulled the sheets up over their heads.

***

Two days later, while O'Brien sat at the foot of his bed, his eyes rolled back in his head as he inhaled while smiling.

"Yes, oh yes, it feels so good!" he carried on while his hormone caused an erection. He could feel the prostitute's vaginal walls as if he was in it himself. Grabbing his genitals, he rolled around on the bed humping and moaning.

***

By November 19th, Sherrod had saved enough money and was leaving his parents place to move into his new apartment. After putting on his coat, he kissed his mother on her cheek and held her tight, shook his father's hand, stared him in the eyes and assured him he was on the right path. He walked out and jumped in the car with Walt. In the car he sighed as he thought to himself; finally my own space, thank God! With really nothing but clothes, Walt's back seat was filled, as was his trunk.

Back home and out on a date with Mya, Elijah was all smiles as she sat catching him up on the things she had going on. He missed her beautiful face so much; he barely heard a word she spoke.

Siege of Darkness/Robert Taylor

"This being my last year in school, now I'll have my B.A. finally! My dad wants me to go to law school and I do too! But right now, I'm going to take a year off and have some fun. What you think?" she happily carried on.

"Whatever you do is fine with me, as long as I'm part of it," Elijah told her.

"You're not even listening to me!" she shouted as she leaned across the table and kissed him. Elijah leaned in for seconds.

***

Friday after work, Sherrod walked through a dark street where hustlers hung out. Tired and worn, the only thing on his mind was reaching home so he could rest. As he passed a porch with guys hanging out, one stood up and had something to say.

"Hard working nigga, huh?"
Sherrod ignored him and continued walking.

"I guess he can't hear me with that hard hat on!" the hustler shouted as he stepped from the porch and chased Sherrod down.

"Hey, I know you heard me! What's your deal kid? You can't come through my block without speaking."

"Well, I don't know you and I think it's best to keep it that way!" Sherrod told him as he stepped harder.

"What? Suck my dick, you ain't nobody! Broke ass, good for nothing, nobody! I get money!" the dealer ranted loudly, as he held up a knot of cash as he felt disrespected. Sherrod ignored him, as he walked on shaking his head in response.

"You betta ask around about Dre," the hustler continued on yelling.

Siege of Darkness/Robert Taylor

About a week later on the first of December, at five o'clock, Sherrod stood on Broad and Market looking around. Taking notice to his presence, one of the other ladies approached him, pinched him on the butt and smiled as he turned to see who it was.

"Hey, Donna's busy, is there something I can do for you?" she looked into his eyes and asked.

"No, I'll wait," he answered with a frown as he walked away and across the street.

Twenty minutes later, he spotted Donna as she walked up and started talking with the others. He trotted across the street and right up on her, interrupting the women's little gathering.

"I need to see you," Sherrod announced fiendishly. With a bottle of milk of magnesia in her hand, bags forming beneath her eyes, she faced him and spoke.

"I'm done for the day, shops closed! I'm not feeling well, so catch me tomorrow."

"I can't wait until tomorrow; I need just a few minutes that's all!"

"Okay, but no sex!" she agreed and walked away with him.

"Why are you still looking so worn out?" Sherrod asked. She coughed as she fixed her mouth to answer.

"I don't know. I still haven't been to the doctor yet. My appointment is for next week. I feel terrible!" she stared at him and pointed out. Sherrod stared back as he reached for her right hand to console her. She immediately moved it and backed away.

Later that evening, as he was unaware that he was traveling down that same dark street where the hustler's hung out, Sherrod paused as he thought about turning around. Choosing to continue on, he hoped that they weren't out there, but they were. Out on the sidewalk, the dealers were making transactions and running in and out of allies. Sherrod moved through them and it came;

"There's that whack dude, right there!" a voice yelled from the street. Sherrod kept stepping as he didn't want any trouble.

"Yo, didn't I tell you not to come through here?" As the person grew near, Sherrod stopped and turned to face him. With his fist tightly closed and his face expressionless, he waited.

"Oh, you bad now! How's that gone help you against this?" he asked Sherrod as he whipped out his gun. Sherrod just stared at him fearlessly. Waving the gun in Sherrod's face, he laughed and told him, "Get out of here before I smoke ya ass!" Sherrod walked off angrily, hard and stiff.

Finally home, Sherrod sat on his bed pounding his fist into his hand. He tossed things across the room and yelled as he thought about what had just happened.

After allowing his anger to get the best of him, Sherrod flew out the door, around a few corners and back onto the dark street where the hustler's hung. Seeing the one he had words with, he watched until he saw him shake a few hands and head around a corner. Sherrod ran through a few allies and ended up on the street where the dealer was. Seeing him walking up on his truck, Sherrod ran up behind him. Before he could react, Sherrod had him in a chokehold.

"When you disrespect someone, you can't slip! Especially when you pull out a burner and tell him to suck your dick! Open the car door and let's go for a ride," Sherrod rambled in the guy's ear as his own skin hardened. The guy tried to resist, but found Sherrod's strength unmatchable. Sherrod smacked him unconscious, ran through his pockets, found his car keys and threw the dude in the vehicle.

Siege of Darkness/Robert Taylor

An hour later in an old apartment building, Sherrod had the dealer tied up and hanging from an old pipe. The dealer woke up and after seeing his dilemma yelled,

"Do you know who I am? My boys gone find you and kill you! Who the hell do you think you are?" On that note, Sherrod pulled a hunting knife from a pouch about his waist and walked right up to the dealer waving it. The dealer, sweating and silent looked Sherrod dead in his eyes.

"You like inviting men to your dick, huh?" Sherrod stated angrily as he unbuckled the man's belt and stripped him of his pants and underwear.

"Look man, it's not that serious! You don't have to do this...I can give you whatever you want!"

"You don't have nothing I need!" Sherrod gave him a brief stare, and clenched his teeth. With one swift motion, he cut off his dick, back to his testicles. The dealer screamed as blood poured and Sherrod yelled along with him.

Fifteen minutes later, Sherrod raced out of the building as blood fell from his closed right hand. His senses were heightened as if he was strengthened by the act itself.

O'Brien in the shower with the water lightly hitting his face, suddenly began to breath heavily as he looked into the palm of his right hand. He saw blood briefly and then it was no more. He closed his eyes and he could see Sherrod racing through street after street. Jumping out of the shower, he wrapped a towel around his body as he sat on the end of the bed. There, he could see what Sherrod had done.

For the next week or so, all around town in every store window, Christmas decorations were displayed. People greeted each other. Inside a small quaint diner, Marie sat alone. Near a window, she slowly nibbled away at a turkey burger and fries. Sherrod, at the counter, was placing an order with the waitress when he turned around and noticed her. He watched her for a few minutes, before walking over to her table.

"Do you mind if I have a seat?" he asked. She never looked at him or responded. Sherrod sat down anyway. She immediately dropped eight dollars on the table, grabbed her coat and purse, rose up and walked away and out the door. Sherrod watched her through the window.

As the snow started falling lightly, at a crime scene in an old abandoned building, one of the officers was directed to collect blood samples. They figured some of them had to come from the killer, because of how fresh they were. As soon as the officer went to retrieve one, it jumped onto the plastic glove he was wearing. He jumped back as the sample clung tightly. He pulled the glove off and dropped it into a bag another officer gave him.

"Did you see that?" he asked.

"Yeah, what and the hell! We definitely have to have that analyzed." The two baffled officers gathered all the evidence and hurried out as they ducked beneath the yellow tape.

Not even two hours later Dre's entire team was being hauled into the police station. Not knowing what it was about, they all seemed irritated. Separate, they were interrogated and released.

That same afternoon, sitting at his desk in that same facility, a neatly groomed black detective named Lewis called out to another, "Now, the guy they picked from the photo line-up, Sherrod Tillman, just came home a few years ago. Guess for what?" Detective Lewis asked.

"Murder."

"Exactly, all of them said they saw the two have words on more than one occasion. He's definitely capable, let's just find

Siege of Darkness/Robert Taylor

him and bring him in and see what's what!" Lewis finished as he got up.

"Okay boss, I'll have the boys bring him in," the younger Spanish detective Gomez answered and exited out into the hallway.

The very next day after work Sherrod arrived at the diner around the same time, but this time Marie wasn't there. He sat waiting for three hours watching television and making small talk. After the place emptied out, he decided to leave.

Just about two blocks away, he spotted her exiting McDonald's and smirked. He immediately began rushing through the crosswalk and people to the side of the street she was traveling on. He eased up alongside her; a smile canvassed his face as he did so.

"You should let me cook for you, so you don't have to eat out so much," he started up startling her. With an angry stare, she walked on, as she tried ignoring him and seemed to quicken her pace.

"Oh, I get it; you don't want to talk to me because my breath stinks!" Sherrod yelled jokingly as he blew into his open right hand to make sure. She sighed and rolled her eyes as she stopped in her tracks.

"No, I'm just not in the mood for any men or their bullshit!"

"Wow, who hurt you!" he carried on as she began to walk again. Leaving well enough alone, he shook his head, turned and headed home himself as his stomach started bothering him.

Just as he turned a corner, a patrol car pulled up on him and the officers jumped out with their guns drawn. Sherrod saw this and immediately threw his hands in the air.

"What's this about?" he asked as they searched, cuffed and marched him toward the car.

"It'll all be explained to you at the precinct. Now get in the car," the officer told him as he shoved him along.

About thirty minutes later at the precinct, being pulled from a cell, Sherrod was angry and beginning to feel weird. A sharp pain caused him to stop in his tracks as he was being escorted through the station. When he finally reached a room where Detective Lewis sat, he smirked.

"Have a seat Mr. Tillman," he offered with a smile.

"Don't you guys have anything better to do than to arrest innocent people?" Sherrod quickly spoke as he sat down and looked him in the eyes.

"I don't know that you're innocent just yet! What...I'm supposed to believe your word?" the detective answered back. With an angry expression, Sherrod grunted right before he placed both hands on the table out in front of him. Cuffs were dangling from each wrist as the chain that bound them had been broken. Astonished, the detective jumped back slightly and looked at him.

"How did you do that?" Detective Lewis asked and motioned for the guard that was standing at the door to come to the table.

"Are those your cuffs that he just broke out of?"

"No, but they were definitely secure on his wrist. I don't know how that was possible," the officer told Lewis as he examined them.

"You want me to place another pair on him?" the officer questioned.

"No, I should be all right. Right, Mr. Tillman?"

"Yeah, It was just that my wrists were hurting, that's all." Sherrod explained as he opened and closed his fist repeatedly.

Siege of Darkness/Robert Taylor

"Look, let's get this over with, I wanna get home and get some sleep," Sherrod stated a little annoyed with having to go through all of this.

"Do you know an Andre Mills, street name Dre?"

"Never heard of him,"

"Well, his people said you and him had some words on several occasions."

"Who, the dealer? I never knew his name! Why?"

"He was murdered a few nights ago."

"Wow, can't say I care, but it wasn't me!" Sherrod answered emotionless.

"Where were you around the weekend of the first?" The detective asked.

"The first of what, this month?" Sherrod asked.

"Yes, the first of December!" the detective clarified.

"Well, I went to work, then after work I went home, showered and got in the bed. Why…is that a crime?" Sherrod asked.

"Didn't you have an argument with Andre that evening?" the detective asked.

"He said something to me. I ignored him and headed home. It wasn't much to it!" Sherrod explained.

"Was there someone at home that can corroborate your alibi?"

"No, because I live alone. Look, he's not worth going to jail for! Every time he came at me, I walked away. Now, can I leave? I got plenty to do!" Sherrod finished as he stared into the detective's eyes. The detective waved him on and the guard let him out.

After he left, Detective Lewis sat thinking momentarily, got up and headed out of the room himself. Walking into his office, he called to his partner.

"Gomez, get me the results of that blood sample. I need to find out who it belongs too!"

"I'm right on it!" he replied and hurried out the office into the corridor.

Siege of Darkness/Robert Taylor

20

Spring of 1999

While sitting in a grass-filled area just beyond a small cluster of trees; Chris was reading the Bible. As he mumbled, "Lord, please guide and protect me." O'Conner appeared as the light became blinding.

As I have told you, I'm here to ensure your safety. You have to believe; otherwise, the forces at work will twist you into a fate fitting only to those of a destructive and evil nature!

"But I have failed my son as his father, as I have failed you and the word. I am but a shell of the man I once was."

You must stop blaming yourself for the misdirection of a lost soul! You are only responsible for passing on wisdom and knowledge, beyond that is up to the individual. Do not let guilt destroy you!

Later at home in his room, Sherrod seemed to be in serious pain as he lay curled up in the bed, sweating heavily.
"Oh, God help me!" he forged as he agonized and out of nowhere a heavy voice answered,
I'm glad you recognize who I am. Now, in order for the pains to seize, you must impregnate a woman. Messing with these less than desirables and their polluted wombs will not

Siege of Darkness/Robert Taylor

do! For the womb that is to carry the foretold ones must be of a certain purity. Every woman you become sexually engaged with from now on, with the transfer of your bodily fluids, the plasmic companions will find passage into the female, therefore, seeking to nest and bring about the ultimate life forces. Your blood will be transferred to the unborn fetus and the rest you will be informed of, when the time comes.

"What is this pain? What is going on inside of me? Oh, it hurts!"

Do as you are instructed and the pain will subside, if not you will perish, you fool! Sherrod, who lay soaked as his body temperature rose, went over to the sink and ran cold water over his head. Walking back to his room, he fell to his knees and fought to get back on his feet. Feeling dizzy, he stumbled once he was almost upright.

After seeing Marie on several occasions, one day she showed up while Sherrod sat in the diner in deep thought. To his surprise, she walked in with a slender, light-skinned woman. They sat in her usual booth. She ordered her usual turkey burger with lettuce, tomatoes, and mayo. The lady with her ordered, eggs, beef-bacon and toast. There was something different about Marie on this day. She seemed a little upbeat. After being shot down, Sherrod was in no rush to speak though.

The waitress stood in front of him as she pulled her pen and pad from her apron and smiled. "What are you having today, Sherrod? Oh, and by the way, the lady's paying for it." She pointed to Marie as she popped her gum.

"Really?" Shocked, he turned and looked her in the face. Marie smiled and nodded, motioning for him to come have a seat at their table. The other young lady grinned as Sherrod got up and moved toward them.

Siege of Darkness/Robert Taylor

As the three of them looked across at each other, there seemed to be a presence surrounding them, a supernatural presence.

"I'm Sherrod Tillman and you are?"

"Marie Childs, and this here is my sister, Michelle, but we call her Missy."

"Glad to formally meet you Miss Childs, and you, Missy."

"So, Mr. Tillman, why are you interested in me?" Marie caught him off guard with that question.

"Because you're beautiful and I see you all the time by yourself."

"Well, I am single, but my last relationship was abusive, and I just took a hiatus from men for a while to get me together," Marie explained. "What about you?"

"Ah hum, well, I'm lonely, like to have fun and if you give me a chance, I'll make it my business to make you smile every morning."

Missy blushed because of how cute they sounded.

"Slowdown, who said I was even interested in you like that?" Marie said, putting on the brakes.

"Well, you're paying for my meal, you asked me to come to sit with you, and you can't stop smiling. I think that's reason enough to believe," The two stared into each other's eyes. An unmarked police vehicle cruised by slowly and the waitress brought three large plates to the table. She sat them out in front of each of them. Marie immediately removed the top bun from her burger and started soaking it with ketchup, while Missy scooped her eggs and Sherrod pulled the skin from his juicy tender chicken breast and bit into it.

"So tell me about this ex-boyfriend of yours?" Sherrod questioned.

"Well, he was a total jerk! Selfish, self-centered and lazy! Not to mention he had a hand problem!"

"He used to hit you?" Sherrod questioned in shock.

"Yeah, he believed in the old fashion way, do as I say and don't question me!" she spat animated.

"Wow, now I understand why you run from men and was so anti-social."

"I'm not anti-social; I just don't want to waste my time dealing with a lot of these fools!"

Sherrod smiled and looked into her eyes.

"Well, I hope you don't think I'm like that!"

"Tell me about you?"

"Well, where should I start? I'm a construction worker in the downtown area. I keep to myself. I love sports and spending time with my woman, when I have one."

Marie listened and looked across at him with a half-smile.

The two gazed into each other's eyes, trying to figure each other out. Missy decided to head home, but before she departed, she told Marie, "He's a keeper, girl!"

After she left, Marie asked Sherrod to walk her out. They said their goodbyes and headed their separate ways.

.

****

For the next three weeks, the two grew close. They went to plays, movies, skating and even took long walks. Sherrod introduced her to his parents and she introduced him to hers. In a short time they became inseparable and that's when the romance began.

One night after a nice comedy show and dinner, Marie invited Sherrod back to her place. Just before she put the key in the door to enter, she turned to face him as he stood close

Siege of Darkness/Robert Taylor

behind breathing on her neck. The chemistry was thick as she looked him in the eyes. Sighing, she cupped his face with both hands and gave him a soft, steamy, wet kiss. Placing his arms around her waist, Sherrod pulled her close and kissed her back as she closed her eyes, surrendering her soul to his passion. Giving up her keys as he held her in his left arm, he opened the apartment door. She led him in, flipping on the lights, bypassing everything and headed straight to her bedroom. There she dragged him over to the bed where she began to undress right there in front of him. Sherrod's eyes grew as the hairs in his nostrils danced and the mesmerizing scent of her perfume filled the room. Her eye contact and nude body prompted him to push her down on the bed where he started kissing her neck. She arched her back as she opened and threw her thick pecan colored limbs in the air. Aggressively, Sherrod maneuvered between them while unbuckling his jeans. In that split second, he was reminded of what the overlord had told him and he reached in his pocket for a condom. After positioning himself, her face personified pleasure as she welcomed the penetration of his girth.

"Ohhh, yes, I like what I feel already!" Marie whispered, making Sherrod's erection even stiffer. Every time she thought he couldn't go any deeper, he dragged the bottom, rotating his pelvis, causing the juices in her walls to flow.

"Owww, where you been all my life?" she questioned. Sherrod, equally amazed, thought he was in a water park, because of how wet and wild she became.

"Damn!" he shouted, as he locked his arms, braced himself and continued on. Suddenly, as he got excited, he became angry and began to act like a dog in heat. What started out so beautifully had turned into something else. His eyes flipped from one color to the next, his back expanded and hunched.

Siege of Darkness/Robert Taylor

Marie's face revealed pain as she opened her eyes and started punching and pushing him. He was solid and impossible to stop or move.

"Please, baby, stop, you're hurting me!" she shouted as he sped up and seemed to become even larger within.

Seconds later, he started to shake as Marie lit up and could feel his warm sperm burst through the already shredded condom.

"Sherrod, get up, I can feel you cummin'! Get up!" she shouted as tears dressed her pruned up face heavily.

After a few loud grunts, he rolled over on his side with his eyes closed. Marie reached down between her legs and could feel the torn and sore flesh. There was an instantaneous tingle within her uterus and spine. Her stomach swelled and got tight also. She was bewildered by it all; she had never encountered sex as wild and animalistic as that. She touched and rubbed her stomach as she turned to look Sherrod in the face and in that instance, his eyes popped open, but sat still. He smiled and kissed her on the cheek. Suddenly, she felt a sharp pain in her stomach, which provoked her to get up and rush to the bathroom.

Minutes later, as she sat on the toilet she leaned over clutching her stomach tightly. She could feel something growing inside her. She assumed it was gas as she rocked back and forth, hoping it would subside and eventually it did. Thinking it was the deep penetration that caused it, she cleaned herself up and headed back into the bedroom, into bed where Sherrod lay out cold. She looked under the sheets at his nude body, She lightly touched his genitals and couldn't see anything out of the ordinary. She looked at the size of it and questioned why it was so painful, it was quite normal.

Siege of Darkness/Robert Taylor

Just outside the window, after jotting down a few notes, the unmarked patrol car pulled off, shining a light in the doorway.

***

The prostitute was curled up in a hotel bed with heavy bags under her eyes, with veins protruding through her flesh and drenched in her own sweat. Saliva ran from both sides of her mouth as her swollen body was black and blue. She cried out loudly as a bottle of gin sat on a nightstand alongside a container of Midol. Within that hour, her body became still, her heart frozen, her stomach rippled, as a tiny hand print surfaced from beneath the flesh.

***

The next morning, while Marie hobbled around in the kitchen cooking, Sherrod lay sleeping with his arms wrapped around a pillow. Waking up, he found himself in the bed alone, so he called out.

"Marie!" Hearing him, she came through the place to stand in the doorway. With her stomach even larger, she looked in his face. "Why do you look pregnant?" Sherrod sat up.

"I don't know! After we had sex, my stomach got bloated. I'm getting sharp pains and my spine feels funny."

"Seriously, your stomach wasn't like that last night!" Sherrod thought about what the overlord had told him.

"I know, but, no more sex for you, until you learn how to respect my wishes and my body! You were trying to tear out my insides! It was like you turned into an animal or something," Marie spat as she stared at him with a serious expression.

He smiled."You enjoyed it!" he stated with an air of cockiness. Marie stared at him momentarily and walked away, still mystified. He fell back into the bed and pondered further.

That weekend, inside Sherrod's apartment, Marie was cuddled up in his arms as the two lay comfortably on the sofa. They were watching *The Cosby Show* when she looked up into his eyes.

"You do love me, don't you?" She smiled.

"Yes, I do. You sexy thang you!"

"You never gon leave me, are you?"

"No, baby, I'm here to stay! As a matter-of-fact, why don't you stay here with me."

"What? You want me to give up my place, and come live with you? I don't know if that's a good idea. What if you get tired of me, or vice-versa? What if, we don't work out? I won't have a place to go too." She answered.

"I really like you, and it seems like you like me, too! Let's try it out and if it doesn't work, you can have my place."

"It's against my better judgment, but okay!" she reluctantly agreed.

"Let's go to church tomorrow!" she blurted out of the blue.

"I don't know about that one." He looked stunned.

"Why not?"

"I'm just not a believer in God right now. Because, if there is a God, why is this world going to hell? I refuse to believe He would allow such."

"You gotta keep the faith. He will prevail!"

"Yeah, whatever! Pass me the phone, I promised my father I would call him."

That next morning, as the sunlight lit up the room, Sherrod was grinding up against Marie. She remained still in her sleep, though he was slowly removing her panties. Rolling her over on her back, he eased her legs open and climbed between them. As soon as he penetrated, her eyes popped open and she looked up into his.

"Baby, get up!" she told him as he continued as though he didn't hear her. She began to beat him in the chest to no avail. She yelled loudly and finally his eyes opened and he stopped.

"What is wrong with you?" she shouted as she jumped out of the bed and ran into the bathroom.

An hour later, Sherrod woke up only to see Marie had left and placed a note on the pillow beside him. *I'm going home to get dressed for church and I'd love it if you came with me. I love you!* Smiling and rolling out of the bed, Sherrod headed into the bathroom and turned on the shower.

Fifteen minutes later, his doorbell rang repeatedly. Wrapping himself in a towel, he hurried to the door assuming it was Marie. Buzzing her in, he listened as she climbed the stairs. She walked into the apartment wearing a nice tan colored pants suit. Sherrod, who stood drying himself off, smiled at the sight of her.

"You look amazing! Even with the bulge."

"I don't know what's going on. I barely got in my clothes. This is crazy!"

"I've never seen anything like this. You should go see a doctor."

"I will. Now, come go to church with me!"

"I'm not going. So, please stop asking!"

"Just this one time and I promise I won't ask you again. Then maybe we can come home and finish where we left off, or should I say where you left off, but only if you're gentle."

"Okay, just this one time." He smiled, after touching her stomach and walked over to his closet.

Siege of Darkness/Robert Taylor

An hour later, the two of them were entering the church, walking hand in hand. Marie looked over at Sherrod and asked, "Why is your hand sweating and why do you look like you're hurting?"

"I'm okay, my stomach's bothering me. I'll be all right in a minute." He took a deep breath and continued on.

Minutes later, as the pastor preached, Sherrod was quite bothered and couldn't sit still. He could feel his body heat up as he began to sweat heavily. Marie checked his forehead for a fever. Looking in his eyes, she wondered what was going on with him. Stretching out his collar, Sherrod was unable to take it any longer, so he got up, walked up the aisle and out the door. Marie jumped up and followed.

Fifteen minutes later, she re-entered alone and sat on a pew near the exit. Sherrod never came back inside. He sat in a shaded area on the steps.

Later, as the church was emptying out, Marie was now standing with Sherrod. She stopped the preacher as he came out and they began to talk.

"Loved your sermon, pastor!" she told him as Sherrod stood by her side.

"Thank you, Marie, and who is this gentleman? Hopefully someone who wants to be part of our church?" He smiled and pointed to her belly. Marie looked at Sherrod, smiled and kissed him on the cheek.

"This is my boyfriend Sherrod. This is his first time here. He got a little sick and had to rush out. I'm hoping he'll join us too."

The preacher looked at Sherrod and extended his right hand, in which Sherrod shook. The pastor's body heated up instantly as he stared at Sherrod, causing him to pull his hand away. "That was weird! Anyway, you know, son, when you accept God, you are cleansed of all your sins. I don't know what you have done, but He is there for you. Hope to see you soon!" He walked away as others warranted his attention.

21

Weeks later, Marie began to experience severe pains, so at her next doctor's visit she questioned her status. The doctor examined her and explained that the pains were normal for a pregnant woman and that there was nothing to be alarmed about. Marie looked at him surprised.

"Doc, please tell me it ain't so!"

"I wish I could."

She began to look worried as she fixed her clothes and got ready to leave.

That afternoon as three patrol cars sat outside a hotel, two officers stood in a room with the owner and a housekeeper. Everyone covered their noses with their shirt collars, as the body of the prostitute, Donna, was pale and bluish as it lay sprawled out across the bed. The paramedics raced in and right away pronounced her dead. Noticing the movement in her stomach, they realized there was a life within her. A conscious decision was made to hurry and get her to a hospital. There, they would perform an emergency C-section.

Thirty minutes later, as a doctor had cut through the layers of skin and tissue, he pulled a two-headed baby boy from Donna's womb. Speechless, nurses stood frozen. The doctor clipped the umbilical cord and passed the baby to an awaiting nurse. As the child screamed, the nurse made her way over to a nearby table.

Siege of Darkness/Robert Taylor

"I don't even know how the child survived as long as it did, inside the womb of a deceased mother with no air circulation or blood flow. It's miraculous to say the least!" the doctor expressed as he walked from the operating room along with a nurse.

Later on that day, Sherrod worked on a construction site alongside Walt who had got him the job. He was a productive person in society

As the sun beat on his back, he was hard at work, six stories up when a supervisor walked up on him and said, "We don't work half naked around here! You want to show all, become a lifeguard or something!" Sherrod gave him an evil stare and went back to doing his job. The supervisor threw his shirt at him.

"What's that about?" Sherrod asked as he closed his fist.

"I told you to put ya damn shirt on or leave the fuckin' site!"

Sherrod walked up on him and when they stood face to face, he told him, "I'm not to be played with, so if you like the way you look, leave me the hell alone!"

"Boy, you work under me, so if you value your job, you'll put your shirt on and get back to work!" he smiled as he finished.

"You're an asshole!" Sherrod told him as he put on his shirt and walked away.

Later, before he got on the bus to head home, a prostitute called out to him from across the street. He marched across to see what she wanted.

"Donna was found dead in a hotel room this morning. The dumb bitch was pregnant. Now, tell me how stupid is that? She had unprotected sex with one of her tricks. She was looking real bad and drinking heavy, I knew something wasn't right!"

"So why are you telling me? I always wore protection!"

"Because I know you were one of her regulars, that's why! You need to go get checked out! The bitch mighta had AIDs or something! Rubbers don't stop everything!"

"Yeah okay."

"Get checked mutha fucka, okay? All I'm sayin'," she finished as Sherrod headed back across the street. He seemed to be in deep thought as a speeding car damn near hit him as it blew its horn.

In Sherrod's apartment, Marie stood in the kitchen cooking and looking up at the clock, wondering what was taking him so long to get home. She had made his favorite, steak and rice. He loved it medium rare. She thought it was nasty because she liked her food cooked until it was done. The front door opened and slammed and into the kitchen came Sherrod as he followed the aroma. He pulled a chair from the table and dropped down in it. Marie turned to face him. He held his arms out and she walked over as he embraced her. With his arms around her waist and his head resting against her stomach, he relaxed.

"What's wrong baby?"

"I'm just tired. Tired of working for jokers half my age and have them play me out like I'm stupid or something. I do my work baby, but it's the way they talk to me! I'm a man just like they are. I ain't gon' be able to take much more of this. Police bothering me and all kinda shit!"

Marie smiled and looked down into his eyes and said to him, "Remember what the preacher told you. He told you if you accept God, you will be cleansed of your sins. Don't let temptation make you backslide. We gon' get you baptized!"

He looked up at her, smiled and expressed to her, "Not a good idea," He hugged her tighter, while he continued to rest against her stomach.

"It's funny that you're head right there." She smiled.

"Why?" Sherrod looked up at her.

"It's crazy, but, I'm pregnant!" she blurted with joy.

"Pregnant, as in with child?" He was stunned.

"Yes!"

Sherrod smiled, stood up, looked her in the eyes and kissed her. In his mind lay the thought of what the overlord had told him.

***

That evening, Willie convinced Chris to take a ride with him to see Jason. Once they reached Jason's place, Willie called Jason on the phone. Upon him answering, he seemed agitated.

"Yes!" he shouted.

"Jason, it's me, your uncle Willie. Your father and I are outside. Is it all right for us to come in?"

"Yeah, I guess so." He reluctantly gave in.

When Jason opened the door, Chris and Willie walked in. Willie hugged Jason while Chris walked in without acknowledging him and sat down on the couch. Linda came into the room from the bedroom, greeting everyone with a smile. Chris greeted her with half a grin. Willie sat down next to Chris while Jason and Linda sat across from them in the loveseat.

"Now I want all this feuding to stop, today!" Willie demanded of everyone.

Siege of Darkness/Robert Taylor

"Who's feuding? I haven't said anything to him or to anyone for that matter! I'm actually in a good place," Jason clarified.

"You know what I'm talking about. You're not speaking to your father and he's not speaking to you. God forbid, what if one of you dies tomorrow? This is crazy! I'm not leaving here until you two start being a father and a son again!" Willie inserted in the air angrily.

Chris spoke first. "Well, my only problem with him is his hatefulness and him drudging up all this demonic stuff."

"Look, I'm out of your house and I don't ask you for anything, so what I do shouldn't bother you," Jason stipulated.

"Jason, I see you're not going to give this up, so I wish you the best." Chris got up to leave. "No I don't, I wish you'd come to your damn senses!"

Jason smirked as Linda looked at him like he was crazy. The door closed behind Chris as Willie watched and turned to face Jason.

"You gon' kill your father with your stupidity! How could you do what you're doing knowing what it's doing to him?" Willie asked.

"I'm not doing anything to hurt him, I love him! I just want him to respect me as a man, and my decisions!"

Willie looked him in the eyes and shook his head. He also, got up and headed for the door.

"Love you nephew!"

Once the door closed, within seconds the truck was heard as it pulled off. Jason watched from the window as Linda got up and went back to what she was doing.

Hours later, as Chris sat quietly in his living room, O'Conner made his presence known.

Siege of Darkness/Robert Taylor

You must let go, for he is too far-gone! He has every intention on following through. Do not blame yourself; the guilt will suck the life out of you! You must become stronger in the face of adversity! I am here as always. O'Conner disappeared.

A teardrop sprang from Chris's right eye and within seconds his eyes froze, he grabbed his chest and fell back onto the couch. Willie walked into the room and after seeing him gasping, he ran to his aid.

Twenty minutes later, in the emergency room, Chris seemed to be breathing fine and he muttered, "Let me go, I don't want to be here when they destroy the world. Let me go!" Right away, his pulse faded and the doctor yelled,

"He's having a relapse! We got to stabilize him, before we either lose him, or he goes into a coma. Come on people, let's go!"

Two hours later in CCU, Chris was stable and being monitored. Out in the waiting area, Willie and Jimmy looked worried as Jimmy reached out to Jason again and again. Finally, Jason picked up half asleep.

"Hello," he greeted.

"Hey, Jason, get your behind to the hospital! Your father had a stroke!" Jimmy shouted through the phone.

"What?" Shocked, he sat up straight and couldn't believe what he was hearing. Hanging up and quickly jumping in the first thing he could find to put on, he ran out the door, leaving Linda watching as she had heard the whole conversation.

Thirty minutes later, Jason pulled up at the hospital. He barely let the truck come to a complete stop before he grabbed the keys and jumped out. Through the emergency entrance, he sprinted, as he darted to a desk to get information.

"I'm looking for Mr. Christopher Milosky. He was brought in a few hours ago," he said totally distraught. After being informed of where to find his father, Jason raced through the hospital.

Twelve o'clock, noon, the next day, Jason, Jimmy and Willie were all twisted up in the chairs in the waiting area. Willie and Jimmy were sleeping, while Jason sat up staring at the wall and the clock from time to time. Minutes later, the doctor came out of Chris's room with a serious expression as he approached.

"You guys are his family, I presume?"

"Yes we are," Jason answered as Jimmy and Willie fought to wake up.

"Well, he's quite lucky. He must have an angel on his side, because two strokes like that back to back should have killed him! He's gonna be all right. You can go in to see him, but not too long. He needs to rest. You guys have a nice day." The doctor walked away down the hall.

***

That same afternoon, Sherrod was at the clinic awaiting the results of an HIV test. As he sat, he looked around and into the faces of some of the people there. Some were drawn up, faces sunken in and frail. Others were coughing and breathing heavily, while sores and scars covered their skin.

Breaking his trance, a nurse came through a door and called out,

"Sherrod Tillman?" Hearing this he got up and followed her into an office. "Now Mr. Tillman what brought you here?" she asked as she took a seat behind a desk.

Siege of Darkness/Robert Taylor

"I just want to make sure I'm healthy, so I can move on with my life!"

"Well, I got good news and bad news. Which do you want first?"

Thinking momentarily, he was shook. "Give me the bad news first," he answered, fearing the worst.

"Well, the bad news is, you have to come back and be tested again in three to six months, to be sure you haven't contracted anything. The good news is that, as of today you do not have AIDS or any other STD." Relieved, Sherrod sighed and smiled.

***

In his bedroom, Elijah stood pinning pictures and articles along the wall. Staring at them, he was trying to find some type of linkage between Byron Malic and the beast, the beast and the wolf sightings. Carefully analyzing the information, he pulled out the book; *The Roman Catholic Church and Its Demons.*

In the early 1800s, a stage coach was attacked by a wild pack of wolves. One of them jumped on the bull whacker (driver) and knocked him off and to the ground, where he was killed. The rider, a Mr. Jenson, struck a few of them down with his musket, but he was eventually overcome by them and killed also. In later months, it was said that a beast surfaced clothed in Jenson's garments and was said to be him. He was known to be a rich and evil man, who many felt made plenty of deals with the devil to acquire his wealth. After reading that, he flipped through to a chapter that talked of Byron Malic and he read on for hours.

Siege of Darkness/Robert Taylor

***

That night while lying in the hospital bed, Chris's spirit had left his body. As it walked into the light, being guided by O'Conner, Jason sat in the room watching over his flesh in tears. Trailing O'Conner, Chris's spirit was taken back into the early eighteen hundreds, back into the woods, where a young Byron Malic was approached by Lucifer. As Byron walked reciting scriptures, the voice of Lucifer startled him.

I see you are a devoted and trustworthy servant of the word. I'm impressed, but yet astounded by your loyalty to a faith that's filled with hypocrisy.

"What? Who? Lord!" Malic uttered confused by the sudden intrusion.

I can give you things your faith cannot, immortality being the greatest of them all! Join forces with me and we will blaze a path to a prophecy that will have this world at our very feet.

"I want not for power or riches. Revelations 5:12, worthy be the lamb."

I know the scriptures far better than you ever will! Do not recite them to me or in my presence, you fool!

After that vision, O'Conner walked Chris through a fog and into another. This one was of Malic calling upon Lucifer while standing in the darkness.

"I have pondered long and hard, and I find that only a fool exists without purpose! I have also found that to achieve honor, sometimes you must shed light and triumph by walking the path deemed less desirable."

You are extremely wise, my young prophet! I applaud you for coming to me and recognizing what shall be a rewarding alliance for you and I!"

Siege of Darkness/Robert Taylor

Back in his body, Chris's eyes popped open and he sat straight up and looked around the room. Jason had left and the only noise was a sporadic cough from a sick roomie.

"Why am I so cold? Whew, I'm cold! Why is it so cold in here?" he spat as he pulled the sheets up over him and curled up under them.

***

Two days later, as Sherrod stood in the mirror shaving, one of the overlords spoke to him.

You have impregnated two, one of which has died because her womb wasn't suitable to carry the lord's children, but yet there is a life. That life is of no use to us, because of the tainted womb from which it came and will be destroyed. The other who has only been with one other than yourself, has been chosen to cradle the seeds of the forth coming prophecy!"

"How is this so, when I, in both cases, wore protection?"

"Ha, ha, ha. Did you think those mere feeble elastic contraptions could contain the embryonic force of a god?"

"What? Are you're telling me that Donna gave birth to a child that's alive and well?"

That's exactly what I'm telling you, but that has to be destroyed!

"This is crazy!"

I told you in order for you to rid your body of all that ailed you, you had to impregnate a woman, and for that you would be rewarded. But by trying to avoid impregnating them you have proven to be disobedient and that is punishable by death!

"You must not do this! I love her!"

Siege of Darkness/Robert Taylor

She will not perish; she is just the incubator, as you were the vehicle. Together the two of you will bring forth the miracle of all miracles!

"You cannot do this! I will have her abort it!" At that moment, Sherrod caught himself gasping and struggling to breathe. Grabbing his throat, he stumbled and fell to the floor.

You will obey my wishes or I will take your insignificant life! Do you wish to remain with her during her pregnancy or leave her to bear what is to be, alone? It is your choice, because your usefulness has long been expired!"

"I, wish to be there beside her. I promise you, please!" At that moment as if a dam broke and water began to flood in, air filled his lungs and his body once again as he lay there choking.

Around that same time within the hospital, the premature two-headed newborn that was cut out of Donna, lay resting in an incubator labeled, John Doe. The light complexioned baby was hidden from the view of the public. A doctor stood over the incubator staring down at it, from its two heads to its twenty toes. He placed his stethoscope against its chest and began to move it around to locate the heart. After hearing a fast-paced rhythm, he wondered if the child was at risk or born with some sort of defect. Unsure, he walked over to a nurse.

"I need to do more tests on this child, something's not right. Get it ready for me, I'll be right back!" He exited the room with a confused expression.

Later that day as Sherrod and Marie lay in the bed together, he placed his arm around her and kissed her on the cheek.

"You do know I love you?" He looked her in the eyes.

"Yes," she smiled. Hearing her answer seemed to only make how he was feeling, worse. How could he allow her to give birth to what is to be the devil's prophecy?

22 THE RITUAL

Now the cool winter of 1999, Jason was twenty-nine years old, and he was much more obsessed and knowledgeable of Malic than in his younger years. Everyone in the township of Highpoint, where he resided, thought he was weird and somewhat crazy. The stories his uncles and father told him were truly no more than an old folk tale as they were discussed and often laughed about. But regardless to the fact, Jason continued his research and kept them alive. He refused to let people's disbelief derail him. He often told the stories himself, mostly when he was drunk. No one really paid him any attention or believed him. He showed articles from different publications and so forth. They laughed at the thought of supernatural beast roaming the earth. Even his uncles stayed away when they saw he was adamant about proceeding with his madness. Jason grew furious with everyone and secluded himself. He moved again, but this time he found a place far away from everyone and everything. He stayed up day and night until he broke down the scrolls, which were written in Hebrew and read;

The dark overlords will reign with double the force. The dark age will be ordained upon their coming about. Death to he who is chosen, chant thy words, death to he who brings life, chant thy words. Life to the double forces of darkness!

Siege of Darkness/Robert Taylor

Reading further, he reached a paragraph that read; evil beings shall roam the earth day and night. Stopping temporarily, he rubbed his eyes, refocused as he went into deep thought. He pictured himself as an immortal with powers unimaginable. He could stare at a person and they would either explode or drop dead right on the spot. He had the psyche of a Greek god and his appearance was youthful. Coming out of thought, he read on and as a few hours passed he fell asleep.

***

At the clinic where Sherrod was tested, the doctor was viewing a portion of his blood sample. As she examined it through the microscope, it seemed to moving about rapidly. Baffled by this, she called out to another for a second opinion. By the time they came back, the sample had disappeared.

That evening, Sherrod lay cuddled up with Marie as she slept. With his eyes open, he thought about what was soon to be and the fact that he could do nothing to derail it. He also thought about what the overlord told him was destined. Looking down into Marie's peaceful face, he envisioned her giving birth to two monsters. He desperately wanted to tell her, but knew his life would be taken before he was given a chance. Running his fingers through her hair, she moaned from how soothing it must have felt. At that moment, Sherrod tried whispering in her ear and immediately his voice went mute as his face grew tight from some intense throbbing that ran through his head. He fell back onto his pillow and it all came to a stop.

***

Around eleven o'clock that same night, Jason ran around town, in and out of stores, searching out all the items he needed to orchestrate the forthcoming prophecy. He bought everything from candles to chalk. He knew he had only one chance to get it right and didn't want to mess it up. So as he sped around town his mind theatrically played out scenario after scenario as he saw the future of mankind. This was what he waited all his life to see and now it was finally happening.

***

At that same moment, Elijah sat in his study watching raw footage of scientific mutation experiments, the mixing of human DNA with animal DNA. He saw humans with tails and claws jumping about in cages erratically. After removing that disc, he put in another titled; *The Bible vs. Greek Mythology.* He was stunned as he listened.

***

Back at the hospital, the baby named John Doe with every breath became stronger and larger by the day. It was diagnosed with *progeria,* a disease as rare as it was, which speeds up the aging process and ultimately leads to the child having a stroke or heart attack before the young age of thirteen.

Fearing the tabloids and newspapers getting wind of the child, Baby John Doe was confined to a room within an institution deep in the woods. There it stared up at the ceiling wondrously. Not old enough to walk yet, it rolled around in the enclosed bed, wrapping itself in a soft white comforter. Frustrated, Baby John Doe began to scream at the top of its lungs. An aide came and peeked through the small picture window making sure everything was okay, watching as it rocked the crib back and forth.

***

Siege of Darkness/Robert Taylor

Back in Sherrod's place, Marie lay on Sherrod's chest, she breathed softly as he looked around the room. Suddenly in a darkened corner, a hooded figure appeared as it was illuminated in an orange colored light. A voice began to speak capturing Sherrod's undivided attention;

You are trying my very patience with your constant disregard. Next time I will be forced as you leave me no choice but to drain the life from your frivolous body! You must know that there is nothing you or anyone else can do to stop what is to be.

"Why her of all the women on this earth? Why?" Sherrod asked.

Why not? Like I told you, her pureness and untainted soul is perfect to carry forth healthy life-forces. You were chosen because of your rebellious nature and behavior! You chose her, not I! You can blame no one but yourself! Not uttering another word Sherrod held Marie, closed his eyes and when he reopened them, there was nothing but a chair where the figure once stood.

***

That next morning, sitting at the kitchen table Jason and Linda were eating. He chewed on a slice of toast as he read from a book and mumbled to himself. Linda watched from across the table curiously.

"Jason, I know you're doing this to prove a point, but I really think you should give it up. A lot of strange things have been happening ever since we found all those old artifacts. I know you see it too! Now, your father's had two strokes. You need to be by his side right now!"

"Linda honey, I can't and won't stop now! I'll reach out to him tomorrow, I promise! But right now, I can make history by uncovering one of this world's great mysteries! Can you imagine..."

Linda just stared at him as she sipped from her coffee mug. He sat there with an undistinguishable fire in his eyes as he turned the page and read on. Suddenly, there was a news interruption on the television.

A man said he saw a beast like creature toss a man against a wall and while he was unconscious, rip his head from his shoulders. This is not the first time someone has reported something of this nature. The witness is being held under suspicion, but is not yet being charged with the murder! Stay tuned for more on this story...

Afterwards, he turned to Linda and stared. She parted her lips. "Do you see all the strange things that are happening around the world? Do you?"

"What that have to do with me? I'm not causing any of that!"

"You may not be, but you doing isn't going to help the world any."

"Linda, I"ve told you again and again, if you want to, you can go. I love you, but I'm not going to keep doing this with you."

Linda got quiet and started walking from the room. Jason stood shaking his head and watching as she did. The bedroom door was heard slamming and to break the trance of the moment, the phone rang.

***

That afternoon the four overlords stood in a graveyard in the heart of Newark. As a ray of light shot from beneath the soil, they continued to stand still with their heads bowed in allegiances. A faced formed in the light and addressed them.

I am more than pleased with how you've aligned my homecoming with the birth of my children. The darkest hour is upon us and I have you to thank. Yes, yes, upon their birth I shall exalt myself high above the throne of my brother, for I will claim my position as the almighty! After that thunderous recital, the light disappeared as did the image and the overlords. The wind made the leaves dance and it whistled as snow began to fall lightly.

***

Back in the city, outside walking with Marie along the sidewalk in the downtown area, Sherrod smiled as she had a glow about her. She stopped at street vendors admiring purses and hats. Sherrod's thoughts were all over the place as he wished there was some way out of the mess he created. Marie planted a soft kiss on his cheek and he woke up from his misery stricken trance.

"What's on your mind?" she asked.

"Nothin, jus' thinking 'bout a few things."

"I love you and I'm glad we're having these twins!" she went on.

"...me too," he added after holding his tongue momentarily. The glow in her eyes and the happiness she projected only made Sherrod feel worse, so bad that he threw up right there on the spot.

"Honey, are you all right!?" she questioned worried. Shaking his head signifying yes, he wiped his mouth with a napkin that he pulled from his pocket and turned to face her as he coughed.

Siege of Darkness/Robert Taylor

***

Hours later that evening, Jason was up in his attic where he lit candle after candle. Placing them all around the room, he turned out the lights as he clutched the book under his arm. Pulling the shades down, he closed the curtains, so that no light would seep in. He pushed everything from old furniture to tools and miscellaneous junk out of the way, clearing the center of the floor. Prancing back and forth enthusiastically, he mumbled to himself. He seemed to be memorizing as much of what was to be done as possible.

Setting the old altar in the middle of the room facing west, Jason began to sweat as Linda watched curiously. She hurriedly helped him prepare for the ceremony, fatefully assisting him without question. Now a short pale woman with short hair, frizzy about her face, she looked older than her thirty-seven years. She even dressed somewhat older, long flowered dresses or loose fitting jeans worn just above the ankles with t-shirts.

"Linda honey, come on!" he shouted. In that moment she rushed to finish setting things up.

"We are about to begin the first phase of Malic's work; the revival of the spirit and the release of the dark forces onto the earth." Jason told her indirectly and loud as if he had an audience.

"Jason, how are you going to get a body for the spirit?" she asked somewhat baffled.

"Malic is not the key! The key is the double forces of darkness, the foretold ones that will do battle against all that is holy and righteous!"

"What are you talking about?" Linda asked riddled.

"Malic was no more than a pawn. He had his time. He was used to help the overlords fulfill their prophecy of reaching into the new millennium. See here in the scrolls, where it says, something holy and righteous must be transformed into something of great evil. Malic was priest of the cloth, a devoted servant of god. He fell into the evil web of the fallen one, Satan himself!" He carried on. Linda listened though confused; she did not sway from doing what was asked of her.

"What time is it? he asked immediately after realizing it was getting close."

"It's eleven-fifty," she answered after looking at her watch. "See tonight, December 31, 1999, or more specifically the first of the year, at midnight, at my summon, the double forces of darkness will be given life. They will be able to endure daylight on earth and the fires of hell. Linda honey, it's almost time! They will be born as death straddles their bloodline. We must hurry, time's running short!" They scrambled to finish preparations.

"It's time! It's finally time!" Jason shouted as his eyes widened with anticipation.

***

Chris was relaxing and watching television when O'Conners appeared.

Your child is defiant and shall burn in hell for his actions! He is aligning what will cause the second dark war.

"So why can't you stop him?" Chris asked curiously.

We have spoken with him to no avail. If we take his life, the devil will make him immortal. Judgment is near and all who are not just, will perish. As it is God's will.

"So, you mean you cannot stop this madness?"

Siege of Darkness/Robert Taylor

Madness, is that of which the devil lives for, as much as he has power on earth, he also has power in heaven. He is still an authority; God has not taken that from him.

"What is this you tell me? Did God not create him?"

Though that is so, God allows Satan to remain so we learn to fight temptation and evil. So, when we embrace him and all of his glory, we have been tried and tested. In this more so, God's glory will shine as if he took Satan out yesterday!

***

Meanwhile in the city of Newark, on 14th Street and Madison, at the bar called *The Last Stop*, Sherrod entered. He looked more rugged than usual, his curly afro scattered about his head. He was wearing Timberland boots, jeans and a black pea coat. In this hangout for the local dealer, thugs and girls looking for a good time, Sherrod sat down and showed a sigh of relief as he thought to himself. He had mixed emotions about Marie having the twins in the weeks to come. He knew she was about to give birth to great evil. He couldn't help but feel like he was totally responsible.

Simultaneously elsewhere, Marie called Sherrod back to back as she sat in pain, but he didn't answer. She called the paramedics and while she waited, she called and talked to her mother. Her water broke causing her to yell as her contractions intensified the pain. She screamed at the top of her lungs, the movement in her stomach was heavy and could be seen through her gown. Her mother called out to her trying to get her to calm down.

***

Siege of Darkness/Robert Taylor

Elsewhere, moving about underground was the loud thunderous sound of a train racing to its next destination. In one of those nearby tunnels, six black men walking single file along a wall in the darkness. The tallest and the most muscular of the group lead as they reached a set of concrete steps. Climbing them, they all walked across an empty platform as music, horns and loud yelling seeped down from the streets and filled the cavity.

***

At that precise moment, Maria Childs yelled from a gurney being pushed by a few nurses as her contractions caused her to scream ferociously. Being rushed into the delivery room, she chanted Sherrod's name. The lights within the hospital dimmed temporarily as everyone looked around wondering what was going on.

***

Far away, in the institution, Baby John Doe's eyes lit up bright red as its body turned a fiery orange. It began to squeal like a pig in the darkness, which echoed throughout the facility. Other patients rushed to their doors curious to see what would make such a sound.

After flipping out, Johnathan Walsh (Jason's great grandfather) was placed in a padded room within the asylum. Trapped in a straightjacket, he sensed something was going on as he stood twirling around in the center of the floor. A few of the nurses watched from the small caged window, as they, too, could feel the presence of something as the lights flickered.

"Something strange is happening…I can feel it! Lord expel all evil spirits and demons from the earth. Let not Satan bring about darkness…" Walsh carried on as he fell to his knees and continued. The nurses scared themselves ran down the hall, grabbed their belonging and made their exit.

***

Back at Jason's place, he sat in the center of his attic chanting the satanic ritual loudly and with great conviction. In the midst of that, the winds shifted without warning, the sky darkened as roaring thunder could be heard throughout. Everything in the room in which he sat shook as pictures and things fell from the walls.

***

Closing in on Time Square, as they stared up into the sky, the six Black men moved quickly. The wondrous lighting and shoulder-to-shoulder crowd seemed to be sickening to them as their facial expression revealed such. Without warning, they began fighting through the crowd. Elbows and forearms were landing everywhere, as they heading to the large celebrity filled stage.

***

At the bar, Sherrod, who was already pissy drunk, continued to drink even more as he seemed to get angry. At that moment, he looked at his watch and decided to give Marie a call. Just as he raised his phone, a young thug who had been eyeballing him the entire time sat down across the table. He stared Sherrod down and took his shot glass. Sherrod closed his phone and watched angrily.

Siege of Darkness/Robert Taylor

"You don't mind? I didn't think so!" the thug followed up.

Just as he turned up the glass, Sherrod drew back and punched him, breaking the glass along with his nose. As the thug fell back and hit the floor hollering, Sherrod watched. Afterward, he rose and stood like a gladiator prepared for battle as some others saw their friend stumbling about. They approached, and Sherrod immediately pulled out his knife. Watching it all, the bartender panicked and quickly went for the phone. It got real ugly, real quick. As fast as they charged Sherrod, he left them lying in the floor with their guts hanging out. He moved like a possessed and crazed animal, leaping and slashing as he did. In the midst of the madness, through the door came two police officers and upon seeing all the blood and destruction they pulled their guns out. After a loud scream and another falling out, Sherrod had one final guy in a chokehold. The officers approached walking lightly and cautiously, hands wrapped tightly around the handles of their guns as a shadowy figure appeared.

***

In Time Square, in the midst of all the hooting and hollering, the ball was falling as the countdown reaches four, three… People began to blow their noisemakers as confetti fell from every window and everyone began to count in unison. Unbeknown to the world a dark figure laughed in the crowd.

***

Back in the hills, flames filled the room that housed Baby John Doe. His screams pierced the eardrums of all those in the vicinity causing their heads to explode.

Siege of Darkness/Robert Taylor

Finally reaching the stage area, the six men grew wings and transformed into gargoyles. The security team, horrified, froze just before they all took off running into the crowd. People started screaming and running for their lives. The largest of the gargoyles squealed drowning out the music. Police officers came from everywhere, halted by what they saw.

***

As Jason began to bring his chant to a close, just over his shoulder the last of the overlords appeared in the room where he and Linda sat.

As soon as the clock struck twelve, Chris woke up wide eyed and sat straight up in his bed yelling, "No!" The darkened sky became lit with loud roaring thunder.

***

Sherrod was murdered by the police after cutting the last guy's throat. Maria gave birth to two twin boys. People were left trampled on as the crowd continued to run wild in Time Square. Y2K was no more than a host. The gargoyles hung in the sky as people trampled over each other. Cars crashed into one another as the horrific site was nothing like anyone had ever seen. Jason had seemed to become possessed. Lucifer's illegitimate child returned to dust! The overlords took their position at the four corners of the world and the new millennium gave birth to the Dark Age!

The End

Siege of Darkness/Robert Taylor

Testament of Evil Vol.2

The Devil's DNA

NEW YEAR'S DAY 2000

That Saturday morning, the sun gradually claimed its position, shedding light on the confetti and trash filled streets. Colorful banners were strung up everywhere, boldly welcoming in the New Year. Ripping winds intensified the cold air, leaving it brisk and unfriendly. The hollow emptiness of allies filled with broken liquor and champagne bottles, revealed how chaotic the night passed had gotten. The sanitation department straddled both side of the street, hard at work with the clean-up detail. Street sweepers and garbage trucks were everywhere, cleaning and washing down everything. During all of this, the beaming sunlight bounced from O'Brien's bare-chest, as he stood erected on the roof top of that old thirteen story hotel. With his arms outstretched, he embraced the new day with a huge smile. While taking in the moment, the four overlords came to appear before him.

It is done! The twins, the double forces of darkness have given us passage. They have opened the gates of hell and from here on, we shall reign like nothing has ever before us! one of them spoke proudly.

"…aaaah, mmmm do you smell that? It is so fresh, so invited is the scent of conquest! " O'Brien shouted smiling and self-absorbed.

You have been a warrior of the ages, one of great loyalty, but there is a much warranted task…we seek of you. one of the

Siege of Darkness/Robert Taylor

overlords continued as his voice barreled about drowning out everything in the vicinity.

"What is it?" O'Brien asked inquisitively.

We need your assistance in watching over the twins, so that no harm comes to them; for there are forces that seek to destroy them! These forces will go to any length to bring about their demise. That must not and cannot happen!

"I am at your disposal, use me as you see fit, for I am forever indebted to you!" O'Brien spoke and bowed in submission like an obedient slave.

We are pleased to hear this! one of the overlords expressed and on that note they all disappeared. O'Brien sighed heavily, walked over to the edge of the roof and looked down. There after closing his eyes and thus taking another deep breath, he grinned, turned and headed back across the rooftop toward an open door.

Simultaneously, within the heavens as God and the angels witnessed the meeting, the angels address God with the issues of Satan and his devastation upon the earth.

"Lord, he has overstepped his boundaries. He is disrespecting all you have created. He and his disciples must be destroyed! Are you not witnessing what we are?" they carried on enraged.

"Yes I am! But understand…those that he can sway were doomed anyway. They are weak! Those that are confident and stead-fast in their belief in me, shall not perish. I will wage war once, hear me! Once only…and then I will cleanse the earth of him and all his followers, leaving only the chosen, faithful and few!"

But lord, we cannot sit by idly and watch him make such a mockery of all you have created," the angels continued their plea.

Siege of Darkness/Robert Taylor

"Man has done that, themselves! Since before the very first sin, Satan has won over so many." God pointed out with great calmest. The angels sat there trying to get an understanding.

"So why didn't you destroy him then?" one of the angels asked.

"I gave man free will, the opportunity to think for themselves, so if it hadn't been Satan it would have been someone or something else somewhere down the line. I allowed Satan to enter the garden, but I also instructed Adam not eat from the tree of Knowledge. With the aid of Satan and Eve, he made the conscious choice to disobey me!

(to be continued)

Siege of Darkness/Robert Taylor

Vol. #1 Fingered for Murder
Vol. #2 One in the chamber
Vol. #3 Somebody's got to die!
Vol. #4 Dirty's Shot
Vol. #5 Savage / The Jasiah story

Bigger fish to fry pt.1 Money or murder
Bigger fish to fry pt.2 Corruption
Bigger fish to fry pt.3 Murder game

The Devil's DNA (Siege of Darkness)
The Devil's DNA (Prophecy fulfilled)
The Devil's DNA (Loyalty or Death)
The Devil's DNA (Coup de Grace)

God I finally found my way

Hood Money Millionaires

Bounce

Meat Factory

Fetty Boy

Siege of Darkness/Robert Taylor